THE
LAST GET

Copyright © 2014 James E. Edwards
All rights reserved.

ISBN: 1450549144
ISBN 13: 9781450549141

Dedicated to:

Peter H. Morley

The Reverend Ralph Urmson Taylor

Donald L. Paige

PROLOGUE

"The left hand of God," Allie used to say, "that's the one you've got to look out for."

With his head cocked so far sideways it made his neck look out of joint, Allie would be staring straight into the eyes of Tate or Moller or Joey and delivering his exhortation with all the authority of the Pope on amphetamines. "Without the slightest hint or clue," he would continue, "this one they call the Lord of Glory will pull the world out from under you like the tablecloth at a third-rate magic show."

Allie's voice would strain higher with the intensity of his words as his friends nodded their bemused approval. "I'm serious," he would say, "He's got this heavenly host of banana peels spread out beneath the feet of your best laid plans and I mean it, man, He will reach down out of the clouds and pop your jockstrap into the middle of next week."

After a short pause for dramatic effect, Allie's voice would level out into the tone of a television newscaster. "Just face it boys," he would say with quiet authority, "we're nothing but straight men for the everlasting King of Comedy."

Then Allie's voice would change again, transforming him into a wise professor as his eyes betrayed the strangest sense of understanding. "But, it's okay," he would say, "it's cool, because the bottom line is this: He only makes you laugh . . . to keep you from crying.

"Trust me, boys," he would whisper, leaning in closer, "the greatest moments in life come down from the left hand of God . . ."

Taking out a quick bit of vengeance on the gas pedal of his car, Tate Henry nursed the ancient pain in his heart as he pulled out into the traffic. Behind him a towering wall of thunderclouds hovered between the houses and the tree tops and billowed up into the open sky. The first strong winds of the impending spring storm beat against the back of his car, as if pushing him impatiently towards his destination that afternoon. A jagged streak of lightning lit up his rear view mirror and then announced itself with a clap that seemed to vibrate the steering wheel in Tate's hands. Just as his thoughts began to drift off towards the drive ahead of him he was startled by an object flying past the front of his car—a cardboard box rolling like a foreboding bundle of tumbleweed caused him to slam his foot to the brake momentarily before he let off with a quick sigh and settled into his journey. He was on his way to his first major rendezvous with his old friends in more than twenty years.

Allie's words were never far from Tate. It had been a long time since the left hand of God was the guiding force in the lives of their childhood, still Tate could recall Allie's speeches on a moment's notice. These principles had been their creed; this theology was its own justification for a reckless testing of its very limit. It was a brilliant theory played up to an end both bitter and sweet in Tate's memory. Smiling as the pain in his heart grew warm again, Tate took a breath and began to relive an entire tumultuous year from long ago.

Indian summer, he remembered, it had been so hot at the first.

In Tate's mind, Allie's irresistible smile played against that look of deep, boyish sorrow in Joey, while Moller's inquisitive gaze peeked out from behind his dangling swirls of black hair. How quickly the images of hilarious pranks and long, wistful car rides gave way to the accelerated scenes of Joey's nightmares and the aching memory of the Mayor in the hospital bed and the Safari Wagon spinning out of control with the four of them inside.

Feeling himself about to begin that spin again, Tate had to pull himself up short and demand order of his thoughts. What was the message of these memories from a childhood never finished, a youth interrupted by a tinny announcement over some primitive public address system crackling with words Tate could never quite make out? What did it all mean?

The years had yielded no answer, even after some twenty-five of them had passed. So here was Tate now, returning again to the scene of all that great drama, as if the stage sets and scenery were left up long after the production had left town. He pulled into the parking lot of Somerset School, steered his car into his favorite old parking space and turned off the engine to his car. Outside, the thunderclouds had almost outpaced him. The entire sky was filled with black and gray moving clouds, and the wind around him was pelting his car with little bits of sand and chat lifted from the asphalt parking lot. Tate gazed across the parking lot at the silent school building awaiting his return.

PROLOGUE

Like fellow actors returning to an empty theater, Allie and Moller would be there too, summoned to the school by their old mentor and friend, Father David Miles, whose retirement as chaplain of Somerset School was the official occasion for the reunion of the three old friends. The unofficial and more compelling reason for their presence was, of course, the ongoing mystery of Joey. The notes from Father Miles to Tate, Allie and Moller had promised new information about the tragic events of their senior year. Tate had no doubt that Allie and Moller would be there and that the mysterious news would be about Joey.

Before he could open the door to his car, Tate felt his thoughts returning yet again to those haunting and familiar images. As if preparing himself for some command performance before that ever-present and invisible jury of his peers, Tate allowed himself to recreate the earliest scenes of a play that had long been absorbed into his innermost being. Closing his eyes, he leaned against the accepting leather seat of his car and drifted back to those days with Allie and Moller and Joey, to a time when the creativity of a child still occupied a stronghold against the dark, encroaching forces of the times, and the universe was ruled, however tentatively, by the left hand of God.

CHAPTER ONE

THE MAGIC EMPIRE

A red plastic disk sailed over the heads of three hundred bored students toward the beloved target of their death wish. Headmaster Martin droned on with his speech. He was oblivious to the violent emotions stirring in the impatient hearts of his captive audience. He was unaware of the shiny red expression of those feelings now sailing smoothly towards him. He was completely engaged in his self-congratulatory speech, bidding "Farewell to the Old Campus" and saying "Hello to A Bright New Era," but he was about to be interrupted by a humble intruder from the nearby regions of the Unexplainable.

"Duck!" shouted the Dean of Students, but it was too late. The red blur struck the Headmaster on the center of his forehead and bounced off to one side where it landed neatly in the lap of Father David Miles. Father Miles smiled in spite of himself and handed the object apologetically to the headmaster, stating the obvious in a way that made it seem helpful:

"It's a Frisbee, sir."

Behind the mass of students, near the point where the Frisbee had appeared, Allie Reed retreated swiftly from the borders of the Unexplainable and cut quickly through the woods behind the amphitheater. A few moments later he casually re-entered the World of the Normal and, escaping notice by way of his sheer gift for nonchalance, took an aisle seat near the front of the amphitheater.

"Great speech," he would tell Mr. Martin later, as if he had been hanging onto every word.

In the meantime, however, Allie had more pressing matters on his mind. It was Indian summer in Oklahoma, and it was hot. He and his classmates were seated on folding metal chairs in the full noon-hour sun, dressed in the kinds of clothes you buy for the fall season, when the hopeful visions of brisk autumn days loom more real than the blistering summer heat just outside the air-conditioned unreality of the clothing store. Allie had taken a seat next to his best friend and accomplice, Tate Henry. Leaning toward him, he whispered in mock earnestness, "Tate, I'm frying in my seat."

"It's jumpy underwear to the max," agreed Tate. "I've heard a guy won a case for justifiable homicide under conditions no worse than these."

"It's worth a chance," said Allie. Suddenly he jumped from his chair screaming "Fire!" and throwing the metal contraption into the air as if it were some sort of Age of Technology hot potato. There was a universal sigh of relief from the students and then a great outburst of laughter as they realized Allie had escaped the fictitious blaze and was frantically working his way toward the fountain at the front of the amphitheater, tossing the chair in front of him. So convincing was Allie's charade that as he dropped the hot tempered steel into the cool water, a cartoon sizzle seemed to emanate from the fountain. With a burst of spontaneous applause, the crowd acknowledged its gratitude at having witnessed that diabolical device of slow torture tossed into the drink.

Allie beamed with satisfaction even as he was silently addressing himself to the very delicate problem of fitting his explosive vignette into the otherwise dull flow of the Farewell to the Old Campus Ceremony. Three hundred students and faculty members had just been jerked from the silent spaces of three hundred separate universes to focus for one fleeting moment on the same ridiculous bit of life on earth, and that was Allie's goal. But now it was part of the trick to return everyone to the World of Normal in a way that avoided any serious repercussions. This Allie did by simply fishing his chair out of the fountain with such an air of, "Well now, that's better", that everyone had to agree and the meeting was quietly resumed.

With the exception of the permanently annoyed Gabin Stone, the teachers and administrators seemed predisposed that day towards giving the likes of Allie a break. There was a certain awareness among them that the transition to the new campus might be more difficult for the older students, and this awareness translated into a kind of leniency, particularly as regards the various forms of creative tomfoolery for which the school had always exercised some restraint in terms of discipline. A few of the teachers might have been seen smiling wistfully themselves at Allie's antics, as even some of the faculty wondered how the transition would play out in their own lives.

In any case, with his first two strikes of the year having met with such success and no sign of immediate reprisals, Allie was glad to endure the rest of the Headmaster's speech, shouting a pleasantly sarcastic "hooooray" when the meeting ended and the students were sent to buses and cars waiting to head for the new campus. Feeling euphoric over his direct hit with the Frisbee, Allie was walking with Tate to his car, explaining to him in a melodramatic monologue the subtleties of the fountain performance and the wonderful reception it had received from an audience not always so sensitive to his efforts. He was working, of course, to convince his friend that the whole thing should be featured in the inaugural edition of the school newspaper at the new campus. Tate was the editor-in-chief of the highly acclaimed tabloid, a position he at least pretended to defend against Allie's otherwise complete occupation of his life.

"It's copy, Tate. First class copy. It has all the elements of a great story and I know you can pull it off. "

Suddenly a familiar face distracted Allie's eye across the courtyard. "Moller! Hey, Moller! Welcome back to reality, boy!" Allie was waving to their friend Michael Moller, who answered from the distance with a slightly raised eyebrow and the faintest of smiles. "Hey, Moller, did you get any pics this morning?" Allie was gesturing with eyes toward the scene at the fountain. "You know, prize-winning photos?"

From beneath long black hair that curled down and wrapped around most of his face, Moller cracked a slightly more noticeable smile and, hardly looking up, raised a couple fingers of acknowledgment to his friend as he nodded a mystically charged "yes" to Allie before he disappeared into a group of passing students.

"There, you see?" shrieked Allie, turning back to Tate, "Moller's even got pics! Tell me it isn't meant to be! What do you say Tate? Is it page one or what?"

At that, Tate stopped and looked at Allie as if he were crazy.

"Okay, Tate, maybe not page one, but it's good copy. You can find just the right spot for it. Think about it. It's great public interest. I mean, how many times have you been fried in one of those worthless metal chairs, you know? You could come on to the reader like, 'At the new campus there will *never be* metal chairs out in the sun again.' Think of it! Old alums would read it and say 'hurray for that!' Parents everywhere would want to send their kids to a school where they could count on climate control. All the good teachers would want to teach there. Why, Headmouster Martin would probably put you on salary as his new head of Public Relations, start letting you go to all the cocktail parties and stuff. I'm telling you man, it would be a great career move for you. So what do you say, Tate? Four-column pic plus story?"

"You're crazy, Allie." Tate was smiling and shaking his head. He knew all Allie needed at this point was a little resistance and the scene would be complete.

"Crazy? What do you mean crazy? Who am I talking to here, Citizen Cane? Is this some sort of conservative creep cover-up or what? I mean, this is news, buddy, news! And...and"—now Allie was shifting gears—"this is our year." Allie turned away for a moment, shoved the heels of his hands into his eyes and rubbed them until they were red with Hollywood tears. Then he turned back around to his patiently waiting straight man and continued. "This is our year, Tate. It's been twelve years in this place and finally we're seniors, do you know what that means? Do you know what a big deal that is? It's our Grand Finale, our Magnum Opus". By now Allie's chest was heaving with painfully restrained fake sobs. "It's our day in the sun. Our fond farewell." Then he straightened up a bit. "And, plus," he continued, "it's the first year of a whole new era. Think about it, man. It's like we're the Last of the Mohicans, except we're Mohicanning on into the next phase. Yeah, it's like a movie sequel—Sons of the Last Mohican—and we're it. We're the guardians of the Old Regime, pioneering our people into this whole new era, carrying the torch of old Somerset School and all that it stands for, carrying the Get itself like the Arc of the Covenant and it's important. So we've got to start it off right. If we don't tell them, how are they going to know?"

"You could always take out an ad."

"Funny. Very funny. My best friend is the editor of the freakin'school newspaper and he wants me to buy an ad about myself. I guess if I died you'd want my parents to spring for the space for my memorial. Great pal."

"Cheer up, Allie. You'll probably be up for boy of the Month by April or May at the latest. We'll run a story then."

"Oh, hilarious. Maybe you should just step down as editor and do a cartoon strip or something. No, I'm serious, man. I'll be very disappointed if we don't see some ink on this one. I mean, all these oaths about the true Gets winning their just acclaim this year. You know? Where's the All-for-One and One-for-All, already? I mean, Hi-o Silver, Tate, let's have some copy!"

By then they were at the car and Tate dodged the end of Allie's rampage by ducking into the passenger seat. Allie's car was one of those old flat-topped Volvo sports cars that looked and felt like an airplane cockpit on wheels. Lowering himself into the driver's seat, Allie abandoned his campaign with Tate in deference to the sound of his engine firing up. He put the air conditioner on full blast and cranked up his radio. Then he put the car in gear and they were off. Charging through the gates of the old campus they went rolling through the tree-lined neighborhoods laughing and then silent, leaning into the turns and, soon, thinking and talking about the past.

"Somerset School," Allie was saying, "the Country Club approach to education. It's been great, man."

Tate's thoughts traveled with Allie as they wandered back through the filtered light of their common past. Long ago, the two friends had together stepped through the heavy gates of pre-memory childhood into the clear light of the schoolyard. There was a classroom there, and the striking image of a woman's face atop a friendly, but imposing, frame. Stern and larger than life, she was in the throes of a good scolding when suddenly her expression froze in pure shock and then melted into a smile she could not restrain. Allie had earlier replaced the prized antique flower vase on her desk with a cheap glass one, which was then "carelessly broken" by Allie. With her in mid-tirade, the poker-faced young Allie had quietly produced the real vase and smiled. He had tricked her: the whole thing was a set-up. The teacher could not help but be impressed by this seven-year-old's ability to perceive—and deflate—her mild material obsession.

She could not help but laugh.

So had begun Allie's long and legendary career. With Tate and the others there to support and inspire him, Allie had taken up the mantle of his older brother and their friends in pursuing a combination of comedically induced social reform and artistic expression known as the Get. The ultimate weapon for pulling down the Strongholds of the Serious, the Get was there to search out and destroy the dark bastions of human hearts trapped in empty traditions and unhealthy attachments. It existed to undermine the rules and regulations of good intentions gone astray or outdated, setting itself against any individual or institution who denied the simple truth that life was ultimately good and meant to be enjoyed. The Get was the practical joke par excellence. It was the ticklish thorn in the flesh, the punch line at Custer's Last Stand. It was the wink at the world's end.

THE LAST GET

Tate smiled as he and Allie daydreamed together. By the time they had entered their freshman year, their many exploits earned them full status as Keepers of the Get, an unofficial honor bestowed upon younger pranksters by the upper-class guardians of the tradition. Willingly enlisted in the upper ranks of this informal army of clowns, Allie and his peers had joined in the war waged mainly against the group they called the "Slumberset." This enemy camp was inhabited by most of the Somerset teachers and administrators plus an always-alarming number of students, and it had long been the main mission field for the Keepers of the Get. All that was about to change.

"We'll be fighting a battle on two fronts, man," said Allie in the midst of their long journey of thought. "All the usual elbow-heads in the Slumberset will be trying to lay the same old stuffiness on us—and then we'll have all these new kids who won't know a Get from a hand grenade."

"No kidding," agreed Tate, shaking his head. "I still can't believe they're doing this to us. Twelve years in the hallowed halls of our forefathers and then they toss us out onto the streets and into the bowels of an academic factory. They could have at least waited for our class to graduate."

"Seriously," said Allie. "All this 'Dawning of a New Era' stuff is the biggest joke since the Edsel. The seventies are going to have a hard enough time following the sixties without getting us all hyped up about—what was it the Headmouster called it?—the 'emergence of new values and a new agenda.' Agenda, my ass: the way I see it, they just needed some new angle for raising money. Why didn't they just have a couple bake sales and car washes, for Christ's sake, instead of coming up with this jillion-dollar-campus-and-a-bunch-of-new-kids-idea? Man, I'd have baked a couple dozen brownies personally just to avoid this mess."

"Definitely," said Tate. "We could have car washed to the max all summer . . . you know, put the cheerleaders out on Riverside Drive in their bikinis. Sex and Suds Fundraisers . . . man, it works every time. They should've asked us. We could have pulled it off without ruining the whole school."

"No lie," continued Allie. "Instead, it's the Stalinization of Somerset School. They're bringing in the Public School proletariat so we better get wise. If we don't get counter-revolutionary quick we'll be mug shots in the history books of the future: 'Former Members of the Now Defunct Aristocracy in America . . . the Displaced Ruling Class . . . Figureheads We Have Known . . .' Man, I hate the way all that sounds."

"Yeah, and while we're fighting off that threat, " said Tate, "we've got to keep up the internal vigilance on the Old Guard. They'll be trying hard themselves to stifle things in all the usual ways."

Allie nodded as they fell back into thought. This had been the plan since that summer, when the reality of the impending changes at Somerset School had finally begun to break through to Allie and the others. With an unspoken sense of ceremony that was their trademark, Allie and Tate and their closest friends had joined together in a solemn pact. In celebration of their senior year as faithful guardians of the Holy Grail known as the Get, they would launch an all-out offensive against the usual bastions of Seriousness among the Old Guard while addressing as diligently the imminent attacks of an over-achieving enemy sending fresh troops into the fray. And the war, it was agreed, was to begin at the opening ceremonies.

Though it had begun well-enough, what with Allie's success at the "Farewell to the Old Campus" speech, that was still the old campus, and here they were now, driving away from the safety of their domain, rolling inevitably into uncharted regions of their rapidly expanding city. As they drove towards the edge of their neighborhoods, Tate and Allie fell deeper into their reverie about all those things they might be leaving behind. All around them the towering oaks and arching elms created a massive vaulted ceiling of feathery green leaves and thick brown branches broken only by the occasional opening where cotton white clouds sailed dreamily against the rich blue sky. Underneath this windowed canopy, huge expanses of lush green lawns and long driveways carried the eyes of Tate and Allie to the beautiful, architectural facades of the familiar mansions and estates of their storied childhood.

This was the residential heart of a place called the Magic Empire, an unlikely oasis of incredible wealth carved out of the rolling hills of northeastern Oklahoma. Here the wide, muddy waters of the Arkansas River made a gentle bend through the center of a tiny city where the skyscrapers on one bank looked out over a vast borough of oil tank farms on the other side of the river. Like a set of regal chess pieces overlooking a humble game of checkers, these glass and concrete towers ruled over their ironclad subjects with dignity and grace. The names on the buildings downtown corresponded with company logos attached to each of the refineries across the river: Skelly, Phillips, Sinclair, Getty. This was Tulsa, a place many still called the Oil Capital of the World, a city once inhabited by more millionaires per capita than anywhere on the planet.

At the beginning of the twentieth century, the area that would soon become the state of Oklahoma was a sprawling badlands of traders, homesteaders and displaced American Indians. Throughout the eastern half of the area, Irish immigrants slightly outnumbered their English, French and Spanish counterparts. The western half, known officially as Indian Territory, was divided among the tribes native to the surrounding regions and their tragically transported cousins from the Five Civilized Tribes. The latter had been forcibly removed by the geniuses of the US Government from their homes and sacred hunting lands in Florida, Georgia and Tennessee and shipped off to their newly allotted lands in "The Territory."

In the rolling hills of the northeast part of the state, a small town had sprung up along the Arkansas River, first as a trading center and then as one of a hundred little centers of commerce for the ranchers and farmers surrounding it. Originally called Tulsey Town, the name was shortened to "Tulsa" just in time for its emergence as one of the most famous towns in the history of American business. What put Tulsa on the map was oil.

The year was 1905 and America was just getting its footing in the age of fossil-burning fuel. The tarry stuff called "crude oil" had already proven itself as a source for lamp oil when the tinkering inventors of the internal combustion engine made a startling discovery. It seems that the liquid waste created in the refining process for lamp oil was perfect for igniting in the chambers of those little engines that were about to make America great. Gasoline was born and with it the already growing demand for crude oil became instantly insatiable. In America, the golden ring was suddenly coated in petroleum.

Significant oil finds in Oklahoma had been sporadically earning the attention of dreamers and promoters for some years, when a strike just west of Tulsa created an oil boomtown overnight. A few months later a massive "pool" was discovered beneath the dusty earth of the widow Ida Glenn's acreage just ten miles south of Tulsa. A black fountain of oil gushed over 200 feet in the air and took three days to control. Within days the word of the so-called "Glenn Pool" had spread to both coasts and the boom became a lasting economic windfall for the entire region with Tulsa at its center.

The grandparents of both Allie and Tate played dramatic roles in the early days of Tulsa's glory years. Allie's paternal grandfather, Whitman Reed, was an independent oil producer with a string of luck that came just at the peak of Tulsa's first boom. He was one of about a dozen so-called "wild-catters" whose success spawned the names of many oil companies still operating today. Known as "Whit", he grew his early successes into a five-state kingdom of drilling operations and retail gas stations before deciding to sell his company to one of his friends. As hoped, the bidding war for his operation came down to a "pissing contest" between his friends, Bill Skelly and J. Paul Getty, that pushed its selling price well beyond fair market value. In the end, Reed Oil Company was bought by Skelly Oil and absorbed into that venerable brand, and Allie's grandfather walked away with enough stock in Skelly to allow Allie's father a life of passive investing and philanthropic endeavors.

Tate's maternal grandfather was an attorney who specialized in the oil business at that same time. In those days, lawyers would often forego their legal fees in exchange for a share of the profits should the well "come in". His fortune was established by a string of these kinds of deals and then greatly multiplied when he became a capital investor in many more wells. His only daughter married a bright young lawyer named James Henry, who also happened to be the nephew of another pioneering oil man, Frank Phillips. Soon after Tate was born, his father's mild political aspirations culminated in a tenure as the Mayor of Tulsa, at which point his love of public life, in his own words, was outmatched by his love of leisure. And so he retired. "Hey," he would later explain, "I already had the title," a fact that allowed all his friends—and Tate's as well, to refer to him simply as "The Mayor."

The silent reminders of Tulsa's unprecedented days of wealth were everywhere as Allie and Tate as they made their exodus through the beautiful neighborhoods surrounding the original Somerset campus. They had already rolled passed the Sinclair Mansion and the Getty Estate just beyond the driveway of the old campus. By now, they could see the tall white columns of the Skelly Mansion ahead on the right, towering behind the wrought iron fence surrounding it. Their last stop before leaving these hallowed streets would be the sprawling grounds of the Waite Phillips Estate, former home of Frank's younger brother.

A few moments later, Tate and Allie found themselves at a stop sign on the far edge of that estate. Pulled from their pleasant musings by the noticeable rush of traffic on the thoroughfare leading south, the two friends couldn't help but stare into the future for a moment, pondering the rise of the middle class like a couple of princes about to be exiled. Aristocracy and tradition, wealth and position, these were things Allie and his friends had always assumed they could take or leave. But that was before they began their exile to south Tulsa.

"This is it," said Allie with a sigh. Then, with a final glance into the tiny world of his rear-view mirror, he took another deep breath, put his foot to the accelerator, and turned his car out onto the open streets.

Allie stared ahead at the wide road taking them out of the old neighborhoods and pointing them towards the campus that was to be their new home. He pressed his lips together and leaned forward a bit. Tate knew his friend was about to wax poetic in one of his rambling monologue pep talks and he shifted in his seat, glad to listen in.

"Well, remember, Tate," Allie began, "no matter how many new kids are out there, it's still our place. This may be the end of an era, but it's still our era, right? The Arab sheiks are building golf courses and country clubs in the desert, and the tour buses are circling over Woodstock like buzzards, and here we are about to be over-run by overachievers with pocket calculators and fast-food coupons, but we've still got a few tricks up our sleeves. The Divine Right of Kings thing is on the ropes again and Survival of the Fittest is getting another day in the arena, so it's time to show 'em how we princes got here in the first place. We'll pull out the Get and give them Survival of the Shrewdest one more time, Tate old boy, and then we'll lock 'em up in fast food concentration camps and throw away the key."

At the mention of his name, Tate realized his mind had been wandering. "Right," he said quickly, but he had missed Allie's last few sentences. For the past few months, he had been less able to lose himself in Allie's visions, and that made him sad and even a little scared. He shook his head and tried to concentrate as Allie took up his oratory again.

"This is not a democracy we've got going here, pal," he continued, "so let's hear it for the ruling elite, which is us. No matter how many of theses public school plebes they have to let in to fill all the empty space out there, we're still the school, the Keepers of the Get, right? I mean, most of those new kids are younger anyway, since they had to let in mostly underclassmen, and what are underclassmen anyway but part of the prep school peasantry? More subjects . . . a bigger following . . . a larger audience . . . more targets for the right Get. It'll be great. And all in honor of our senior year. What a deal . . . "

As Allie went on with his dreamy monologues, Tate was smiling, nodding, quietly leaning into the curves with his friend, but he was also somewhere else. Allie had most likely noticed the whole time, but he wasn't letting on that he knew what was happening with Tate. Things were a lot more serious than Allie and the others ever talked about and they all knew it, but that was part of the deal: it wasn't any good to let on.

As they saw it, things were better kept light. The world was full of people who spent their lives overwhelmed by the heaviness of it all, and Allie and the others felt this strange sense of responsibility not to give into that sort of thing. Somewhere along the line they had all picked up the unspoken understanding that they of all people should be able to keep things light. After all, they had everything. It was theirs without asking and they usually felt that enjoying it was the least they could do. They were at times very aware of the poverty and pain in the world, but they had resolved not to let the heaviness of it all overwhelm them. And so they fought it off with every joke and stunt they could come up with.

That's where the Get came in, and there was some zany sense of righteousness to it all, as if the best Gets were sobering blasts from heaven itself, little reminders from the left hand of God, administered by their merry band of Episcopal misfits, too old to be choir boys, too young to be priests. Not that the Keepers themselves would ever speak such ideas out loud. These things were rarely discussed in those terms at all. It had always been understood that saying too much could somehow threaten to entangle even the Get itself in the whirlpooling madness of a world lost in its sense of self-importance.

No, for this life at least, the essence of the Get could only be shared in that certain twinkling of the eye, in the eternal Moment of Impact of a great stunt or punch line, in the hilarious realization that someone had been caught taking himself too seriously. That was indeed the calling of this little foursome entering their last year at school: to spread the joy of life's most inspired banana peels beneath the unsuspecting feet of the world's tyrants of the Serious, to proclaim belly-laughing liberty to the captives of that ego centric system, and to keep themselves unstained by the heaviness that had set in like a cloud upon their civilization.

This was the plan. And Tate tried hard to keep all these things in mind as Allie paid homage to them again in his eloquent way. As for the other things beginning to weigh so heavily on Tate's mind, it would not do to bring them up now. If there were a dark specter of seriousness hovering on the horizon of his life, they would have to deal with it later. For now Tate would have to laugh off his fears once again and be with Allie in his cockeyed pep talk, pretending that such things were all they knew.

CHAPTER TWO

THE SLUMBER SET

"There they are, Tate: the Enemy. Take a good look at 'em and tell me what you think." Allie was peering over his steering wheel as he cruised through the parking lot of the new campus. Three public school defectors, new members of the Slumberset, were climbing out of a shiny GTO and getting their first lasting look at the new Promised Land.

"Serious, Allie," Tate was saying. "They look serious."

"Yeah," said Allie, "Check out the guy with the madras sports jacket. Don't anyone tell him he's about two years late with that get-up. Other than that, he looks like a real ladies' man."

"Yeah, and his buddy's got him his first double-breasted jacket," Tate observed. "Luckily, I heard that they're coming back in."

"Great! And the car, man! Can you believe that hot-rod?" Allie leaned his head back and laughed. "These guys must get their kicks . . . on Route 66!"

"Wait a minute, Allie, give 'em a break," said Tate with mock compassion, "Maybe they've got summer jobs making beach movies or something." They both laughed and then Allie sat up straighter, watching.

"Boy, they're sure checking things out," said Allie a little more seriously. A group of freshman girls walked past and the three new students were giving them a long once-over, and somehow it bugged Allie. Never mind the fact that he would have done the same thing in the situation—this was different. And it was a call to action.

Allie wheeled right up in front of the main doors to the school where the new guys were still primping for their grand entrance. He stopped the car just within earshot.

"All right," he said quietly, "We need to Get these guys right here." Then he rolled down his window and yelled a happy, "Say fellas! Pardon me, boys! Yes, you guys. Could you come here a second?"

They eyed Allie inquisitively as the guy with the madras jacket led the way for his friends to the window of the car. He was a little nervous, trying to get his bearings on his first day at Somerset School. "Uh, yes, did you want something?"

Allie smiled innocently and in his friendliest voice said, "Yes, I was wondering if you could tell me where to find the gabala."

"The what?" replied Mr. Madras.

"No, the where," said Allie.

"The what where?" asked the guy.

"No, just the where," said Allie patiently.

"I know," said the guy, getting a little exasperated, "but where is the what?"

Then Allie smiled. He had him. "Well, I don't know," he said, then he pointed towards Tate, "you'd probably have to ask my friend here...he knows more about that than I do."

Now, this poor guy was trying so hard to make good on his first social encounter that he wasn't giving up yet. He looked at Tate and asked him, "Do you know what he means?" like Allie was a foreign exchange student from Russia or somewhere, and Tate looked at him with big, open eyes and sort of half-screamed a very friendly litany of fake Russian explanations, "Oi! Alga van mrishkatov! Illya emish kraektow mikihlta va," all the time grinning and nodding his head like the good old Russian boy that Mr. Madras had in mind for Allie.

About that time Allie was hitting the button for the window washer on his Volvo, which he had long ago modified to spray in an arching shot outward from the hood of his car. From that angle, Mr. Madras was getting light spray from directly overhead, which can only feel like fly-by bird droppings when it's too clear a day for rain, so by now the guy was looking up for birds, which were nonexistent, and looking for his friends, who by then had gone in, and looking back at Allie and Tate, who were happily gazing back at him with the blank gaping cheerfulness of a couple of over-eager immigrants.

"Well, thanks anyway, man," said Allie finally. Then he slipped the car into gear, looked up at Mr. Madras and, with a twinkle in his eye, added, "And welcome to the Slumber Set."

After finding their way to the section of the parking lot marked "Seniors Only"—"It's the least they can do," griped Allie—the two friends made their way across the newly laid gravel and fresh black asphalt towards the main building of the new campus.

The largest of the four sprawling buildings comprising Phase One of the school's Ten-Year Plan was the Upper School building. At two-and-a-half stories tall, the only gesture towards grandeur was the expansive roof space above the huge central room about to be introduced as "The Commons." Otherwise, all of the buildings were designed in the understated style in vogue at the time. Exposed steel beams supported long, low rooflines. The walls were brick in some areas and fashionably unfinished concrete in others. Long rectangular windows adorned mostly the upper third of each floor, letting in lots of light but not allowing for the kind of view most suited for class time daydreaming. To soften the somewhat stark appearance of the buildings, there were terra cotta lamp sconces along the outer walls, teakwood benches here and there, and extensive landscape plantings throughout. Still, Allie and Tate were not impressed.

"It's Frank Lloyd Wright meets the Berlin Bomb Factory," observed Tate as they approached the building.

Allie nodded thoughtfully in agreement. Then, as was his gift, he summed it up even more succinctly. "Yep," he said, "it's Blank Lloyd Wright."

Inside the main entrance, the huge Commons was overwhelming in sheer scale. Towering columns of unfinished concrete rose some thirty feet to support the steel beamed roof of the giant, square room. A wood parquet floor warmed up the room a little bit—as did the rather impressive copper and terra cotta lamp fixtures hanging from the steel rafters—but the overall feel of the room was provided by its sheer size.

"It's a barn," exclaimed Allie.

"Hangar Number One," chimed in Tate.

After a few moments of disbelief, however, Allie and Tate quickly began to wake up to the possibilities of the place.

"It does have some serious playground potential," said Allie as he eyed the columns in rows, the mezzanine that overlooked the main floor, and the many nooks and hallways at the outer perimeters of the room. Spotting a large hallway that disappeared around a long curve, Allie gave Tate's arm a tug and said, "Come on, let's check this place out."

Looking like a couple of casual bloodhounds on the scent, Allie and Tate made the rounds through the main building, quickly realizing that an enormous amount of thought and financial resources had been poured into the new school.

"Somebody spent some money in this place," said Allie as they surveyed the new chemistry lab.

"Man, I hope they're not expecting us to find a cure for cancer or something," said Tate.

"Come on," grinned Allie, "we'll be lucky to find the gym."

From the beginning, Allie had been the fearless leader. As a young boy, he had never been pushy or overbearing but was instead just so animated in whatever he was doing that others were drawn to him without effort. As he grew older, his lean, tall frame added to his natural attraction as it helped him to rise aristocratically over most situations, even when the gentle mayhem he created was clearly his doing. He had a thick head of brown hair that called to mind the Kennedy's, whose golden age of Camelot had come and gone during Allie's middle years. His brown eyes were handsome but not extraordinary – until his crooked smile ignited them into an irresistible glow of earnestly offered friendship and adventure. His keen sense of observation informed these friendships and endeavors with an intellectual sensibility, but it was his pure comic genius and timing that were his greatest trademarks.

Tate, meanwhile, was the perfect straight man and accomplice. He had a broad, soft face and gentle blue eyes that conveyed a certain sincerity, even vulnerability. Despite the fact that he came up with some fine pranks in his own right, Tate generally played the part of willing assistant. His look of natural innocence was often commandeered by Allie for use in his more elaborate pranks. If there was much serious groundwork to lay for a Get, Tate was the man for the job. If it was necessary to convince someone that they were really shooting straight, it was time to send in Tate. For better and worse, this probably worked so well because Tate actually was sincere: while some people were nothing but punch lines looking for a sucker at all costs, Tate was more apt to be looking for sincerity and just couldn't help giving in to the Get side of the situation, if it came up. And with Allie around, it usually came up.

"Check this out," exclaimed Allie. They had burst into the doors of the new gym at full speed and were genuinely impressed.

"Helloooo in there," shouted Tate, listening for the echo of his voice from the towering rafters above them.

"This place looks like the damn Astro-dome," yelled Allie. Completely awed, it was suddenly too much for the two of them to experience alone. Then Allie had a thought. "Hey, Tate, this place is an indoor Frisbee Heaven," he shouted to his friend. "Let's go get the Fris' and try this out."

"Right." agreed Tate, "but let's round up Moller and Joey first."

"Good point," said Allie.

Back in the Commons, Allie and Tate were awed again, this time by the flash of so many faces, old and new, populating this place that was to be the new Somerset. At first, their friends were nowhere to be found.

"I can't get over this building," said Allie as they continued their search. "It's as ugly as an ape, but the scale is just so impressive."

"Maybe they didn't have time to finish it," suggested Tate as he pointed to the open rafters and unfinished concrete that were the strange rave of a period of architecture perhaps by now forgotten.

"Maybe so," agreed Allie. "Classic architecture it certainly is not, but there's something kind of compelling here . . . "

"Speaking of classic architectural features," interrupted Tate, "here come a couple wonders of the world." He was beaming at someone approaching him, and Allie turned to see the bright smiles of Emily and Sarah, arms swinging, hair and skirts bouncing.

"Hi, you guys!" they were saying as they wrapped their arms around each of their old friends and exchanged warm hugs. Emily Stone and Sarah York had been around since Day One. Along with Tate and Allie, they were the only other Somerset "Lifers" in the present graduating class. By now, they were all the best of friends. As it worked out, Tate and Allie didn't have steady girlfriends that year. They had each had their share of long-term romances over the years—given the fact that anything over six months was considered long-term—but somehow they were both "between relationships" at present. This was all right by them, partly because they found Emily and Sarah to be much better friends than a girlfriend could seemingly be. They had found things much easier without the strange possessiveness that seemed to come from trying to make a steady go of it, which all seemed to add up to nothing more than make-out privileges anyway, which by then wasn't worth it. They could always get a few good kisses off Emily and Sarah at a party or out cruising in the car, and the rest of it just didn't seem worth it right then. And somehow, not getting too close seemed to keep them all a lot closer in the long run.

"So what do you girls think?" Allie spread out his hands to the vista of the new school with genuine interest in the girls' opinion of the deal. He was sincerely charming, as if the girls' approval of the place would totally determine its acceptance by he and Tate, and the girls loved to play the role.

"Well, it's pretty nice," said Emily first.

"Needs a woman's touch, maybe," said Sarah with a flair for playing out Allie's scene, "But I like it."

"Well, if *you* like it," said Allie with all his heart, "then we'll just make the best of it, too."

The girls just smiled and ate it up.

"Men of Destiny! Control your Fate!" It was Michael Moller, and he burst onto the scene with uncharacteristic abandon. He was glad to see his friends.

"Moller!" shouted Allie back. "You drugged dog, how are you doing?"

"*Doing*?!" shrieked Moller in reply. "I am not *doing* at all, my poor, imprisoned slave of Western Thinking." He was shaking Allie's hand and pushing his friend playfully. "I am *being*!"

"Yeah, right, guru-boy," said Allie dryly. "So how are you *being*?"

"Fine, thanks," said Moller quickly and, with his point apparently made, he smiled brightly at Tate. "Hey, boy. What's news?"

"Not much, Michael," Tate said, shaking his friend's hand.

"And our lovely Guinneverian friends?" asked Moller without sarcasm as he turned to Emily and Sarah.

"Hi, Michael," said Emily. "How have you been?"

"No, Em," interrupted Sarah sternly. "It's how are you being. Always in the present, honey, gotta keep it in the Here and Now.

"Right!" said Moller, beaming with the feeling that his latest philosophical stance had been so quickly grasped by his feminine friend. "Always a pleasure to re-unite with a fellow mystic, Sarah, and how are you?" He had taken her hand and they were sharing a warm look between the lines.

"Oh, this *fellow* mystic is fine. It's always good to be one of the guys again." She smiled in a way that qualified her as one of the guys and then some. "And how are you, really?"

"Fine, kid, thanks," said Moller quietly. When all was said and done, Michael Moller was probably the most purely intellectual member of the group. He had come to Somerset in his freshman year, a product of a well-traveled childhood, his father being a brilliant petroleum engineer whose talents were highly sought by corporations near and far. Moller's variety of experience far surpassed that of his friends, but it seemed to humble him more than make him into some sort of expert, in the offensive way some kids in that situation turn out.

Moller's long, curly hair was his calling card. He was always pushing it back out of his face as a token social gesture of some kind, since it immediately fell right back where it was, hiding him from view once again. He looked like some sort of French prince come to modern times—royalty and intelligence framed with a certain disheveled look. That was part of the basic Somerset profile really, the kind of European-prince-in-beat-up-sneakers look, but whereas Allie and Tate leaned toward the British side of the bloodline, Michael Moller looked like he should have been riding a skateboard through the halls of Versailles. Being a little smaller, perhaps, had something to do with it, but the black, curly hair closed the case. For a time, Allie and Tate had called him "Louis" in honor of familiar portraits of Louis the Sixteenth, although there was also a reference to Louis Pasteur in the title, in reference to the scientific slant of their friend.

That was the other side of the coin. To get the complete picture of Moller, some mention must be made of the Einstein side of him. There was a scientific look about Michael Moller, the look of a guy that at any given moment was processing a mass of information on several different levels at once. At his best moments, Moller looked like a teen-aged version of Einstein himself, slightly slumped over and moving across the floor, as if in a low tunnel of thought, off to see if any clues had been missed. And even though the French prince side of the guy could not be ignored, Michael Moller was as American as it gets. He seemed to exude that American kind of curiosity and sense of adventure that somehow came across in the way he dressed and walked and even just stood around. He was always on the lookout for some latest piece of the puzzle in a life he was usually trying to figure out. And though he enjoyed a certain hermit-like, mad scientist persona, he often proved to be more deeply aware of the feelings and opinions of others than were his more gregarious running mates. For Moller, it was all about observation and information, but it was always meant to be shared.

"So what's the latest from the Old Country?" asked Allie with a grin. "Are our ancestors holding out, or are we looking at the Commies crossing London Bridge? Let's have the Full Report."

"So far, so good, boys," announced Moller on cue. "In fact, I think we'll have to worry about McDonald's taking over Europe before the Commies do. At least that's the way it looked in circles my parents drug me around in, I—"

"'*Drug*' you around in?" interrupted Allie. "Did you say they *drug* you around? Is that your grammar failing you or have we got some sort of Freudian slip there, son, a little wishful thinking maybe?" Allie was zeroing in on one of his favorite topics with Moller, namely his friend's extensive experimentation with various drugs. This was one area of experience that Allie and the others were only familiar with by way of the "Full Reports" of their friend. Allie loved to grill Moller on the subject somewhat mercilessly. "It must have been rough on you, Moller—nine weeks without pharmaceuticals of any kind—"

"Well, there was a fair amount of wine," interrupted Moller. "And although I'm not much on alcohol as you know, I think a little wine has its place... and there is quite a precedent for its use as a tool of philosophical exploration. Do you realize that wine is all Solomon used in his so-called 'experiments with folly.' Just think if he had the drugs we have today, the man would have—"

"The man would have had nothing more than another chapter of 'vanity and striving after wind,'" Allie interrupted in a hurry. "Now, come on, Moller. Sober up, son! It's school time now. Would you give us a break?"

Michael shrugged with an undaunted smile, "Well, you asked."

"I asked about the Commies, man—I want to know if the crummy Commies are taking over like the Weekly Reader warned us or not."

Willing to take his friend at face value all over again, Moller gathered his observations of the summer into a concise statement delivered like a veritable press release: "Well, the Communist threat may yet prove to be a factor in denying much of what is valuable in Europe's culture, but as I said, I would keep my eye on McDonald's."

"Big Macs in Buckingham Palace, eh?" asked Tate.

Moller nodded. "It could be bad, you know, but what are you gonna—"

Moller was interrupted by an electronic pop that cracked the air from across the Commons and was followed by a thin, reverberating voice.

"REPENT AND ESCAPE THE WRATH TO COME."

Tate and Moller whipped around and Allie put his head in his hands and groaned, "Shit. That's gotta be Joey."

"ALLIE REED, PREPARE TO MAKE AN ACCOUNTING FOR YOUR SOUL."

Laughing, Allie looked up just in time to see Joey dodging the Great Stone Face for one more blast on the bullhorn:

"THE TIME IS AT HAND, PREPARE T—"

The sound snapped off as the Great Stone Face caught hold of Joey's neck and jerked him away from his mission. Joey let his body go limp—one of his favorite tricks—and chuckled an unconvincing, "Hey, you're killing me . . ." as his captor shook him violently and dragged him to the nearest conference room door. Allie and the rest of them cracked up and shook their heads with the usual mixture of admiration and disgust.

"The Fanatical Radical rides again," said Allie.

"And he's back in the lion's den already," added Tate.

"No kidding," agreed Allie, "the Great Stone Face was hot!"

"But Joey was hanging loose!" said Moller.

"I think he's crazy," said Sarah suddenly. "Why do you guys hang out with such a dork?"

"Cause he's a great guy," said Allie without hesitation. "You just don't happen to understand him."

"Yeah, right," said Emily. "And I guess you're Mr. Spiritual yourself."

"You bet, baby," said Allie, lunging for Emily. "Come with me into the woods and I'll show you spiritual."

"That's right," said Moller, jumping in and grabbing Sarah. "It's all sin and redemption according to Joey. Let's chalk up a few on the sin side so you'll be ready for redemption."

"You freaks," shrieked Emily with a final slap and shove to Allie and Moller. "I take it back, you do need someone like Joey just to keep you in line."

"Now you're getting it," said Allie, backing off. "It never hurts to have a friend in high places, you know."

About that time, Joey re-emerged from his encounter with the Great Stone face, sans bullhorn but sporting a wide if ever tentative smile. Across the giant room that would become the Grand Central Station of their senior year wandered the final and most unlikely member of the merry band. Looking a little alone in his world as usual, Joey Liptisch made his way through groups of other students, on his way to joining his only friends. The girls excused themselves and slipped away as Allie and the others greeted their friend.

"Young Joey!" shouted Allie with a melodramatic tenderness. He waved a hand to Joey with an enthusiasm that betrayed himself—Allie had a soft spot in his heart for Joey that even being cool could not disguise. Joey was small and frail; his wire-rimmed glasses encircled deep brown eyes that mixed pain with hope in a most unsettling way. Behind his clear glasses, flashes of fear alternated with looks of profound certainty. On the surface, Joey's great internal struggles tended to make their appearance in waves of nervous banter and social awkwardness. Luckily for Joey, his oldest friends had known him from the beginning of his complicated life.

THE LAST GET

Joey was the prodigal partner of Allie, Tate and Michael Moller. He had left Somerset School in the seventh grade on exile with his newly divorced mother, not to return until the summer of their sophomore year. His mother was from a prominent Jewish family and had more or less fled the city to escape the crossfire of the ugly divorce proceedings that left scars on everyone, not the least of whom was Joey. When she returned, it was worse. In a move which was either one of the boldest or most ignorant attempts at conquering kosher condemnation, Joey's mother came back to Tulsa to face the beast of social acceptance with a new husband who was, by birth, more Catholic than a fish fry. Although the man had an obvious ambivalence for the religion of his forefathers and possessed the kind of vast wealth that normally smoothed over the worst of social outrage, the couple wasn't winning any contests with the city's Jewish culture—or the WASPS and Catholics for that matter. But there they were, back to make a go of it anyway, and here was Joey three years later, back from another predictably disastrous summer with his real father, who had himself left the city some years after the divorce.

"Hi, you guys," Joey said as he reached his friends.

There was a warm chorus of "Hey, Joey!" and "Young Joey!" and everyone was shaking his hand and pushing him around a little bit.

"Survived it again, huh, buddy?" said Allie.

"Yeah, we made it through," Joey replied with a good humor that hid all but the tiniest hint of pain.

"Hey, hold on," shrieked Allie suddenly. "What is this?" He grabbed the wooden cross that hung from Joey's neck and feigned horror. "My God, son, it's grown. What's the deal Joey, have you got yourself a religion or a disease? This cross is like a goiter. It gets bigger every time I see you."

"Lay off, heathen," cracked Joey. "With werewolves like you around, I need the biggest weapon I can get."

"But, hey, you could hurt somebody with that thing," laughed Allie.

"Guess it's his cross to bear," chimed in Tate.

"You guys are killing me," complained Joey. It was his classic line, a comically pained refrain that he seemed to sound in thanks for the attention. He held his frail chest in feigned suffering and prepared to wheeze his weak reply, but was glad to be interrupted by Michael Moller.

"Okay," said Moller suddenly, "so how *was* the summer?" Joey's summers in Michigan with his father were strange ordeals, about which he usually shared only partial information. The little bit that Joey had revealed had earned his father the title of "The Czar" among Joey's friends. Indeed the old man was a czar of business and industry—and apparently life in general. The designs he had on Joey's life were as mysterious as they were omnipresent. Joey couldn't help but hope that it was some sort of love, but his friends were not so optimistic. Whatever the situation was, they were always glad to get Joey back in one piece.

"It was alright, really," Joey said. "Really."

Allie eyed him slowly like the older brother he may as well have been. "Good!" he said at last, giving the situation the benefit of the doubt for the present. "That's good to hear, Joey."

Michael Moller, however, was not so easily convinced. "So how is the old Czar?" he continued. Even though he was at first glance the most different from Joey, Moller and Joey were closer than they appeared. "Still ransacking the hills and dales of corporate America, is he?"

Joey smiled. "I don't know, Michael," he said, "I couldn't see any dried blood under his fingernails or anything, so it's hard to say."

"Maybe he's finally mellowing then," interjected Allie. "Every great leader eventually learns to stay off the front lines."

"And how about with you, Joey?" insisted Moller. "Is he staying off the front lines of your life these days?"

"Well, we had our skirmishes," said Joey, fumbling around in his pockets, as if to find some confidence there. Then he straightened up a bit and smiled faintly, "I decided to take the offensive a little myself," he said.

The others all rallied behind that.

"Good show, Joey!" said Allie.

"Yeah, that's great," Tate was saying, but Moller smiled a bit tentatively.

Allie was grinning thoughtfully and patting Joey on the back. "Well isn't that interesting?" he mused. "Joey takes the offensive."

Slowly Moller realized what Joey meant. "Hey, wait a minute," he exclaimed with a laugh, "you don't mean you . . ." He glared at Joey with a knowing look trailed by a question mark. Joey looked him back right in the eyes and nodded his head rather emphatically.

"Yep," he said. The others began to catch on. Somewhere in the long chain of sad and bizarre events that made up Joey's life, their young friend had picked up a baffling belief in a God of love, strangely evidenced by Joey's even more bizarre expressions of what he claimed to be true Christian faith. Needless to say, these things had not visibly helped relations around the home front, and Joey's fanaticism, which was know to run rampant elsewhere, had long been held in check by the unspoken threats of his mother and stepfather. Around The Czar himself, his faith was not even an issue, so great was the terror of the Czar's wrath. At least, that's the way it had been until now.

"You mean you gave The Czar a Little Dose?" asked Allie incredulously. When Joey answered Allie's direct question by continuing to nod, Allie and company went crazy.

"That's great!" shouted Tate. "The Czar gets a Little Dose of the Truth." Allie and Tate were grinning away, and Moller was especially animated by the news.

"Joey gives the Czar the ol' Turn-or-Burn," exclaimed Moller. "I can't believe it." But he did believe it, at least he was having no trouble imagining the scene in his mind, smiling at the images he saw. "Man, that's like preaching to the Emperor of Rome, Joey! No, it's like going up against the head Pharisee, man. I can't believe it. But, really, it's about time."

"It *is* about time," said Allie, smiling and giving Joey a gentle shove. "Now maybe you'll lay off *us* a little bit. The Czar is the kind of guy you need to be getting anyway."

Moller was still musing. "The Czar repents. I can see it now. What I would have given to be there . . ."

Joey mumbled something, and he was smiling, but he was drifting away. He was heading for the safety far behind those deep brown eyes and the others knew what that meant. Joey could hang out for awhile, even when the joking started getting close to home, but before too long he would start reeling his heart in and he'd be gone again. Sometimes this would make Allie and the others a little mad, and their playful persecution would cut a little deeper, but by then Joey would be miles away behind his more sadly wheezed "you're killing me . . ." and the others would have to write off their strange little friend until next time.

"What was that, Joey?" asked Tate, not wanting to lose Joey just yet.

"Oh, nothing," said Joey. "I was just saying Moller probably wouldn't have wanted to be there that badly, really." There was something in Joey's eyes that let the others know it hadn't been quite the scene of victory they were painting for him.

"That's all right, kid," said Moller quickly. "You wouldn't want to conquer the whole world by age seventeen anyway. Look how bummed out Alexander the Great was when he figured out he didn't have any other lands to conquer."

"Yeah," said Allie. "The best defense is a good offense anyway. At least you got the ball in his court for awhile."

Joey smiled and Moller took the opportunity to move the subject onto less painful grounds. "So, meanwhile, kid, what do you think of the new place?"

Joey answered him happily and again all was well. There was no reason for a rapid retreat after all, and the others were glad to have him with them all the way for the time. It was no good digging up a lot of pain for Joey anyway, when all the guy really needed was a couple of friends. That's how Allie and the others figured it, and they were glad to keep Joey around.

"Joey's alright," was all that Allie used to say. And that was all there was to it. By the start of their senior year, Allie and Tate and Moller couldn't imagine life in the Slumberset without Joey, and it was good to have him back. What with the new school and the invading foreigners, they would need all the help they could get. In the meantime, it was—

"The gym, Moller!" remembered Allie suddenly, "You have *got* to check out this gym. It's Frisbee Heaven down there, man, now come on, you guys. Tate, go for the Frisbee and we'll meet you down there." Then Allie turned to Joey to make sure he was still with them. "Let's go, Joey, you've got to check this out, too. It's like heaven on earth in there, it really is . . . come on, man, let's go see if you've still got the touch."

Joey smiled and gladly followed, his wooden cross bouncing happily on his bony chest as the Keepers of the Get wove their way through the sea of new students. "Out of our way . . ." shouted Allie with a smile, "were on our way to Frisbee Heaven, you heathens . . . clear the way, you Philistines . . . we're on a mission here, clear the way . . ."

Looming tall above the other students, Allie waved his hand like a modern day Moses and watched with a grin as the Sea of Change seemed to part in front of his merry band. "Come on, you guys, the coast is clear," he shouted behind him, and then he plowed ahead, Joey's hand resting on his back and the others close behind.

CHAPTER THREE

RENDEZVOUS

"It's a nebula, Joey," Moller was saying, "but it's just a baby."
Michael Moller had his eye stuck to the end of the powerful telescope set up on the deck of his parents' lake cabin. Joey was squatting in the back end of a lounge chair at the other end of the porch, munching potato chips and squinting at a pocket-bible in the light of a gas lamp, acting disinterested in his friend's activities. Tate and Allie were in-between, lost in a combination of two-handed poker and Twinkies.

"A dwarf nebula," continued Moller, "That's what they call it, and man, is it a midget! Only a couple light years across it—a real punk, you know?'

It was around midnight on the first Saturday night of the school year. A summer away from each other and three days of classes in their strange, new environment had left the four friends primed for a rendezvous. The obvious spot for such a meeting was the Mollers' "fashionably rustic" lodge at Lake Hawthorn. A sprawling affair in rough wood and stone, the cabin had three bedrooms and a sleeping loft, a massive kitchen, several porches and patios, and the infamous "Trophy Room" where the stuffed heads of big game and exotic animals bagged by Mr. Moller seemed to gaze upon the human festivities with noble indifference. The main deck was outside the huge glass wall of the Trophy Room, by day overlooking the lake and by night offering a stunning view of the sparkling heavens.

"Ooh, Joey, check this out," said Moller. "Come here, look at this," he said. He was motioning blindly behind himself, until his friend knew he may as well forget reading until he looked through the telescope.

"Okay, okay," said Joey, not really too upset about giving into Moller's enthusiasm. "Yeah, so what is it?" he asked, a little unimpressed as he put his eye to the scope.

"What is it?!" Moller screamed. "Joey, haven't you been listening to me? It's a dwarf nebula! Right before your eyes: a bona fide, billions-of-light-years-away, dwarf nebula."

"Looks like a bunch of stars to me."

"It is, Joey, it is!" But it's a very special bunch of stars." For a moment, it seemed as if Moller was about to go into one of his long scientific explanations, but then he decided against it. "Oh, never mind. I can't get into the deep-space physics of astronomy with you guys so caught up in grazing down here on planet earth. So, what are you guys eating, anyway?"

Owing to a family get-together the previous weekend, the cupboards at the cabin were especially well stocked, so Allie, Tate, and Joey had been helping themselves to the vast array of lake food, the sum enjoyment of which was one of the few things the four friends could always agree upon. On this particular evening, Michael Moller had been temporarily foregoing the all-night feast in deference to higher stratospheres.

"Well," reported Allie, "I think we've demolished a case of Twinkies and Joey's wolfed a couple hundred of those chips in bean dip and then—"

"Hold on, hold on!" interrupted Moller. "Why are you guys going for that light-weight stuff anyway? Come on." And with that he swung the telescope away from him and headed for the patio door. "Let's do some serious grazing."

His friends quickly agreed, knowing this was Moller at his best: combing the cosmos for his friends and coming down just in time to treat them to the best the earth had to offer as well. Moller was the perfect tour guide and host.

"As long as you guys are gonna be so earth-bound," he was saying as he flipped on the lights to the kitchen, "we may as well make the best of it. Now then . . ." He flung open the door of the refrigerator and surveyed the scene. He grabbed four or five containers, lifting the lid off one, shaking a couple others, rejecting yet another and then turning around with the top choices and spreading them across the counter like a chemist lost in the makings of a formula. Then he began opening and closing the cabinet doors, grabbing seven or eight more boxes and small bags and laying them out on the counter with their comrades from the refrigerator.

"Okay, boys," he finally announced, "here's the deal. We're looking at the leftover roast, lamb chops, and a couple of already grilled burgers. There's corn soufflé in this little bugger," he said, tapping a green Tupperware dish with his finger, "and another delegate from the vegetable group, Sir Cauliflower, dressed in cheese for tonight's event. Homemade biscuits here, a little gravy of uncertain ancestry, the usual chips, cracker and dips—may I recommend the shrimp?—and, of course, dessert. Now, Allie and Tate have been bad boys and spoiled their appetites with Twinkies, so we're gonna punish them with a five-brownie limit on Barbara Mae's delicacies"—Barbara Mae being the Mollers' maid and cook back in town—"after which you will each have to write a letter of apology to Mae asking forgiveness for woofing down Twinkies before meal time."

"But, Michael," Joey protested, "It's after midnight—how were they to know we'd be digging into the serious stuff?"

"Anticipation, Joey! They've got to anticipate. We all do! How many times do I have to explain that to you? I mean, that's supposed to be part of your doctrine, isn't it? Waiting for the Lord to come back and all? I hope you don't have your mouth full of Twinkies when he shows up. A fine hallelujah that would be: Twinkie crumbs flying out of the mouth of an angel trying to blow the trumpet."

"Moller . . . " Joey was cracking up in spite of himself, but his broken laughter let on that he wasn't quite sure if it was "okay" to be making light of such things, which was obviously and exactly where Moller loved to get him.

"Uh-oh. Uh-oh. Sacrilege alarm! Approaching heresy! Danger, danger." Moller was waltzing around in the kitchen in the throes of his drama. "Come on Joey, lighten up! You've gotta get this Gestapo God concept out of your mind. You think God was born in Germany or what?"

"You're killing me, Moller," complained Joey, stalling for a clever answer, but all he could come up with was, "He probably doesn't woof down Twinkies."

"How do you know?" retorted Moller instantly. "I bet he would. Why, if Jesus had only come to America instead of Palestine, we'd probably break Twinkies instead of bread at communion. Twinkies and Dr. Pepper. You know, something the common man could relate to."

"Moller!"

"Okay, okay. But think about it man. Some people got upset because Jesus went to all those parties, you know, at tax gatherers' houses and so forth. What do you think He'd do if we invited him to a grazing party?"

"He'd probably recommend the roast beef," interrupted Tate, "which is a suggestion I will take at this point. Now where's the mayonnaise?"

"Right, right, Tate," cracked Moller. "Always the peacemaker. You oughta suggest spreading mayonnaise across the faces of all the U.N. delegates. That would smooth things over."

"It certainly would," replied Tate. "Now where is it?" But by then he had found the mayonnaise himself and the graze had begun. Moller gave up theology as quickly as astronomy when his appetite was on the rise, and the conversation turned to exclamations about the sheer quality of the grazing grounds that night and, then, to the inevitable issue on everyone's mind.

"One hundred twenty new kids in four grades," said Allie out of the blue. "They almost doubled the size of the school in one cruel blow." He pulled a small nut out the brownie he was eating and zipped it across the table where it made a direct hit on Tate's forehead. "What do you think of that, Tater head?"

"Scary, man," said Tate on cue. "The odds are way too even for me."

"One hundred twenty 'Publics' invading our turf on the eve of our senior year. Now I know how the Angles must have felt when all those Saxons showed up."

"And here we are as Anglo-Saxons," observed Moller. "Does that mean that future graduates of Somerset are gonna be some weird hybrid of ruling elite and middle class plebes?

"I hate to think about it," groaned Tate.

"So much for the pure bloodline," said Allie. He dunked the next brownie into his mug of milk, and left it in a long time, as if soaking his sorrow. "Just doesn't seem right . . . "

"Well, Allie old boy," said Tate, "I guess it's just like the Mayor has always said: Life isn't fair." It was a standard line from Tate's father, but this time it was followed by a sigh and the loaded comment, "and he should know."

There was that tone again and everyone noticed it. No one said anything about it—that was part of the deal—but there it was again, this time attached dangerously close to the topic that was perhaps its main source: Tate's father was sick, really sick. He had suffered several strokes and a heart attack and most of his friends were surprised that he was still alive.

Mayor Henry was something of a patriarch to the oil and banking tribes of the city. A hog-jowled old guy in a pinstriped suit, the Mayor was kind and soft-spoken and possessed a sense of humor as dry as the martinis he championed. He had a love for Tate and for all of Tate's friends that was well understood. The news of his decreasing health seemed, ironically, to canonize forever one of the Mayor's great mottos: listening to the usual complaints of spoiled adolescents, he would stir his drink with a stubby finger and say in his gruff baritone, "Hey, fellas, nobody said life was gonna be fair . . . " How true that would turn out to be, it seemed, for the kind old Mayor himself, whose life was apparently being cut short, despite all his good will.

Allie broke the short silence with a calculated, "Well, I know it ain't fair, but at least it should be fun for awhile. We're gonna have our hands full keeping things in perspective out there."

"Well, so far, so good," chimed Moller, and everyone was quick to agree. The first three days of classes had been a complete success. Following Allie's antics at the ceremony and their first informal encounter with the new students, there had been a series of maneuvers designed to test the new balance of powers at the school. As Allie had been careful to point out, it would be important not to lose touch with the need to keep the old administration in line. Foes such as the Great Stone Face could not be allowed free reign, even if the challenge of simultaneously conquering the new students kept them busy for a while.

And, along with their initial successes in carrying the Get forth into the new era, it was good to be re-united with their other friends and with those few special teachers they considered to be allies to their cause. "Was it great to see the Magnificent Bolo or what?" said Allie.

"No kidding," said Tate, and the others smiled in agreement. Mr. Don Bolin, a.k.a The Magnificent Bolo, had been a major attraction at Somerset School since the day he had arrived there several years earlier. Bald and big-lipped, the man had at first seemed an unlikely addition to the Somerset faculty. His raucous style and rambling lectures were a far cry from the distinguished bedside manners of the traditional Slumberset teacher. Before long, however, it had become quite evident that he was too brilliant and too likable to write off. By the end of his first semester, he had earned an affectionate nickname that would stick, and his classes in both Sociology and the History of Western Culture had become favorites among the Keepers of the Get.

Allie and the others had latched onto the Magnificent Bolo as quickly as possible. It was, in fact, one of Allie's older brothers who had first compared the classroom antics of Mr. Bolin to the garish showmanship of a locally televised professional wrestler known as Bolo the Magnificent, and the legends of this newly-christened teacher's outlandish approach to teaching were soon well-known among the younger Keepers. When it was announced, therefore, that Mr. Bolin would be teaching a middle-school course in Civics, the boys had been the first to sign up. Their eagerness to get to know the Magnificent Bolo had not been disappointed and their initial sense of delight with his classroom antics had worn well over the years, particularly as the more loosely structured class schedules of the upper school allowed them many informal hours at the feet of their gregarious guru of modern culture.

Hailing from Chicago, Mr. Don Bolin had admittedly been raised in an environment where the supremacy of the loudly spoken word could only be challenged by the powerfully exaggerated details of the inner city Tall Tale. Carrying this approach into the realm of academia, Bolo the Magnificent had developed a unique style of teaching, to say the least. The Keepers were soon to find out that, for the Bolo, all analysis took place in terms of sweeping generalizations and absolute judgments. Vastly complex historical developments and sociological phenomena would be reduced to a crassly stated oversimplification which was, if not completely accurate, extremely effective in stirring up heated debate among the normally listless ranks of otherwise spoon-fed students.

The Magnificent Bolo might, for example, reduce the entire political system of the Roman Empire to a "bad joke on the rest of the world," while the Civil War became "a bunch of red-necks getting their dose of comeuppance," and Byzantine art was likened to a "kid with the 64-Color edition of Crayola's but only one eye." This was hardly the stuff of conventional prep school instruction, but the disturbing truth was that it worked. Students subjected to his explosive lectures mixed complete outrage with irresistible admiration in a complex response that the Magnificent Bolo adamantly defended as the "greatest kind of learning experience available in the Western World." Ultimately, even the administration could not resist the persuasive powers of the Magnificent Bolo.

Pondering now their first day of Senior Sociology with their beloved teacher, the Keepers chuckled among themselves. "Could you believe we got a 'Final Word' out of him so early in the going?" laughed Michael Moller.

"He was primed for it," smiled Allie. "He couldn't wait."

To understand the effectiveness of Mr. Bolin's approach to education, it is necessary to see the importance of what Allie had dubbed early on as the "Final Word." Delivered as a sort of insider's monopoly on knowledge, the Final Word was the main weapon in the rhetorical arsenal of the

Magnificent Bolo. "It doesn't matter whether it's true or not," Allie had explained. "Everybody wants a Final Word so badly that they'll believe anything as long as it's stated in absolute terms."

Judging by the Slumberset's reaction to the Final Word, Allie seemed to be right. It wasn't long before students locked in the throes of any kind of debate would find themselves heading for the hallowed office of Mr. Don Bolin determined to have the dispute settled by a Final Word from the Magnificent Bolo. Given his limited knowledge of a very vast number of topics, it was one of the greatest ironies of life in the Slumberset that a Final Word from the Bolo was considered Truth, at least for the sake of an argument between students.

It was in this spirit that the Keepers of the Get had purposed to elicit a Final Word from the Bolo on their first day of Sociology class. Reveling in their success as they made a final tour of the grazing grounds in the Moller's lake cabin, Allie led the others in a living color replay of the event.

"It was great," Allie was saying, hand wrapped around a huge sandwich. "The Magnificent Bolo barrels into the class like he just came from a convention of prophets. His books are falling out of his arms like bombs and then he drops the big one on us. What was the line—"let's hear it for—"

"No, no," interrupted Moller, and then he quoted Mr. Bolin word-for-word from three days earlier. " 'So much for the Sixties,' was what he said . 'Every radical in Berkley is enrolling in computer courses so they can get a job in the anthill after all.' "

"Yeah, that was it!" agreed Allie, and they all laughed.

"Classic line," chuckled Tate.

"Quintessential Bolo," declared Michael Moller and Joey nodded his agreement.

"And that was only the beginning," said Allie. Indeed, what followed had been a veritable barrage of gross generalizations and comically sweeping overviews, at the climax of which, Allie had raised his hand to address his teacher.

"Mr. Bolin," he had begun, "Tate and Moller and I have been having some discussions lately about the sociological implications of a certain historical figure's lifestyle. We were wondering if you could shed any light on the topic."

The Magnificent Bolo had eyed his pupil and said, "Well, Mr. Reed, although one of the great introductory lectures of the era stands waiting in the wings, I'm sure your studied curiosity merits an answer. What's the rub?"

"It's Gandhi, sir," Allie had said. "Do you think Mahatma Gandhi treated his wife like a dog?"

The Magnificent Bolo had leaned back in his chair as if remembering the happy times he and the Mahatma had spent playing badminton in the back yard. Then he had answered with all the authority of Gandhi's first cousin and said, "No way. Are you kidding me? The guy had an absolute reverence for life. There's no way he beat the old lady. That was obviously a charge trumped up by his competitors. They were sick and tired of trying to fast as much as him just to keep up. No that was totally bogus."

"Of course, sir," Allie had nodded matter-of-factly, and the laughter he had soberly stifled then, he now let out in a great belly laugh shared with his friends at Moller's cabin.

"Was that perfect or what?" exclaimed Allie as they finished recounting the event. "A Final Word in the first ten minutes of class. What more could you ask for?"

The others agreed and the laughter continued until the wages of too much food and folly began to take their toll, their stomachs aching both from their gluttony and the uncontrollable fits of laughter brought on by their recounted exploits.

"Okay fellas," said Allie finally, "we've gorged ourselves long enough. We've had our laughs and then some. Now we have to do the penance of merciless physical exercise. Moller, where's the Frisbee?"

Moller's lake cabin featured an enormous back lawn, not really plush like in town, but nicely level beneath big oak trees and covered with enough grass to make it smooth for running and soft for diving, when necessary, for that great object of their athletic affection, the Frisbee. The whole area was lit up by gigantic flood lights hung in the tress, creating a canopy of reflected light from the tops of the towering oaks all the way to the shimmering grass below. Allie had christened the place the Cricket Cathedral and the championship matches there pitted Allie and Tate against Joey and Moller in an ingenious game of "skill and supernatural sport" invented and modified by the four friends over several years of play. The otherworldly qualities of the place elevated the game into a dimension of mythic battle, an Olympian arena in the truest sense. It was, Allie insisted, Sport as it was created to be experienced.

"Dive, Moller!" screamed three ecstatic voices, and dive he did, at full speed extending his right arm and then his entire body to a position fully horizontal to the ground. Snagging the Frisbee at the last possible moment before it hit the lawn, Moller pulled it into his body and prepared for a full-impact landing in the soft grass of the Astral Plane Arena. The ground met him with a firm but playful smack and he screamed with delight. "Yes!" he said, leaping to his feet in a triumphant show of the rescued Frisbee. The boys had taken the field.

In an age in which a certain Triple Alliance of Sports still reigned supreme, youths ungifted in the sacrosanct games of football, basketball and baseball had long awaited a deliverer. Many a healthy but athletically ungifted lad had cried out for an end to his plight as a "wheeze-bag" in a world of macho sport. How long would guys like these have to spend their youth along the Sidelines of Life, unable to do battle with the elemental things of Sport? How could they ever have their turn at developing the hand-to-eye mastery over Mass and Motion that was so much a part of existence on earth? Where was the playground for the Olympian fantasies of the non-varsity sportsman? For millions, the end of athletic exile sailed in from the netherworlds of play as a little piece of plastic. The savior for these countless generations of sports wimps was none other than the Frisbee.

Despite the Machiavellian moaning of every known champion of the old Alliance, it was soon clear that the Frisbee was here to stay. As simplistic and silly as the game appeared from the sidelines, there was something completely and irrevocably contagious about tossing a Frisbee. The scenario was happening a thousand times a day, in each and every corner of the Western World: a behemoth of the old Alliance makes his way across a playing field when suddenly a round, plastic disk glides to a stop at his feet, mistakenly sent his way by a couple of early prophets of the game whereupon the angry behemoth considers stomping it into oblivion, but the deep-seated curiosity leads forces him to pick up the Frisbee instead and lamely tossing it to its apparent owner, at which time a subtle but magical bell rings somewhere deep within him, and he ends up spending the rest of a long, golden afternoon trying to learn how to throw and catch the Frisbee.

And, how much more eagerly would those uninitiated into the inner circle of the old Sports Alliance seize the chance to play Frisbee? For them, it was just too good to be true.

The four current champions of the Astral Arena, of course, fell into this second category. Joey and Tate were completely lame with regard to conventional sport of any kind. Allie was a good tennis player and

Michael Moller was more than accomplished at the game of soccer, but both of these sports were distant indeed from the mainstream of Triple Alliance glory. Thus the four friends found the Frisbee to be their ticket into the higher regions of sport.

"Let the games begin," bellowed Allie, and suddenly a deeply charged silence fell over the Astral Arena. Even the crickets seemed to sound a lull for a magical moment as the four participants prepared themselves for tournament play.

"We are ready," shouted Joey soberly.

"Then begin," beckoned Allie.

Joey and Moller walked out into the light, silently studying the field of play. They held a brief conference and Joey took off on a dead run. At the point where Joey passed the first of the giant oak trees spread randomly across the lawn, Michael Moller let loose with a low, straight fling of the Frisbee. Immediately, Joey began weaving in and out of the oaks as Allie counted off the trees passed by Joey. "Four . . . five . . . six—go for it." As he came around the sixth tree, Joey looked up one last time and lunged for the Frisbee.

"He got it!" shouted Moller. "Six!" It was a great score for the first round and everyone knew it. "Nice job, Joey."

Flinging the Frisbee to Tate and Allie, Joey glided across the Astral Arena back to his partner. Sharing a charged handshake, Joey and Moller turned to watch Tate and Allie. Stepping out onto a slightly different spot on the lawn, Tate and Allie exchanged a few quick words, as Tate pointed off to the left side of the arena. Then it was Allie who was off through the trees, Tate flinging the Frisbee when Allie reached the first oak, and Michael Moller on the count.

"Two . . . three . . . better hurry . . . four . . . look out"

The Frisbee had made a sudden descent with Allie rounding the fourth tree. Diving out vainly, he fell to the lawn a few feet from the grounded Frisbee.

"Tough luck, boys," shouted Joey.

"A big zero," chimed in Moller.

And so the game went. For reasons long forgotten, they called it the Celtic Weave, and their contests in this simple game took on all the importance of the Super Bowl, a certain humorous tone notwithstanding. At its best, it was the "Tournament of Chumpions," "winner take nothing," and "may the best man grin." So went the rhetoric in the Astral Arena, as the four Olympians nevertheless went after it with complete abandon, as if the fate of nations depended on the outcome. Hours would pass, appointments and overdue assignments would go unattended, as the game continued, sometimes into the wee hours of the morning. The winners would have the sole reward of reigning in the glory of self-ascribed supremacy until such time as the next tournament was played. But such reward—as was not so different from all sports anyway—was more than enough.

On this particular evening, Joey and Moller were in rare form. It had been three months since they had thrown the Frisbee together, but here they were connecting on miraculous tosses and heroic catches all the night through.

"Absence makes the heart grow fonder," smiled Moller at Allie and Tate. Allie had been bemoaning the fact that the summer's frequent sessions between he and Tate seemed not to be paying off too well, and Moller and Joey were quick to agree.

"But that's the essence of this game," continued Moller. "It's all about how far can you be apart and still make the connection."

"Right," agreed Joey, his confidence at an all-time high. "Michael and I were in training by being apart. We figured, three thousand miles for a couple months and when we get back, fifty yards will be like inches."

"Oh, I get it," groaned Allie. "Now you're gonna act like you had this whole thing planned."

"Give us a break," added Tate. "Let's just call it dumb luck and forget about it till next time."

Moller looked at Joey and feigned exasperation. "See what I mean, Joey? I told you these guys don't even understand the game."

"Gosh, Michael," said Joey playing along. "And all along, I thought they knew."

"Give it up," snarled Allie with a small, uncontainable laugh. And, to change the subject, he picked up the Frisbee. "Come on, Joey, go deep."

Instantly, Joey bolted out across the lawn as Allie reared back and flung the Frisbee as far as he could. It sailed magically through the trees, the excitement of all four friends mounting with each tree cleared until they burst out laughing as Joey made a leaping catch at the far end of the lawn. "I guess Joey and I have been practicing too," said Allie.

"Exactly," said Moller. And there was something in the magic and power of the toss just caught that made him sound more sincere than he had intended. The mystique of the long-distance connection was indeed what brought such delight to bear on the simple activity of playing

Frisbee. The little piece of plastic could in some mysterious way fill vast spaces between people, guided as it was by some invisible hand past the many imposing obstacles, and this was the essence of their enjoyment. Watching the shiny disk of human intention make its courageous journey through the earth's unpredictable atmosphere into the outstretched hands of another human being, this was the reason for their many hours spent of the Lawns of Life together, testing their ability to connect from so far apart.

Joey ran back toward his friends and, from a more reasonable distance, sailed the Frisbee back into their midst. It was a straight and easy toss, until suddenly Joey yelled, "Blind Man!" signaling the challenge of another of their games. Allie, Tate, and Moller instantly obeyed, tightly shutting their eyes and holding out their gently flailing hands as the Frisbee made its way toward their tight circle. Joey watched with delight as the Frisbee struck Tate in the chest, bounced up into Allie's face, and finally came to rest in Michael Moller's blindly grasping hands.

"Yes!" screamed Joey, laughing hysterically. The others opened their eyes and shared the amazement.

"Too much," exclaimed Allie.

"Nothing to it," smiled Michael Moller. Tossing the Frisbee to Allie, he turned toward the house. "Who needs sight when you've got the Touch?"

CHAPTER FOUR

THE MAYOR

A Black Cadillac rolled through the narrow gate into the back parking lot of St. Paul's hospital, glided to a stop and fell silent. Two figures got out of the front seat and, walking around behind the car, pulled a wheel chair from the trunk. They wheeled the chair around to one of the rear doors and began helping a third figure out of the car.

Taking his seat in the wheel chair, Joey took a box from Michael Moller, who then got out of the back seat. Joey placed the box in his lap and sat poker-faced as Allie and Tate wrapped a blanket around him. "Okay, fellas," said Allie quietly, "let's go."

Inside the hospital, things looked deserted. The round information desk in the center of the lobby was unattended, and the long halls with their tile walls went off in every direction with hardly a soul in sight. An orderly engrossed in his task of waxing the floor certainly posed no threat to the mission unfolding. Two nuns appeared at the end of one hall and approached a bit ominously, but they soon turned a corner away from the four mysterious visitors, leaving a clear path to the elevator.

"Up, please," said Allie to the empty elevator as the doors opened and Moller wheeled Joey in.

"Number Five," said Tate, and Allie pushed the button. Once the doors closed, the boys broke out into an intense, if guarded, burst of hoopla.

"So far, so good," said Allie.

Joey wheezed his little half-laughs and murmured, "This is great, what a plan."

"Okay, cool it," said Tate as the elevator jolted to a stop. Then the doors pulled open for four silent visitors facing the final obstacle of their journey, the nurse's station. As they stepped out of the elevator, a nurse greeted them without looking up.

"Good evening, boys. Can we help you?"

"Yes, nurse. It's Tate Henry. I'm here to see my father."

"Oh, yes Tate," said the nurse looking up quickly. "Of course. And you've brought your friends. Won't your father be pleased?"

"Yes, ma'am, he will," said Tate with a sly look at Allie, "he certainly will."

Allie stood by and gave the nurse a deadpanned, "We hope so, yes ma'am." Joey kept his eyes on the floor, suddenly not sure what kind of sickness would justify the wheelchair he was in, and Michael Moller smiled.

"Well, your father's awake," said the nurse. "You can go on in."

"Thanks, ma'am."

Moller resumed his slow push behind Joey in the wheelchair as Tate led the way. Pausing at the door to establish their sense of timing, the boys then entered into the hospital room with a melodramatic air of professional servitude.

"Room Service for Mayor Walter S. Henry!" announced Allie.

"Dinner is served in the Mayor's suite!" rejoined Tate.

A silver-haired man reclined in three-quarter position in a hospital bed covered with magazines and newspapers. "What's this?" he said, clearing his throat and sitting up a bit. Then he smiled. "Well it's about time, lads."

"Hello, your Mayorness," said Allie. Moller and Joey added cheerful greetings, and Tate smiled at his father.

"What's happened to Joey?" asked the Mayor, staring at the wheelchair.

"Purely cosmetic, your Mayorness," said Allie. "We've got a little surprise for you, and we didn't want the authorities to intervene, sir, if you get my drift."

The Mayor raised an eyebrow of interest as Tate continued. "Yes, Pop. I could not help but notice on previous visits to this fine establishment, the rather severe lack of culinary creativity among the chefs here."

"Therefore," continued Allie on cue, "we took the liberty of contacting the staff of a certain country club with regard to your predicament, and they responded to the crisis in heroic fashion." Then Allie turned to his friends, "Shall we? . . ."

At this point Moller pulled the sheet from around Joey to reveal an impressive array of boxes squeezed onto his lap and wedged into the seat around him. Instantly, a rich and warm aroma began to fill the room, quickly reaching the Mayor's sensitive nostrils with a message that lifted his entire being. "Ahhh," he said gratefully, "you boys are saints."

"Absolutely," agreed Allie, and the hearty response of the Mayor prompted everyone into action. They began pulling the carefully sealed boxes off Joey's lap and cutting the strings that held the thin, white cardboard together. The first box to be opened revealed a dinner salad of epic proportions and impeccable freshness.

"The first course," announced Allie, holding the salad gently in the air.

"The utensils, Master Joey," reminded Tate, and Joey reached gingerly into his shirt and pulled out a rolled cloth napkin wrapped tightly around a set of the country club's silver utensils. "Great," said Tate. "Then dinner is served."

The Mayor was beaming, his great joy being channeled, as always, through the calmest of mannerisms. Pulling his robe more neatly about his neck, he reached for the control on the hospital bed. "Let's see, lads, if I can rise to the occasion," he smiled.

Once sitting upright, the Mayor received his set of silver from Joey and began gracefully unwrapping it as Michael Moller produced a crystal water glass from one of the boxes and filled it with water from a plastic hospital pitcher. Meanwhile, Tate pulled out a dinner plate, wheeled the bedside table into position over the Mayor's lap, and placed the plate on the table. Moller set the water glass in place as the Mayor arranged his silver and then received his salad from Allie as graciously as a host at the head of his table.

With the boys poised around his bed like guests and servants around the great dinning room table in the Henry house, the Mayor stretched out his arms and announced, "Shall we bless the food?" The boys bowed their heads, delighted that the Mayor had completely entered into their plan.

"Great and wonderful God," said the Mayor gently, "I thank you for sending your servants to help me in my hour of need. Even as you fed your servant Elijah from the mouth of the raven, so you have sent these little ravens to bring more than sustenance to your humble servant. Gratefully do we receive this food as evidence of your steadfast watchfulness over the otherwise insignificant lives of your children. In Christ's name, we thank You . . . Amen."

"Amen," said Tate and the others.

"Yeah, great prayer," said Allie smiling. "You really know how to lay it out to the Big Guy."

"No kidding," said Moller. "If God really is an Englishman, you've got it made."

Approaching his salad and the conversation at the same controlled speed, the Mayor smiled. "Is there any doubt in your mind, Michael, regarding the cultural persuasion of the Lord?"

"No sir," replied Moller. "He's a gentleman, a scholar, and, most likely, an Episcopalian."

"Indeed," said the Mayor. Neatly taking his first bite of salad, he held the boys' attention as he deliberately chewed and swallowed. Enjoying the casual banter with Moller, but sensing Joey's discomfort with the topic, the Mayor took a breath and swept the conversation gracefully into a different direction. "Boys, this salad is superb," he said. "You have no idea what a week of hospital food does to a sensitive palate. A fresh salad like this is better than a week in the Bahamas at this point."

The four friends shared a feeling of success. Their plan was working. Tate moved about the hospital room as if he had just been released from prison. The others were relieved to see Tate acting like his old, light-hearted self. They were also glad that the Mayor did not seem as bad off as they had feared. His most recent stroke sounded much worse than it appeared eight days later. Tate told them that the worst danger had passed, still they had not known exactly what to expect on their first visit to the Mayor's hospital room.

"Speaking of great vacations," said Allie, "my folks called from Australia last night. They said to tell you to quit trying to get attention and get back to work."

"Work?" laughed the Mayor. "What would Almand Reed know about work? You can tell them to get back here so we can car pool downtown. We'll see what he has to say about work." It had been seven or eight years since the Mayor had retired from the office that earned him his life-long title among his friends. Since then, the liveliest discussions among the ranks of semi-retired oil men and investors comprising the Somerset Board of Directors centered around who spent the most time on the golf course. Himself never accused of being a workaholic, the Mayor was nevertheless a vigilante when it came to castigating the leisurely work habits of his friends.

"Okay," said Allie. "I'll just tell him you said that you're ready whenever he is."

THE MAYOR

"Fair enough," smiled the Mayor. Having finished his salad, the Mayor laid his fork down and watched as Joey poured soup from a Styrofoam container into a china bowl held by Michael Moller. Tate took away the salad plate as Moller glided over with the soup.

"The second course, your Mayorness," said Moller.

"Thank you, my good man," said the mayor. Reaching for his soup spoon, the undisputed Master of Conversation continued his dominion over the meal. "So tell me, lads, how are things at the new campus?"

"Well, so far, so good," said Moller. "Allie put on a virtuoso performance at the 'Farewell to the Old Campus, Hello to the New Era' ceremony, and we've been on a bit of a roll with some initial Gets for the year, I must admit."

"Yes, Tate told me about the fountain performance," said the Mayor. He savored a taste of the soup with the image of Allie at the ceremony. "Very clever..."

"Thank you, sir," said Allie proudly. "Having had to endure your share of long ceremonies yourself, I thought you might appreciate it."

"Tell him about the skunk Get," said Joey shyly.

"What's that Joey?" said the Mayor.

Joey looked at the floor and nudged Michael Moller.

"The skunk Get, Moller, tell him what you did to 'Dewey'."

"Yeah, Moller," agreed Allie. "Let's give the Mayor the Full Report."

"Michael?" implored the Mayor gently.

"Right," said Moller, shifting in his seat to give the Mayor a better view of his impending presentation. "It's like this, your Mayorness. You see, we're fighting a war on two fronts out there. The obvious threat is all these new students coming in with no idea what life in the Slumberset is all about. So we've got to deal with that. But we can't really slack off on keeping the old administration in line, too. The Great Stone Face could slip in any time and we'd have a military academy before we knew it—"

"Or someone like Quaigmeyer could take over at the philosophical level," interrupted Allie, "And it would be depression of epidemic proportions—"

"If not mass suicides," added Tate.

"Exactly," agreed Moller. "So we've got to fight this war on two fronts—and history has not dealt kindly with those in our predicament."

"Indeed," smiled the Mayor.

"But we have no choice," said Allie. "And that being the case..."

"And that being the case," continued Moller, "we sort of divided up forces: Allie seems to have a handle on the new student situation, so I tried to take up the slack on the ongoing battle with the administration."

By now, the Mayor was equally absorbed in the Full Report and the second course of his meal.

"The Skunk Job, Michael," reminded Joey.

"Right, well I got this idea," continued Moller. "Actually it kind of hit me right in the face when I was going up one of the new back stairwells, and there was this can of paint that must have been left there by some workmen—you know they haven't quite finished up things around there—so here's this can of white paint, and it just sort of hit me: that black dog Mrs. Warner adopted last year just popped into my mind's eye and I thought, wow, that dog would make a great skunk. And you know how Mrs. Warner is, your Mayorness, I mean, that librarian is wound tighter than the inside of a golf ball. Plus which, she has to be one of the most irritating women alive. And here she has this scrawny black dog—named 'Dewey,' for God's sake, after the Dewey Decimal System—and who would miss an opportunity like that?"

"Who indeed," agreed the Mayor.

"So," continued Moller, "with the stellar assistance of your earnest son, we were able to create some pretty darn realistic skunk markings on that little mongrel, if I may say so myself." By now the Mayor had a wide grin on his face. He even laid the soup spoon down for a moment as he pondered the scene in his mind's eye and, then finally, he let out a full-fledged laugh that ignited the whole room.

"It's true," chimed in Joey. He'd been watching nervously until he saw that the Mayor was starting to enjoy the story. "He looked just like a skunk, he really did."

"But that's not all," added Tate through his own laughter. "Allie got in on the plan just in time to suggest they turn the whole thing into a school-wide scare. Always prepared, he came up with one of those cheap stink bombs they sell on the Fourth of July, and he set it off in the girls' locker room with no one around but the clearly incriminated skunk/dog."

Again the Mayor erupted in a good-natured laugh.

"The rumors of a marauding skunk hit the administration with a wave of pioneer panic," raved Allie. "Had they built the new school too close to the boundaries of the wilderness? Would snakes and other rodents soon be invading their territory as well? Fear was on the rampage, your Mayorness. And the ensuing turmoil was only ended by the bewildered librarian having to vouch for the dog's integrity (and his ancestry) before a member of the state wildlife department who had called in to incarcerate the rogue skunk."

"But there wasn't a trace of evidence," said Allie. "It was a perfect Get."

The Mayor threw his head back for one more laugh and then firmly clapped his hands. "Bravo, lads," he bellowed. "Bravo."

Joey beamed as if his suggesting the story was equal to having performed the Get in the first place, but Moller and Allie didn't mind, and Tate was happier than he had been in weeks. "Bring on the main course," he said, "and then tell him the best one, Allie."

"Oh, delightful," said the Mayor, and he meant it. Joey and Tate busied themselves opening the last of the white boxes while Allie and Moller waited in the wings for their cue. The head chef at the country club had sent along a perfect cut of prime rib, "rare just short of mooing" as the Mayor always ordered it, complete with more mashed potatoes, gravy, and squash than one man could possibly eat. When Joey had loaded up the plate to dangerous heights, Tate presented his father with the main course, and Allie began his monologue.

"So it was like this, your Mayorness," he said, "when I was certain that Moller and Tate had the Old Guard under control, I knew it was time to start the Education Process on the new students. I had been studying the situation pretty carefully—research is a strict requirement for our major Gets—and I had soon classified the enemy into two main categories. For the guys, I call em' 'Wheeze-bags' and 'Golden Boys' and they are one or the other: either they are of the super-intelligent, 'our brains are about to evolve beyond the need for our wimpy bodies' category, or they were brought in to bring athletic glory to the school by way of Adonis-like physiques bred to dominate the Triple Alliance of Sports. Meanwhile, your Mayorness, the female version of the Wheeze-bags are known as 'Wheezettes,' and the girl version of Golden Boys, we simply call 'Barbie Dolls.' "

At this last image, the Mayor laughed out loud, giving Allie just the encouragement he needed to plunge headlong into his story.

"I sensed that we would usually have to deal with these categories separately," continued Allie, "but I really wanted to come up with something big early on to Get them all simultaneously. So the first thing I noticed was what a hard time all of them were having with the dress code. I never appreciated the great evolution of our own ultimate response to the coat-

and-tie requirement of the dress code until I saw all these guys showing up in the corniest looking outfits you could ever imagine. Every one of them looked like the main character in one of those Western movies, you know, the ones where some white guy was captured by the Indians as a baby and is raised by 'the savages' and then suddenly he's recaptured by white men and has to fit back into our civilization. Cut to the scene where he's just had his first bath in twenty-eight years and they have stuffed him inside a suit that is two sizes too small and itchy as hell, then multiply this image by about one-hundred kids and you've pretty well got the scene at Somerset school these days. 'Crying Wolf Comes to Somerset.' It's that kind of a deal."

The Mayor laughed again and patted the hospital table in delight. But Allie was on a roll and didn't let up.

"So here's all these guys looking like 'Squaw-Man Goes to an Ice-Cream Social,' and I'm looking around at the Old Guard thinking, 'man, we have really dealt with this dress code thing with some class.' You know what I mean: our approach is to start out with the worst looking corduroy jacket possible and match it up with the ugliest tie and shirt combination you could can up with; then you leave the tie knot hanging about ten inches below the chin—minimum—while you have trousers so baggy you could fit three baby kangaroos inside each leg. And, of course, you finish it off with the most beat up pair of tennis shoes you can find or those standard-issue-shoes of the Slumberset, the desert boot."

Here Allie paused only long enough to punctuate his point by lifting his own trouser legs to reveal the soft-suede ankle-top shoes to which he was referring. The Mayor extended his head a bit over the edge of his bed, nodded and returned to his prime rib, as Allie returned to his tale.

"So I realized that it could take these new guys years to get the hang of this, and I figured I should try to come up with a way of, you know, speeding up the process. I ended up deciding that all personal growth begins by recognizing the error of your present way of doing things, so, I thought, 'hey, why not show these guys how stupid they really look?' If they had to understand that 'coats and ties' doesn't mean you have to dress like a geek, why not just demonstrate how laughable their current condition was? It was that simple."

"So the second Monday of classes, your Mayorness, I showed up looking like a public school poster-boy dressed for Sunday School at Sears. I went out and bought the cheapest polyester suit I could find, a JC Penney's affair in a putrid shade of green, one size too small, of course. The tie was a

THE MAYOR

large-striped monstrosity, just a little too wide and tied in a knot the size of a baseball, and I topped off all this by stuffing my hair up inside a sort of Beatle-wig combed into a public school "flop-top." The subtle finishing touch was a pair of square-toed boots that are in great vogue among the semi-hip middle class. With a pair of phony glasses, I soon found that the new Allie Reed was absolutely unrecognizable."

"It's true," said Tate.

"He really was," said Joey. "It really killed me."

"In this get-up," continued Allie, "I spent most of the day as an ignorant new-comer, pestering the unsuspecting teachers and administrators with questions like, 'How long till we get to play with the computer?' and 'When do we get to talk to those guys from Yale?' I bluffed my way past teachers who had known me for years. I even succeeded in fooling a Somerset Lifer into giving me directions to the headmaster's office. This was all just a warm-up, however, for my formal presentation that afternoon." Here the Mayor shifted in his bed, giving Allie a look of complete attention even as he politely continued his meal.

"You see, Mayor, for the first three days of classes, there was an all-school orientation meeting every afternoon at 2:00. The idea was to get the kinks out of the new class system—rotating schedules, variable class lengths, and all the other great amenities of the 'progressive education' they're suddenly throwing at us. As you might expect, these little get-togethers were wide open for stupid questions and irrelevant rambling by students and faculty alike, affording an opportunity not to be missed by a certain discerning Keeper of the Get, blessed as he was by his condition of being completely incognito. So, halfway through the meeting," and here Allie began slipping into the persona he had up until then only been describing, "halfway through the meeting, I raise my trembling little hand and get called on by Headmouster Martin. So there I am, rubbing my hands together in this pathetic show of fake nervousness like some Beatle-wigged alien from the public school twilight zone, and I start this whiny oration about the urgent need—immediately if not sooner—for dress code advisors.

"For some of us," I say, "fashion is a very important part of school social life." Already, of course, there are a few muffled laughs throughout the room as everybody is checking out this hopelessly out-of-touch guy trying to play it cool. "And though some of the uniform requirements are quite clear," I continue, "I feel there is a lot of room for individual expression, and I just feel there ought to be some sort of guidance available to the new students like myself who are trying to make a smooth transition—as regards fashion—into Somerset culture."

"At this point Headmouster Martin is pretty speechless, and the crowd is getting really interested so I just keep going: 'So what I was wondering was, would it be possible for a new student like myself to start some sort of club or committee? I was thinking we could call it the 'Fashion-Wise Committee' because it's kind of a play on words, you know we're trying to fit in 'fashion-wise' by being 'wise about fashion', if you catch my drift'—at this point, I couldn't help but snort a little self-congratulatory laugh at my character's lame sense of humor—'and this Committee or Club could have meetings and come up with good ideas about how you can, well, stick with the Dress Code, of course, but you know, spice it up a little bit with just some good fashion sense."

By now the Mayor had to stop eating so he could fully observe Allie's performance. Moller and Joey were laughing and adding comments like, "Yeah it was great" and "Fashion-wise! Where did you come up with that?"

Tate was just beaming about how happy the Mayor seemed with the whole thing. "Five-Star Food and Full-Reports, Pop," smiled Tate, "What more could you ask for?"

"What more indeed?" laughed the Mayor, and then he baited Allie to continue.

"So how did the venerable Headmaster handle it?" he asked.

"Oh, he was smooth, your Mayorness," replied Allie quickly. "You guys on the Board definitely picked the right guy. Headmouster Martin looked at me with all the sincerity in the world and said something like, 'That's an excellent point and an intriguing idea. I'd like to suggest that you write up your idea and submit it to our Director of Extracurricular Activities, Mrs. Walsh.' And he was being so supportive and all that I couldn't help but take it to the next level. So I said, 'That would be great, Mr. Martin, and I wanted to say that the club could even be open to faculty members because I'm sure even someone like yourself would want to get a few pointers, you know, fashion-wise, so you could keep up with the times because, frankly your outfit could use a little . . .' and about then is when the Headmouster used his supreme gift for cutting people off by quickly taking the next question and leaving me to mumble the rest of my comments to myself, which fit in just right with my character."

"Perfect," said the Mayor, "Bravo and bravo." He was clapping emphatically and wiping away tears of laughter. "Well said and well done!"

Tate was still watching his father who suddenly seemed as fully alive in his hospital bed as he had ever been on his feet. Flooded with another wave of relief, Tate felt something warm and salty burning at his nostrils and welling up in his eyes. With an awkward cough, his tears came out as a laugh. "He's finished the main course, Joey," he blurted out. "For God's sake, man, what's for desert?"

CHAPTER FIVE

THE GREAT BARGAIN

"The Lord be with you."

"And with your spirit."

"Let us pray." Father David Miles clasped his hands in front of himself, took a deep breath and, with a faint smile, lifted his voice. "Father, protect us from ourselves. Grant us insight and humor in dealing with our many weaknesses. Help us to use our manifold gifts and our unique life stations to Your glory. And, above all, deliver us from junk food and television. Amen."

Allie opened his eyes and smiled across the small sanctuary at Tate and the others in the first pew of the chapel. Dressed in a long, black robe, and standing next to Father Miles, Allie stifled a laugh as Moller and Tate enjoyed a quiet chuckle in the pew. Next to them, Joey stared straight ahead, avoiding or simply missing the humorous side of Father Miles's prayer. Sensing Allie's waning control, Father Miles slid a casual foot over Allie's and slowly pressed down until the pain was just enough to bring his young acolyte back into the fold. It was Sunday night, and this was the gospel according to Father Smiles.

Since mid-way through their sophomore year, the Keepers of the Get had been at virtually every one of the school's Sunday evening chapel services. Certainly not a mandatory practice for the rest of the school, Allie and his friends had taken on the obligation in exchange for a deal made with their long-time confidante and sometimes mentor, Father David Miles. They called it the Great Bargain, and it had to do with the Light Show.

"The Eighth Wonder of the World Music and Light Review" had its origins in Tate Henry's basement some years earlier. Inspired by the psychedelic light shows flourishing on both coasts at the time, the Eighth Wonder was a surprisingly sophisticated version of the extravagant multi-image productions accompanying rock concerts in certain venues around the country. Using multiple projectors and as many stage lights as could be safely mounted, the light show presented life as a barrage of images and events too rapid to consciously comprehend. Artistic defenders of the concept considered the technique a way to bypass the rational mind into the intuitive heart, a proposition that certainly sounded good to the Keepers of the Get. Ultimately, they saw the light show as a way of presenting a full-blown artistic expression of the same philosophical views buried in the folds of a great Get.

On a trip to the West coast in the summer before their freshman year, Allie and Tate had seen several of the best light shows in the world. Immediately upon their return, they recruited the technical talents of Michael Moller to implement their new vision. From that time forward, anything that could not be said in a one-liner or practical joke was turned over for consideration to the Eighth Wonder of the World Music and Light Review.

The Eighth Wonder was built around the fledgling rock band championed by Tate since the eighth grade. Tate was a vastly accomplished musician, whose training in classical music on the piano had been wed to the rock and pop music of his earliest teen years, resulting in a style of music both intricate and accessible. After developing his style as a player, Tate surrounded himself with four other gifted musicians from the school and proceeded to build a band capable of reproducing even some of the most difficult music of the day. Then Tate began writing his own songs.

Drawn from his introspective view of life and seemingly endless musical vocabulary, Tate's music was soon on par with most of the music on the radio. With his built-in skills as a live player and vocalist, he developed a certain talent for arranging and leading his band of gifted players until, by most accounts, he had the best live band in the city. Then they added the light show.

Along with Moller and his technical talents, Joey was allowed to help with the development and operation of the Eighth Wonder. Moller's wizardries as augmented by Joey's sidekick style of shy enthusiasm and occasional insights were critical for handling the various technical demands of the Light Show. And, if Tate was the musical brains of the outfit, it was Allie who served as artistic director for the overall scope of the shows. His brief appearances as Master of Ceremonies set the tone for each production, and his signature could easily be read throughout the flood of film images and song topics in the shows.

For the engineers of the Eight Wonder of the World, the late summer and early autumn of their sophomore year had been a time of great discovery. The year of 1967 was a rare time for music in America and England, making inspiration abundantly available by way of radio and records. Listening to and studying these sounds, the band had buried themselves away in Tate's basement with an ever-growing array of slides, film, and overhead projectors as they experimented with the various ways of combining music and multiple images. Within a few weeks, they had outgrown their workspace and moved their operation into the top floor of the Five Star Auto Hotel, a mostly vacant building owned by Allie's father. The results of their work began to emerge at mixers and dances through that first year, most notably at a stunning New Year's Eve performance where, as the young artists would learn to say, it "happened" for the first time: the product of their endless hours of preparation came across with a sense of subtle genius and complete spontaneity, and it met with a deeply receptive audience. The artists were born.

Present that night to witness this unlikely birth had been Father David Miles. Officially there as a chaperone for the school, Father Miles had instantly recognized the spark of genius in the Light Show. He knew it as the same flame used to ignite the various Gets of his young friends, but he saw in this new form the possibility of expressing things far more clearly—and safely—than the pranks ever could.

Father Miles had always been something of an unofficial sponsor for the Keepers of the Get. Since winning over Allie and the others in his elementary level drama classes, he had nurtured them along through the turbulent middle school years, often acting as "confessor" to their numerous transgressions against the Slumberset status quo. More than once Father Miles had likewise been an advocate of pardon and leniency in pleading their case before an administration not always as appreciative of the humorous side of life as he. For this, Father David Miles had gained the complete trust of Allie and the others, eventually earning the affectionate title of "Father Smiles."

On the first day of classes after the New Year's Eve debut of the Light Show, Father Miles had called Allie into his office and made a life-changing proposition. An Anglican priest from York, England, Father Miles had found a permanent home at Somerset as a teacher and chaplain. He seemed to take delight in using his British accent and studied mannerisms to the utmost, particularly when the drama of a situation called for it. On the afternoon of his meeting with Allie, it was apparently the occasion for full British fare. He seated Allie across a low table set with a silver tea service and, in true British form, pretended to get right to the point. "Allie, my boy," he asked, "how would you like to have an hour and a half of school time every day to work on your light show?"

Allie was stunned, but not too stunned to respond clearly and concisely, "Are you kidding?" he said. "How would you like to be chaplain of the Miss America contest?"

Father Miles laughed. "Well, I'm not sure that's a good parallel," he said, "but I get your drift. You would be in favor of such an idea, then?"

"In favor of it?" repeated Allie. "I would commit misdemeanors at least and probably certain felonies if pressed—"

"Well, hopefully that won't be necessary," interrupted Father Miles, his British accent embellishing his words in a way that helped stir Allie's already pricked curiosity. Father Miles popped his 'p' and 't' sounds and stretched one out of every three vowels sounds and mumbled everything in between; the effect was, as Allie once said, like someone spewing wet oatmeal out of a slow motion machine gun. "I have a proposition for you that could quite possibly make such an arrangement feasible," announced Father Miles.

"What is it, sir?" asked Allie, sitting up straighter in his seat and becoming more animated by the moment. "I mean, hey, enough of this British propriety . . . let's spit it out, American style!"

Again smiling, Father Miles held his ground and continued at his carefully calculated pace. Part of his strategy with his American students, it seemed, was to disrupt their frenetic impatience with the torturously slow tempo of his proceedings. He poured a cup of tea for Allie and, as he poured one for himself, began ever-so-slowly to explain.

"Well, Allie," he said, "it seems that with all the recent developments in what the great modern educators like to call progressive education, there is quite a stir about such things as 'independent study' and 'flexible curriculums' and the like. The idea is to take the student's most passionate interests and channel them through the most appropriate academic structure, in hopes of achieving new levels of learning."

Father Miles interrupted himself to offer Allie sugar and cream, both of which Allie shook off hastily. Taking a spot of sugar himself, the priest continued. "I, of course, have my doubts as to how all that will work in most situations, but I think the theory has some merit. And, in this case, I think it could actually come into play nicely for you and your mates."

"Are you talking about putting the Light Show on Independent Study?" asked Allie, leaning forward.

"Precisely."

"Smiles, you're a genius."

Again Father Miles only smiled. His tentative manner suggested he was not finished speaking. Allie caught himself and quickly tempered his enthusiasm. "I mean, Sir, it sounds like a fine idea."

"Right," said Father Miles. "And, judging by your enthusiastic posture on the matter, I am sure you will be happy to learn that the administration has already approved the idea — on a trial basis, of course. You and your three colleagues have been cleared for full academic credit in a tutorial course entitled 'Multi-Image Art and Modern Music Theory.' Off the record, we'll just call it 'Light Show 101'."

"You've already got it past the Bigwigs?" said Allie, gaping. "Father Miles, this is great." But, again, Allie was quick to respond to the continued restraint of Father Miles. He knew the wily chaplain well enough to know that there was only one free lunch in his doctrine, and this wasn't it. "Okay, okay," said Allie warily. "So what's our part of the bargain?"

"Well, Allie," began the chaplain, "I wonder if you can even imagine how terribly difficult it is to raise the spiritual interests of such happily pre-occupied youths as your peer group happens to consist of. Now I don't mean to imply that your own artistic pursuits—and your philosophy in general—is not as spiritually enlightened as the average armchair theologian, it's just that it is frightfully hard to translate such gems as some of you possess into anything even vaguely resembling church life. And you know how I feel about the importance of the Church."

"Yes, I do," said Allie. His concentration was at an all-time high. Many hours had he and his three friends spent with the earnest Father Miles, considering life from all angles imaginable. Many times had they gone head-to-head on the basic tenets of every major philosophy and doctrine from fundamental Christianity to Hinduism to Existentialism. A casual Christian believer at heart, Allie was opposed to any form of what he called "cattle-guarding" of his faith. So as Father Miles laid out his proposition, Allie knew it was going to force him to the very limits of his feelings about personal freedom and individual expression. His position on ritual and doctrine was mostly at opposite end of the spectrum from that of Father Miles, who had dedicated his life to the notion that certain practices of the Western spiritual tradition were like pillars in the human soul and certain doctrines were like 'stately walls with beautiful windows.' Sensing that Allie was beginning to feel cornered, Father Miles finally got to the real point.

"It's chapel," Father Miles said. "On a weekly basis, you lads simply trade me one hour of your presence—at the Sunday night chapel service—for the seven and one half hours of weekly school time I've won for your light show."

Allie laughed. "You're a cruel prelate," he said. "Are you sure you didn't step straight out of a time machine — from the Inquisition? Father Miles, you drive a hard bargain."

"But it's a great bargain," said the priest, knowing he was right. Despite Allie's renegade style, he had always been willing to listen to Father Miles's enlightening sermons, as had Tate and even Michael Moller. Joey's frequent attendance at the Sunday evening services had at first given a semblance of stability to his otherwise radical brand of faith, until his increasingly intense indoctrination in evangelical circles led him to see most of the organized church as the anti-Christ, a view not helped by Allie's own cautious outlook.

"Joey could be a problem," said Allie along those lines, but he was stalling and Father Miles knew it.

"You have won Joey over to projects much further from his personal beliefs than this," said the chaplain succinctly.

"That's true," said Allie. "But Moller, too. He's still pretty strong on his existential kick."

"No one's asking him to take vows for the priesthood," said Father Miles. "Certainly the experiential possibilities of consistent exposure to ritual could be presented to him as sufficient justification for his time. In addition, he seems to be quite taken by the Light Show, perhaps a bit more than any of you."

"Right again," said Allie and, once more impressed with Father Miles' own powers of observation and negotiation, he smiled. "So I guess it comes down to me."

"It would appear that it does," smiled Father Miles.

"You're a cruel prelate," responded Allie.

"But it's a great bargain," said Father Miles.

"It's a great bargain," agreed Allie. "I'll see what I can do."

In the end, of course, Allie and the others had gone for it. Light Show 101 had begun the following week, as had their formal induction into what Father Miles called the "Smells and Bells" of the Episcopal high mass service. Thus had the happy alliance of art and religion been formed between the wily priest and the Keepers of the Get.

"We believe in one God, the Father Almighty, the Maker of heaven and earth..." On this particular Sunday evening, Allie had successfully sobered his mind to the humble task of an acolyte, a job that he shared with his three fellow conscripts on rotating Sundays. As explicitly outlined in the final terms of the Great Bargain, each of the boys served as the Episcopalian equivalent of an altar boy—known in church terms as an "acolyte." Instantly renaming the position, "act-alikes," Allie and the others had given themselves over to the job in a way that was as surprising to them as it was to Father Miles. By the third year of their indentured servitude, in fact, the task had taken on some interesting aspects of its own, as each of the four novices came to appreciate the various ritualistic, symbolic, and even performance art aspects of the job. Allie, especially, had given great thought, as well as considerable verbiage, to the role of priest as performer, and performer as priest. Increasingly, the fine line between art and spirituality formed a tightrope upon which Allie dared to walk, all along beckoning his three friends to venture with him.

On this evening, however, there was more than performance art going on with the Keepers of the Get. As Father Miles gave the final reading for the first chapel service of the new school year and launched into his sermon, Michael Moller nudged Tate in the pew beside him. Reaching into the deep pocket of his oversized corduroy jacket, Moller produced a box of 35mm slides and a small viewer. Tate nodded and took first the viewer and then the slides from his friend. Lodging the viewer carefully between his knees, he opened the box of slides and took the top one out. When he slipped the slide into the viewer he casually leaned his head down a bit to catch a glimpse of the tiny screen. What he saw was a Fifteenth Century Dutch landscape painting. Nodding his approval to Moller, he removed the slide and exchanged it for another in the box.

Moller sat back in the pew and smiled. Much as Allie and Tate had made their Great Bargain with Father Miles a few years before, Michael Moller had recently struck his own deal on another front. During the first week of their senior year classes, Moller had won a brief audience with the greatly esteemed monarch of the arts at Somerset, Miss Jane Quinn. Known first as the "Mighty Quinn," after a Bob Dylan song of the period, she had then evolved from a Ricky Ricardo-voiced "Quin of Arts" into simply, "The Queen of Arts," or, simpler still "The Queen."

Miss Quinn was a young, sandy-blond teacher of art and art history. She had ascended the throne of the Keeper's pubescent hearts a few years earlier; her arrival had been one of the more pleasant developments in recent Somerset history, as she replaced the ancient and uninspired Johnson Withers as head of the art department. She brought an instant and palpable vitality to an area of Somerset life that had all but died over the previous years.

Though by no means a cover girl, Jane Quinn had a pretty face and animated personality that often shined with a bright radiance. To win her approval was to win a few enraptured moments of basking in this warm light, a reward that did much to draw the attention and effort of her students. Of the four friends, Michael Moller had from the beginning been the most smitten by this potential Madonna of Creativity, although Joey, too, had been accused by Allie of swooning for their teacher. Tate and Allie were apparently not exempt from her charms either, though, since by the time their Senior Year rolled around, all four of them had taken most of the various Technique classes offered at Somerset.

As enlightening and enjoyable as these courses had been, there was a greater glory awaiting the faithful upon the arrival of their final year in the Queen's service. A course called "The History of Art" was offered as an optional class to seniors only, being one of the golden carrots held before the students through their final years at Somerset. This lights-off tour of Europe and beyond was an adventure of epic proportions, and the Keepers of the Get had long awaited their divine appointment. When their hour had arrived, they had not been disappointed. Five minutes and twenty majestic 35mm slides into their first class, Moller had leaned toward Tate and the others and whispered, "Fellas, we're in the Holy of Holies."

The following day Michael Moller had staked out a spot on Jane Quinn's previously researched daily rounds, a well-thought out plan on his mind. As made possible by the flagship benefit of the Somerset "Senior Privileges", Moller had grabbed an Off-Campus Lunch Pass, ducked out of the school around noon and piloted his car to the number one destination for these forty-five minute blasts into citywide freedom. Tomstead's Sundry and Soda Fountain was a wondrous place buried beneath the main corridors of what had been the city's first shopping center; it was an irresistible haven of old books and greasy hamburgers. Universally known among the Slumberset as "Tolstoy's," Mr. Jacob Tomstead's dusty establishment was a catacombs of fine literature, junk novels, magazines, and comic books. At the back was a café counter and several booths where patrons could choose between the sugar highs of giant milk shakes and the longer burning if equally as nutritionless fares of ground beef and white bread. Along with the truly impressive collection of books and magazines, the notoriously capitalistic Mr. Tomstead also featured a vast array of novelty items and bizarre gifts in his relentless effort to see the American dream realized in his own financial life. The result was a veritable museum of modern culture, a drawing card that had long ago secured the almost daily appearance of the Queen of Arts. Or maybe, as Moller sometimes thought, she was just addicted to the chocolate shakes.

On the day Michael Moller waited in hiding among the tall shelves of Literary Classics in paperback, Miss Jane Quinn had arrived as hoped and was soon cornered among the latest old shipment of old movie posters.

"Oh, hi, Miss Quinn," said Michael Moller, feigning surprise at "running into" his teacher off campus. "Checking out the latest in modern art?"

"Well, yes," smiled the pleasantly surprised teacher. "Aren't these great?"

"Yeah, they really are," said Moller, relieved by Miss Quinn's initial friendliness. Despite his mental preparation, it was always a tenuous experience to encounter a teacher outside of the mind-numbing familiarity of the school, and there was more at stake here than a chance meeting. Pulling his curly locks out of his face, Moller's eyes shifted with a believable sincerity to the boxes of partially unwrapped posters. "Hey, here's a classic," he said quickly, picking up a poster from the *Wizard of Oz*.

Without hesitating he launched into his standard cameo portrayal of Dorothy, proclaiming in a comic falsetto, "Well, Miss Quinn, this certainly doesn't look like Kansas."

His teacher smiled appreciatively, happy to get an off-campus glimpse of one of her more intriguing students. "Very good, Mr. Moller. You should try out for the next school play."

"Naa," replied Moller. "I'm not into that stuff . . . it's a little too phony, you know." Gathering his sport coat and shirt into a Shakespearean stance he bellowed a melodramatic, 'To be or not to be' ", and then shifted back into his own cracking voice, "that may be the question but what do most high school kids know about that? 'To be a cheerleader or not to be a cheerleader?'—now there's a question we can relate to."

At that Jane Quinn chuckled aloud, sending Michael Moller into a short orbit above the last of his nervousness. Seizing the moment, he plunged into the heart of his mission.

"Yeah, that's the thing about high school," he began. "You can't just hit 'em with Shakespeare and figure they're gonna get it. I mean, in Shakespeare's time there was not even such a thing as teenagers. Sure, Romeo and Juliet happened to be in their teenage years, but those guys were grown-ups. It wasn't like, 'hey, you wanna go to the prom?' No, it was, 'hey, let's go out and kill ourselves just to make some sort of political statement.' Remind me not to double date with those two. I mean, how can we relate to that? Come on, Shakespeare would have to make Hamlet captain of the football team if he's gonna expect us spoiled American descendants to relate."

By now, the young teacher was somewhat absorbed by Michael Moller's performance. She had put down the poster she had been looking at and was quietly studying her student's monologue.

"So that's why we've got the Light Show," continued Moller. "It's like, let's boil this thing down to its basic, understandable elements, roll them out in some new configurations and see what that triggers in everybody else. I mean, isn't that what art is all about, Miss Queen, I mean, Quinn?"

"Something like that," said the teacher.

"And so, wouldn't it be great—" and here Michael Moller was intensely engaged in making his pre-meditated pitch seem like it was just occurring to him on the spot—"wouldn't it be great if we could take some of these basic American kid things like we've got in the Show so far and mix them in with some classic art stuff like you show us in class . . . "

"Put you right up there with Van Gogh and Rembrandt," interjected Miss Quinn.

"Well, yeah," stuttered Moller. Caught off guard for a moment, he quickly rebounded to his teacher's kidding with a quick burst of cocky energy. "Yeah, you bet! Van Gogh and Rembrandt, Reed and Moller...I like that. It sounds good. No, you know what I mean. There would have to be a way of using some of that great art stuff going on in this century and see if it can hold its own. I mean, if Michelangelo wimps out in the face of the Hell's Angels, why even keep studying his stuff?"

"Why else indeed?" smiled Miss Queen.

"So what I was think . . . I mean, it sort of just hit me . . . what if I could maybe . . . you know . . . borrow some of your slides—really carefully you know and just for a few days—so I could get some copies made that we could use in the Show . . . "

A gently raised eyebrow on Miss Quinn's peaceful face seemed to signal her understanding of the game. "Well, that's quite a little brainstorm, Mr. Moller. And I hadn't even noticed that it was cloudy."

"Well you know what they say about the weather in Oklahoma," parlayed Moller. "If you don't like it, just wait a minute."

"From Shakespeare to Will Rogers," replied his teacher. "You are quite the chronicler of culture." The mock admiration in her voice was outweighed by a gentle sincerity and Moller knew that his request was being granted. He quickly dropped the last of his cockiness and shifted into the most humble tone he thought he could get away with.

"Oh, it's not like that, really," he said. "It's just that a few things have stuck with me."

"Well, then perhaps a few things more would stick with you if you had some classic art in your repertoire."

Moller dropped all his airs and blurted out, "you mean we can . . . you know . . . it's alright if we—"

"Come by my office on Friday and I'll give you a couple sets to get you started."

Thus had the Light Show received the first of its heavy artillery form the annals of great art. Moller had stopped by to pick up the first battery of slides from Miss Queen on Friday afternoon and, after a busy weekend apart from his comrades, was having his first opportunity to share his catch with Tate during the Monday morning chapel. Being careful not to be noticed by Father Miles, Moller and Tate had spent much of the service squinting into their laps at the powerful images of fine art captured on film. The first installation covered mostly European painting from the 14th to the 17th century. So while Allie and Father Miles were performing the various stages of the chapel service, Moller and Tate were taking turns gazing through a tiny lense into the magical worlds of the Dutch, Flemish, and Spanish painters. There were the muscular disciples of Christ in the Rubens paintings and the sorrowful women of Titian. Then appeared the spiritually charged interiors of Van Eyck and the ultra-real rendering of Christ by Rembrandt. "It's like a peep-show into heaven," said Moller at one point.

"No kidding," agreed Tate, already seeing how they could work into the light show. "Nice job, man, these are great."

Meanwhile, assisted by Allie, Father Miles steered the congregation into the peaceful waters of the Prayers and Petitions section of the service. Putting the last of the slides back into the box, Michael Moller could not help but mutter a quiet thanks for the generous aid of the Queen of Arts. Then, as smoothly as a sand-banked river, the service turned a gentle bend into the Preparation for Communion. Closing up the box of slides, Tate and Moller returned their full attention to the front of the church. Allie's dedication to his side of the Great Bargain had him moving like a true virtuoso of the altar boy guild as he followed Father Miles gracefully through the paces of the Preparation. Allie's comically graceful lilt gave this most hallowed of English high-church choreographies an expression that instantly revalidated its meaning for modern man.

"The guy's an artist," whispered Tate to Michael Moller. Allie had just two-stepped his way across the front of the chapel, all the while cradling the Communion chalice with a perfectly sanctified sense of ceremony. Tate just smiled and nodded, breathing in the incense-filled air of the Sunday evening service, finding temporary relief from the ghosts haunting him. In the asylum of the chapel, and in the flow of Moller's forward progress on the Light Show, he could close the door on the lingering images of his fears and drift away from the muffled sounds of the terror he hoped would somehow be gone.

On one side of Tate, Michael Moller was now slumped in total comfort against the end of the pew, eyes on Allie as if he were the lead dancer in a magnificent ballet. Joey, meanwhile, sat rigidly on the other side of Tate, breathing with some difficulty against his allergies and listening intently to Father Miles's every word. Every so often Joey would twitch or lurch, as if prodded by some phrase in the liturgy of which he was not quite sure, and then his eyebrows would furrow as his insatiable mind processed that phrase against every tenet of truth and doctrine he did trust. Allie had dubbed these movements "heresy spasms" and, in accordance with the Keepers' policy on the matter, Tate spent a good portion of the remaining part of the chapel service faithfully elbowing Joey following each spasm—"friendly shock treatments," Allie called them—in hopes of rescuing Joey from his over-active brain and his tortured conscience. Then the Preparation was ending and it was time to come forward for Communion.

At the altar Tate, Moller and Joey met up with their robed friends from the other side of the rail. In the heart of this sanctuary, all the mental gyrations ceased and even the jokes fell away as the perplexities of a world gone askew were put on hold for a moment.

"This is the body of Christ. Do this in remembrance of Me," said Father Miles as he broke pieces of bread from a large loaf and handed one to each of the three friends at the altar.

Then Allie took the cup of wine and held it out to Tate as Father Miles said, "This is the blood of Christ, shed for the forgiveness of sins." Tate put his lips to the cold edge of the cup as Allie tilted the chalice until the wine poured into Tate's mouth. A slight shiver ran through Tate as he swallowed the wine and the mild taste of alcohol hit him. A warm peace settled in on Tate as Allie moved down the altar to their other two friends. Within a few moments, as they returned to their seats, the peace surrounded and filled them all with new hope, even as the flow of new ideas began to brighten up their thoughts.

Benefited by the terms of the Great Bargain, the Light Show had flourished, as had the four friends' tolerance for life in a wooden pew. It seemed that both endeavors were silently working towards weaving their lives together in a seamless bond in a way that might somehow prepare them for the difficult times ahead. For this they could forever thank the wily little Englishman, presently finishing his first service of their perilous senior year.

"The Lord be with you," bellowed Father Miles at the end of their separate meditations.

"And with your spirit," rejoined the four friends in the small chapel.

"Go in peace," said the priest.

"Amen," said his friends.

CHAPTER SIX

PIGSKIN APOCALYPSE

On the following Monday morning, all of Tulsa arose to find that the curse of Indian summer had been broken. The slight drop in temperature was magnified a hundred fold by the much more critical departure of humidity. Although scalding temperatures might return, veterans of the region's dramatic weather cycles somehow knew when the dog days of August had given way to the first hints of fall. Mercy was unmistakable.

"This is great," exclaimed Allie as he and Tate flew down the last hill before the entrance to the campus. Windows wide open, stereo blaring, they celebrated the occasion by hanging their heads out the window and yelling at the cattle, who were enjoying their final days of pastoral roaming before the land developers ground up their grazing land into the chuck-roast size parcels palatable for housing projects.

"Go for it!" screamed Tate at the grazing cattle. "It'll all be driveways and flowerbeds before you know it!"

The atmosphere at school was as much in transition as the weather. The previous week's three-day orientation was giving way to the first full week of classes and the change in weather made it all seem, in Allie's words, "like they're playing for keeps out here."

"There's no turning back now," agreed Tate. They were making their way through the front doors of the school, and the flow of students into the building had a force of its own.

"This is like a real school," grimaced Allie.

"No kidding," said Tate. "It's like, 'hey Beave, did you bring your lunch or are you buying today?' "

Allie laughed. "Yeah, actually I'm taking Lassie home for lunch so you and the Beave will have to go it alone today—u h-oh, Great Stone Face at 10 degrees starboard—defend your tie."

Gracefully the two friends veered off to the left and averted the roaming giant of harsh discipline. Tate and Allie had made it a personal challenge to make it through a given school day with their neckties loosened several notches below school standards. What had once been an insignificant issue of comfort had become a symbol of personal freedom. The trick was to slide the tie into respectable position only when forced by impending circumstances, and even then not until the last possible moment. In this case, a simple re-routing was all they needed and the two friends were off to meet Moller in the media room, ties firmly at half-mast.

"Hey boys," said Michael Moller from behind a stack of slide projectors. "Can you believe this set-up?" He looked up from his tinkering and spread his hands out to the panorama of equipment, cords, and electronic paraphernalia. "It's like audio-visual Disneyland in here. I think Bell and Howell are both buried in a vault underneath this room."

"What are you working on?" asked Tate.

"Oh, nothing much," said Michael Moller. "Just some old stuff, really—some of the cloud shots and the skid row sequence."

"Did you get the still shots back yet on the fountain Get?" asked Allie.

"Not yet," said Tate. "They're supposed to be ready today. I'll pick them up after school."

"Man, I wish we had filmed that," said Allie. He slapped a fist into his other hand and shook his head. "We should have gotten that whole scene on 16 millimeter."

"It would have been some great footage," agreed Moller. "But I just couldn't' get all that together so quick...after just getting back into town and all."

"I know, I know," said Allie sincerely. "I should have gotten everything ready before you got back. What were we thinking, Tate?"

"We just never dreamed it would have come off so perfectly," suggested Tate.

"Yeah, but we should always be ready, just in case. That's the deal, man: you've always got to have those cameras rolling just in case."

"Gets a little expensive," said Moller.

"Since when is money an object here?" asked Allie. "Your dad running low on food stamps this month?"

"Oh, I forgot," snapped Moller playfully. "We've got Rockefeller junior here for our little scout leader. Say, Rocky, can I have GM for my birthday?"

Tate had been wandering around the room, not paying much attention to the usual bantering, when he discovered a 16 millimeter projector cued up with a film he did not recognize. "Hey, Michael, what's this?"

"I don't know what that is," said Moller shrugging. "Maybe Joey knows."

"Knows what?" demanded Joey suddenly as he burst into the room.

"Knows what the meaning of life is," teased Allie, "when he grows up."

"Funny," sneered Joey, "your humor is killing me."

"No, Joey," said Michael Moller, "we wondered if you knew what was on the projector there. On number four, I think."

"Ohhhh . . . ," said Joey, his mood changing quickly as he seemed to be remembering something more pleasant than Allie's last wisecrack.

"On number four, huh? Well, no I can't remember what that might be. Can you, Michael?"

Joey was the worst actor of the group. He had pulled a few fine charades among the many he had been asked to attempt, but for the most part, he just had too much trouble lying, even for a short time, and even when the lie was completely in the best interest of everyone involved, as was the case this morning. As usual, Allie was on to him instantly.

"Joey, you're lying like a dog," said Allie smiling. "What are you guys up to?"

"He's just brain-damaged, Allie," said Moller casually. "We don't know what's on that projector . . . but, hey, we've got twenty minutes till class, why don't we check it out."

"Why don't we indeed," snorted Allie. "You guys have got something going here . . . if it's another porno film I'm turning you both in to the Great Stone Face myself."

"Allie!" protested Joey.

"Sorry, Joey, it's for your own good. I know you weren't in on that last one but if Moller's taking you down the tubes with him, I've got to stop the moral decay before it's too late."

By then Tate was at the light switch, "Ready?"

"Yeah, Tate," said Michael Moller, still playing it cool. "Hit the switch and let's see what we've got here."

THE LAST GET

The magical whir of the projector cast its instant spell on the four friends. A white light flashed onto the large screen at the front of the room, followed by a blurry scene.

"Focus!" yelled everyone at once.

"Okay, okay," said Joey and slowly there appeared a clear image. A crowd of students was packed into the school amphitheater and Mr. Martin was taking the podium.

"Moller!" shouted Allie. "You got the fountain scene! Tell me you got the fountain scene."

Okay," said Michael Moller coolly. "I got the fountain scene."

"You are a prince!" said Allie, eyes glued to the screen. "You are an absolute prince!"

"Just a good nose for news, old boy." said Moller. He leaned back in his chair and put his hands behind his head. On the screen the camera's eye zoomed in on the Frisbee smacking the Headmaster in the face and then pulled back to show Father Miles reaching down to his feet and coming back up with the Frisbee. Then the shot pulled back further to catch Allie sneaking back to his seat. It was a great sequence and Moller had to chuckle with his friends. "Caught in the act," he said.

"This is great," said Tate and Allie together. After a few seconds of Allie resting safely in his seat, there was a short blip on the screen where Moller had shut off the camera to wait for Allie to make his second move.

"There he goes," said Tate. And with great joy and laughter the four friends watched as the monumental event at the amphitheater was replayed before their eyes. Pleading a convincing case for the need for historical documentation, Michael Moller had won permission to set his camera on the roof of the class building overlooking the amphitheater, so the point of view was panoramic and commanding.

"What a great camera angle," said Allie.

"The gallery of angels," said Joey quietly.

"The what?" asked Tate.

"The gallery of angels," said Joey again. "It's like we're looking down on the whole scene from a cloud, you know, like a balcony in heaven."

"Okay, I can see that," agreed Allie. "But do you think angels would pay two dollars for a bag of popcorn?"

Before Joey could figure out if Allie was agreeing with him or making fun of him, Moller interrupted, pointing to the screen and saying, "Alright, now watch this . . ."

The figure of Allie was in perfect view as he approached the fountain. On its last toss, the chair make a graceful arch and then disappeared with a splash, as Michael Moller added the sound effect of the sizzling hot steel in the water.

"Perfect!" shrieked Allie. "Moller, you're the best!"

The others were laughing in complete agreement as the end of the film ran off the reel and the bright light reappeared on the screen.

"It's a masterpiece," said Tate.

Michael Moller calmly nodded his head. "Came off pretty well," he agreed. "I think we can find a place for it in our program . . ."

Just as they began brainstorming about what the best application of this new footage would be for the Light Show, the bell rang and it was time to report to the commons for Announcements.

"Well," said Allie. "Let's go see what else is happening."

When they wandered back into the main part of the school, the Keepers found that the Commons had been transformed by an apparent onslaught of banners and balloons. "Oh, my God," said Allie. "It's a pep rally!"

"Indeed," sighed Michael Moller, "it seems the dark demigod of the autumn world has followed us to our new haunts..."

"The pigskin idolatry continues," whined Joey.

Streamers and balloons filled the high spaces of the room, while banners denouncing the football team's first enemy were strung everywhere. By the time the four innocent observers had walked in, the cheerleaders had already taken the floor and were leading the sleepy students through a barrage of chants and slogans. After a few seconds of gross alienation, Allie turned to his friends and announced, "You know fellas, we're gonna have to do something about this stuff."

With his friends nodding their sober approval, Allie composed himself and then issued the inevitable proclamation: "It's time for us to go up against the god of football," said Allie. "We're gonna launch a Get against this Pigskin pandemonium."

Because of the size and nature of the school, Somerset had a rather unusual football schedule. First they played about five games on what the wisecracking athletic director called the Highway 12 Tour. Being too small a school to play against the city public schools, Somerset had for years gone up against the schools in some of the small towns just outside the city. In reality, only three of the towns were actually on the old Highway 12, but it was clear what the wisecracking athletic director meant.

In Oklahoma, as in certain other states, there is the phenomenon of the football town. It all begins on Highway 12 or some other two-lane state road that turns into Main Street as soon as the first of four traffic lights appear. About twenty or thirty store fronts line both sides of the street, looking like Hollywood facades of an Old West boom town. A speculating visitor might wonder if they kept this part of town crated up in a warehouse for most of the year, just setting it up for football homecoming and Christmas eve, but the sound of pickup trucks cracks through this fantasy—trucks with teenage cowboys hanging out the windows, honking their horns and calling the visiting team all manner of derogatory names which are hardly original but do have a certain local charm to them.

What has happened in these town is this: in the days just after the Oklahoma heat had finished melting the Arctic Glaciers into new rivers, a certain local hero made good on the region's battlefields of high school football and by merit of an uncle-in-law who happened to be a state senator, he won a scholarship to Football Mecca itself, Oklahoma University. There he played out the drama of four years as a second-string guard on a National Championship football team and returns home to parades, slaps on the back, and new elementary school football programs inaugurated in his name. From that day forth, no male member of the citizenry of that town can enter into the joy of small-town acceptance without passing through the formidable initiation rites of two-a-day football practices in the blistering summer heat.

So it was in Odell, Oklahoma. The god of pigskin had been set on the throne of every young heart in that town, dangerously close to the lamb-carrying Savior whose picture shared the dining room wall with the yellowed clippings of Odell's living sacrifice to the OU god of pigskin. Odell's own Joe Grutland had been a linebacker on the legendary OU teams of 1954-57, the pinnacle of the Bud Wilkinson era and the beginning of the end of free will among the male youth of Odell, Oklahoma. Ever since, participation in football was as certain as circumcision in Odell, and by the looks on the faces of their helmeted players, about as painful. "High-school football as a cult religion," Allie once said, "is a bitter way to go."

It was into the mouth of this heathen monster that the baby blue Somerset bus was to venture the very next Friday evening. Everyone knew what to expect. Nowhere on the Highway 12 Tour would one meet with such intensity. Eight-year-olds would yell obscenities and vicious country witticisms at the bus as their parents stood by proudly. Pony-tailed girls in pep-club uniforms would raise their noses in arrogant condescension in a stunning show of denial as regards their own bleak existence. Two generations of former players and their weary wives would line the parking lot in a show of silent solidarity. And then there were the players themselves.

Stories of the kid beaten with an "ugly stick" pale beside the horror wrought on Odell's youth. These poor souls had instead been beaten with a football stick, and it created a subtler yet infinitely more horrifying animal. No neck. Tiny brain. Muscle-bound eyebrows. Iron jaws. There were club-like hands and arms on some of them, strangely large thighs and over-round hips on others. And in all of them, in every face of every once-innocent youth, there was the animal look, the high-school kamikaze look of a youngster robbed of every reason for existence but one: Pigskin Glory! This was a Football Town, this would be a Football Night, and Somerset was the Archenemy, the Specter that threatened to steal away the Golden Ring of Hope from this pitiful town. Somerset was the Visiting Team!

It was against this backdrop that Allie planned to attack the god of pigskin.

"We'll use the launchers," announced Allie at their quickly scheduled strategy meeting. The four friends and a handful of accomplices were at Tate's house, congregating on the rolling lawn by the estate's pond.

Tate nodded in agreement. "It's time we put this technological marvel to its best use," he said.

The "launcher" was a huge, three-man slingshot constructed by Allie and Tate from surgical tubing, leather and stainless steel pipe. They had begun experimenting with the concept as early as the eighth grade, but it was not until their sophomore year that they had come up with the final prototype. They now had three nearly identical models in their arsenal and, to hear Allie tell it, it was now time for "full deployment of this state-of-the-art Get weaponry".

"So what will we launch?" asked Tate.

"Mini-balloons," said Allie.

"Water or paint?" asked Michael Moller.

"Better go with water," said Allie.

"What's the target?" asked Joey.

Here Allie gave way to a slight dramatic pause. He smiled at his three friends and their followers and punctuated his short silence with contained delight: "The Odell Bearcats," he said. "We're going to launch them over Bearcat Stadium into the middle of the game."

"That's crazy," said Tate slowly, then he smiled. "It's perfect, of course, but it's really crazy."

"Bearcat Stadium," chuckled Moller, "the Mouth of the Beast. It *is* perfect." Joey just shook his head. It was three "yes" votes already so Joey did not even bother to object. Instead he just whispered the usual, "Oh God, please forgive us" and it was settled.

Three nights later, the four friends and a group of four other helpers met at their appointed rendezvous spot in the Bearcat Stadium parking lot. It was Friday night. It was a brisk sixty degrees out. There was a strange energy in the air.

"Man, you can feel it," Allie was saying as a group of three straggling zombies from the Odell team crossed the parking lot not far from them.

"It's high-school hypnosis," Tate said.

"It's idolatry," insisted Joey.

"Whatever it is," said Moller, "they have these guys shot up on Pigskin Glory, and there's no stopping them."

"Not by might anyway," smiled Allie, with rumors of his own brand of Pigskin Glory twinkling in his eyes. "However . . . "

Circling around behind the last of the Odell players, Allie led the way to a small fence that separated the stadium from the practice fields behind it. Waiting a moment until the excitement of the Odell team taking the field created a distraction, Allie quickly hopped the fence, followed by Tate and Joey. Michael Moller, meanwhile, headed into the stadium and immediately took up his station on the top row of the bleachers overlooking the practice field behind him and the field of play before him.

On the field, it was Pigskin pandemonium. The opening home game in Odell was like the Fourth of July and New Year's Eve all rolled into one. Moller watched in astonishment as a marching band seemingly larger than the town itself took the field. The pep squad was next and was so big that Moller theorized it could only have been assembled by the taking of virgin slaves from other towns in Pigskin conquests previous. The stands on the hometown side of the field were overflowing.

"They must bus in all their kin from a four-county area for these games," thought Michael. After a brief display of small-town musical wizardry, the band quieted down for the long awaited inauguration of the 1969 Football Season, Odell, Oklahoma.

Across a cool autumn breeze, the deep and reverent voice of Joe Grutland himself re-united the people of Odell with their destiny. His voice wafted mystically through the hazy glow of the stadium lights, his words reverberating with authority against the gently awakening hopes of a town with little else to live for. Here the generations came and went like so many seasons of planting and harvest. The endless cycle of working, eating, and sleeping was broken only by the brief chance for heroism on the region's rich, green fields of athletic battle. The Great Festival Moon for this people was shaped like a football.

From the top row of the bleachers on the other side of the field, the stirring of the souls was clearly apparent to Michael Moller. "I could see goose bumps on those people from eighty yards away," he later told the others. "They were into it."

On the darkened practice field behind the visiting team's bleachers there was profound anticipation of a different kind. "This is gonna be great," shivered Allie as he took the last ammunition from a duffel bag and laid it carefully beside the launchers on the damp grass. "Listen to that guy carrying on over the PA system...there's probably not a dry eye in the house. If ever there's been a case of someone taking themselves too seriously, this has got to be it."

With Tate and Joey chuckling in agreement, they picked up their favorite launcher and began strapping it to their hands, one end in Joey's right hand, the other in Tate's left. Their helpers braced themselves on each side of Joey and Tate and then grabbed a hold of whatever clothing or appendage they could to help hold the two in place. When they were ready, Allie picked up a water balloon and laid it gently into the leather cradle of the slingshot. "Okay," he said. "Practice Shot."

The entire group shuffled around until their backs were to the stadium; then Joey and Tate and their "anchors" braced themselves.

"Ready here," said Tate.

Slowly, steadily, Allie pulled the leather cradle back until the surgical straps were stretched to the limits against Tate and Joey's quivering hands. Allie froze for a moment and then silently released his grip, sending the small balloon filled with liquid off into the autumn sky. With great effort, the balloon could be seen hurtling through the night in a giant arch until it met up with the dark line of the ground several hundred feet away.

"Perfect," whispered Allie. The launcher was indeed an amazing innovation.

Behind them the band struck up the Star Spangled Banner. Unconsciously, all the members of this outlaw band of pranksters stood up a little straighter. Joey even placed his right hand — still wrapped in the end of the launcher—to his chest. They lifted their heads to the great halo of stadium lights hanging over the football stadium and listened to the eternal anthem of high schools and war veterans.

"It's like a hymn to the god of Pigskin," said Joey, and Allie had to agree. With Joey mumbling something about "misdirected hope," Allie's eyes fell on the arsenal of water balloons laid out in neat rows on the ground. These were their missiles of Truth, he thought, and he embraced his mission with a new sense of certainty. "Come on," rasped Allie. "Let's drop one on the band."

The unplanned move seemed instantly appropriate to Tate, and for Joey it was like an answer to prayer. "Yeah, come on," he said as if it had been his idea.

Quickly the launcher was loaded and ready. "Ten degrees right," said Allie, and his human launching pad pivoted smoothly to the right. "Perfect . . . hold it . . . hold it . . . k-plang!"

The black dot made a perfect arch over the bleachers and quickly disappeared into the dark atmosphere above the halo of artificial light. Allie, Tate, and Joey strained their eyes to see it re-enter but failed. Their answer came a moment later, though, as Moller, unaware of their change in plans and deeply engrossed in some Star Spangled meditations of his own, suddenly did a double take in the direction of the playing field and jerked his head around to see if his friends had just fired an unscheduled shot. Seeing them all posed around the still "smoking" launcher, he threw his head back in laughter and then shot them a "direct hit" sign. The Get was under way.

The first scheduled shot was to have been on the opening kick-off. Quickly rejoining their original strategy, the boys began reloading as the crowd roared for the teams to take the fields. Michael Moller signaled to his left, indicating that the Odell Bearcats would be lining up on the North end of the playing field. The human launching pad shuffled a quick twenty yards to the north and prepared for firing. As the teams lined up, Moller waited for the perfect moment and then dropped his hand behind the top rail of the bleachers.

"Fire," said Allie as he released his missile. The whistle for the opening kick-off sounded as the balloon disappeared above the lights. Michael Moller surveyed the field of play intensely until suddenly he jerked with laughter. The balloon had exploded in the white chalk of the Odell thirty yard-line, just a few feet from a profoundly entranced Odell Bearcat. Shocked out of his stupor by this unexplainable visitor from another dimension, he stood upright just as the football was kicked into play. Stranded between two worlds as he was, he made an easy target for the undistracted Somerset attacker bearing down on him. As he watched the Bearcat take a merciless hit from his opponent, Moller waved an ecstatic report to his comrades. It was: The Keepers of the Get: 2, the god of Pigskin: 0.

Having ultimately promised themselves a non-partisan attack on the Pigskin heresy, the next few balloons were intended for the Somerset team. The first shot disappeared into the night, never to be seen again. This mystery was not without precedent in past launcher experiments, however, and simply called for another attempt. The second shot re-entered the atmosphere twenty yards behind both teams. Signaling the degree of error as best he could, Moller directed the third shot while the Somerset team was in the huddle. When the intense concentration of the Somerset team suddenly exploded with a wet cloud of dust in their midst, Moller nearly fell over the rail of the bleachers. Half the team looked up into the sky, as the rest of them muddled around in confusion until a frantic coach regained their attention to the game going on around them. Too late, however, to avoid a five-yard penalty for delay of game.

By now both teams were aware of some strange phenomenon. Because of the deep arch of the projectiles, the unexplained objects seemed to be falling from the sky itself. The ultra-thin balloons purchased by Allie from a laboratory supply house tended to disintegrate during the explosion, leaving no evidence whatsoever of man-made mischief. There was just no explaining these giant raindrops or gargantuan bird droppings, especially with their apparent sense of intent. It was a complete and startling mystery, and it reduced an otherwise ruthless band of single-minded pigskin maniacs into a cowering band of shell-shocked kids.

By half time, the coaches on both sides were raving madmen. No amount of whining explanation on the part of their players could get through to them. Their half-time speeches were nearly identical sermons on the First Commandment of the Pigskin religion: Keep Thy Head in the Game! But it was no use. After the Odell Band and Pep Squad had watched their halftime show turn into the most unnerving experience since the London air raids, the teams returned to the fields with great reservation.

Michael Moller, meanwhile, had made use of a halftime to round up additional recruits for a second-half blitz of still greater proportions. Pre-game uncertainties about the risk of recognition had vanished with the first few shots: the balloons dropped faster and smaller than the eye could see. With the coast thus clear, it had been part of the plan to add two more launching teams to the attack, as arranged the day before with six novice Keepers of the Get from the lower classes. With some effort, Moller rounded up these soldiers from their current dens of high school revelry and sent them to their station. By the time the second half began, three launchers and a second batch of ammunition were ready.

In his wisdom, Allie had decided to wait out most of the second half. The silence, he reasoned, would be as unnerving as the first wave of bombs had been. He was right. By the time the third quarter had ended, the game had been reduced to a tentative affair of fearful anticipation. The power of the Pigskin god had been crippled. The game had become completely irrelevant. This, of course, was not enough. Allie wanted a complete revival. He was out to break forever the spell of seriousness cast over the adherents of high school football. He wanted a Pigskin Apocalypse.

"Patience, lads, patience," he coaxed his allies, as the minutes ticked off the game clock. Finally, with three minutes left in the game, he made his move. "Let's load 'em up." A few brief instructions were given to the others and then the barrage began. They fired in unison, reloaded, and fired together again. Round after round of the invisible bombs found their way to the middle of the playing field. There were direct hits on helmets and numerous near misses. Pandemonium was breaking out. By now even the coaches were becoming believers, but it was too late to forestall the wrath of this new deity so obviously at war with the god of Pigskin. The apocalypse had come.

The game ended with Somerset an incidental winner. This in itself was a miracle wrought by the new deity: Odell was the one member of the Highway 12 Tour who had categorically resisted Somerset's domination. It was the first Somerset victory against them in eight years, but it went almost unnoticed. The players were just glad to get off the field.

The Keepers had made their point: the game really didn't matter.

"Beginning tonight," Allie would later say, "Pigskin glory will fade from Odell, Oklahoma. The yellowed clippings of Joe Grutland's heroics will slowly find their way into drawer tombs and cardboard graves, leaving the lamb-carrying Savior an undisputed place on the mantle of Odell hearts."

For Allie and the others, Odell would long be remembered as one of their finest mission fields. Paganism had been laid to rest there in a big way that night. The captives had been set free from bondage to a system of Pigskin idolatry, never again to be so enslaved.

"What a great night," said Allie as he tossed the duffel into the back trunk of his car in the Odell parking lot. Then, as if the heavens were sounding the amen, he turned to see a small child pull away from a shell-shocked older brother in uniform and jerk him toward the car. "I wanna go home," he insisted. "I don't wanna be football player when I grow up."

"That's the spirit," said Allie quietly.

"Good lad," agreed Tate. Just then Moller emerged from the crowd moving across the parking lot. Pure joy seemed to emanate from every part of his animated body as he practically jumped onto Joey.

"It was a revival, Joey," he exclaimed. "A good old-fashioned fire and brimstone—and water balloon—revival. Could you believe it?"

Joey just wheezed a happy, "Yeah, it was a real killer." Then he added, "And you had the best seat in the house."

"That's right, Moller," said Allie, "we're expecting the Full Report on the way back to town. Now come on, you guys, let's get out of here before somebody figures this thing out and starts a lynching party"

The others happily agreed and piled into the car for the long victory ride home. It was the first full-scale Get of the new school year and it had come off more perfectly than they had even hoped. As their car pulled out of the parking lot onto Highway 12, a beautiful mist was illuminated by their headlights.

"Check it out," said Allie as a tunnel of light opened up through the fog. "We're entering a Cloud of Glory, Joey." Suddenly too pleasantly exhausted to answer, the others just smiled and settled into their seats. The hum of the tires on the smooth asphalt road added to the hypnotic effect of the white stripes appearing out of the mist in front of them. Even Moller's Full Report could wait until the next day. For now the four friends were quite happy to ride silently together through the silvery wisps of clouds hovering low over Highway 12.

CHAPTER SEVEN

WHEEZE-BAGS, GOLDEN BOYS, AND BARBIE DOLLS

Mr. Gabbin R. Stone, a.k.a. The Great Stone Face, stood before the student body and searched them out with a cold stare. Slowly rubbing his hands together as if squeezing some poor student's golfball-sized head between them, he intended to force a confession by the sheer power of his psychic fear.

He wanted to know what had happened at the Odell game. He wanted an explanation. He wanted blood.

Many an innocent student's eyes stared at the floor, unable to face the wrath of the Great Stone Face. The weakest among them had to cling desperately to their clear consciences, resisting the temptation to confess to a crime they did not commit, simply to break the grip of fear clenching the collective throat of the student body. As for the guilty, they seemed by comparison quite secure in their hideouts. Allie yawned and stretched as Tate and Joey quietly continued their game of chess on the floor of the Commons. Michael Moller turned the page of his history book, calmly waiting for the morning announcements to continue.

"We know there is a group of culprits in this room," bellowed the Great Stone Face after a long silence. "We intend to expose the guilty and levy the maximum punishment if they do not come forward immediately. Do yourself a favor and report to my office after announcements and some leniency will be considered."

"Right," whispered Allie. "Castration instead of decapitation . . . 'leniency' indeed."

With a final hexing stare, the Great Stone Face yielded the floor to the rest of the morning's announcements. The usual variety of trivial meeting schedules and project news sounded like elf chatter in the wake of

Mr. Stone's booming indictments. The contrast was so striking it awakened the elf in Allie, who suddenly could not resist baiting the Great Stone Face in front of the entire school. Raising his hand soberly, he was recognized by Headmaster Martin and stood for his brief announcement regarding a fictitious club just concocted.

"There will be a short meeting of the Slumberset Legal Society immediately following announcements. The topic to be discussed today is 'Plea Bargaining with School Administrators.' All inquiries will, of course, be confidential. Thank you."

Taking his seat squarely in the center of the Too Bold to be Guilty section of the student body, Allie breathed a sigh of relief. There was no way the Great Stone Face would suspect him now. He would have to be a fool to taunt Mr. Stone if he were really guilty.

Despite this shrewd maneuver, Allie and the other Keepers found it expedient to lay low for a few weeks. The complete lack of evidence notwithstanding, suspicions ran high among the school administrators. The signature of a Get was easily discernible on the strange events Odell, and only time and the busy call of other duties would completely take the heat off, so a few weeks of dedication to less controversial areas of creativity seemed in order.

As always, there was much work to do on the Light Show. The summer's various activities added much in the way of potential new material ideas to be brainstormed, developed and programmed. Many times before had the deeper things of creativity been a helpful deterrent for the temptation to try one prank too many, too soon. After only a week of attempting to bury himself in such activity, however, Allie was becoming uncharacteristically restless. Much to the chagrin of his colleagues, Allie seemed for a few days to be stirring up a new scheme. Just when the anticipation was about to become too much for the others, Allie suddenly looked up from some work they were doing together on the overhead projector plates and announced, "It's the Great Stone Face. We've got to deal with him directly."

"Right, Napoleon," said Michael Moller quickly. "Let's meet him at Waterloo and slap a great Get on him there. Don't forget to tell the Prussian Army to be there for the laughs."

"Very funny, Mr. History," snapped Allie back at him. "I guess you want to just go out with a big snore. It'll be great to be remembered as the class who graduated from the Slumberset counting sheep instead of Gets. Maybe we can have our Senior Gift be a sleeper sofa for the commons."

"Well, the timing could be a little better," reasoned Tate. But Allie would have nothing of it. In the end the others had no choice but to humor him, at least until they could secretly go for help to the only person in the universe who would understand their plight.

"Father Miles, you've got to help us." Tate closed the door to the chaplain's office and looked to Joey and Moller for support.

"It's Allie," explained Moller. "He wants to try and pull a Get on the Great Stone Face."

"And he wants to do it now rather than later," said Tate.

Father David Miles smiled calmly and tapped his desk top with his thumb. "I see," he said. "A bit awkward on the timing, I agree. Doesn't sound like Allie at all. Timing, after all, has always been one of his strong suits."

"That's what we've been trying to tell him, Smiles," said Moller. "But he just isn't listening. He's into his 'time is of the essence' mode, and we can't seem to shake it."

"I see," said Father Miles again. He offered his visitors tea, but his mind was in deep thought. "Yes, I see." Looking out the window for a moment more, he took a short breath and turned to the boys. "Then I think we need to convince Allie that his precious Time is better spent on other issues right now. We need to direct his efforts to a less explosive battlefront."

"That's right," said Tate, "but what would that be?"

"He seems to make everything explosive," fretted Joey.

"You have a point there, Joey," said Father Miles. He stood up and began pacing behind his desk.

"Wait a minute," said Moller. "How about the new students? There's a less volatile war for you. . . and it is something we need to deal with anyway."

"They seem to be harmless enough," agreed Tate.

"Perhaps so," said David Miles, and, although something in his voice betrayed some undefined reservation, he had to agree that, "for now, at least," the threat of the new students would make for a safer battlefront. "I'll talk to him, lads," said Father Miles. "I'll let him know what the 'real threat' is."

A few days later Allie returned from a conference with Father Miles, unofficial sponsor of the Keepers of the Get, and had a new strategy working. "The new students are the real threat," he said flatly.

The Keepers had gathered at Tate's house for a strategy session. Perceiving immediately that Father David Miles had successfully steered

Allie into safer waters, the others conveniently forgot all previous plans for a Get against the Great Stone Face and diplomatically agreed with their leader.

"They are pretty cocky," said Tate.

"And their numbers are staggering," whined Joey.

"Ah, but the more, the merrier," rejoined Allie. "And the harder they come, the harder they fall."

"So how do we trip 'em up?" baited Michael Moller. Clearly Father Smiles had saved the day and a great sense of relief shined upon Tate, Joey, and Moller. The prospect for a safe Get was suddenly a joyful proposition indeed.

Allie was deep in thought. "First we go for the Wheeze-bags," he said.

"The brainerds?" said Tate.

"Yeah," nodded Allie, "the brainerds, the geeks—those skinny, bespectacled little androids they brought in to fill up the empty spaces in this new academic factory they're trying to build here. We need to let these refugees from the perils of public school persecution know that this isn't their promised land yet. I mean, I'm glad they're not going home with bloody noses anymore, but they need to understand the Slumberset."

"It's true," agreed Moller. "I watched a group of them going giddy in the Commons the other day. They were, like, talking into their little pocket calculators, saying, 'Beam me up, Scotty,' and stuff like that."

"Oh yeah," grimaced Allie. "See, we can't have stuff like that taking over. They need to understand what good taste is. They need to learn a little restraint, channel that super-intelligence through more refined avenues."

"It's true," agreed Tate, pondering the situation. "And maybe at the same time, we could make a statement to the administration," he continued, "let them know we aren't falling for this academic factory thing."

"It *is* a lot like a revolution," said Moller. "I feel like we're being taken over by the rise of some oppressed class of wheeze-bags. It's like Stalinism and the Industrial Revolution and Invasion of the Body Snatchers all wrapped into one." He shuddered at the images and looked to Allie, who was ready with his answer.

"We need a counter-revolution," he said flatly. "And fast."

Everyone agreed and the conversation turned to specific methods. Tate was quick to point out that physical abuse would have to be avoided, less the Wheeze-bags view their Slumberset educators the same as their former oppressors. When Moller stated that the other main tool for revolution was propaganda, everyone agreed that a campaign of bogus propaganda could be effective—and it was not hard to imagine how it could be done.

"What we need is a slogan," said Allie. "Something we could scribble and stamp all over the place, you know, like the 'Kilroy was here' thing only political sounding and to the point."

Before the others had time to think, Joey leaned forward a little bit and said: "Academics is the opiate of the masses."

The room went dead silent for a minute as the phrase sank in and then Moller began to smile.

"Perfect!" he said, then, responding to the puzzled looks on Tate and Allie's faces, he explained Joey's drift. "You know, it's a take-off on that Karl Marx bullshit about - 'religion is the opiate of the people'. And it's perfect, man. We'd be nailing the Commies and the Academic Junkies all at the same time."

"I like it," said Allie slowly. " 'Academics is the opiate of the masses'— it's true, man, there's way too many people shooting up on higher education as the way to salvation these days. As if some big chunk of knowledge is going to give them the key to life . . . yeah, it's perfect."

Moller was nodding in agreement and Tate began to smile. It was just what they needed for the Get, he was thinking, and the Get was just what they needed to keep Allie from confronting the Great Stone Face head on. There was another round of laughter to seal the agreement, and then they began their planning. Within a few minutes, however, Emily burst into the room, looking frantic.

"It's Sarah," she said. "She's in trouble."

"What is it, Emily?" asked Allie. "Sit down and talk to us."

Flopping into a chair and tossing her books down on the table, Emily began to explain. "I saw her crying and running into the girls' bathroom, so I went in and she told me that there had been a big fight at the pep club meeting. Somehow one of the new girls has already gotten herself voted head of the Homecoming Committee and there was this huge argument over who was going to, you know, bust through that big banner at Homecoming, and when Sarah tried to tell her the head cheerleader had always done it, this girl pulls out some Somerset Pep Squad Rule Book published in the year 500 BC, which says they always have voted on such big deals, and guess what, we must be outnumbered because the new girl won out."

"Holy shit," said Michael Moller. "The dike is starting to give."

"I can't believe it," said Tate.

"We better believe it," said Allie. "This is what I've been trying to tell you guys about. If those guys want democracy, it's time we showed them where the balance of power lies in a true democracy. You think Tommy Jefferson would have rolled over and let some Middle Class Joe be president? Hell no. Those guys understood the concept of the ruling elite, and it's up to us to carry the torch on all that. Don't worry, you guys. Let me handle this one. You all take care of the Propaganda Campaign and I'll deal with this Barbie Doll parading as a girl. Moller, just be sure to be set up with the 16 millimeter at Homecoming. Get us a Gallery of Angels shot on the north goal post before the game. We'll give this chick the debut she deserves. Now somebody tell Emily the other good news. I've gotta go find Sarah."

The next day, the mysterious slogan began to appear at Somerset School. It began with a simple graffiti campaign. Some unsuspecting Wheeze-bag would open his locker and the immortal words would be written on the inside of the door: ACADEMICS IS THE OPIATE OF THE MASSES. Likewise for the covers of their books, the rear view mirrors of their cars and the backs of their tee-shirts in gym class: ACADEMICS IS THE OPIATE OF THE MASSES.

The following week the slogan magically appeared in glowing green letters on the entry program of the new computers purchased for the students. The computers were, according to Allie, "a symbol of everything we have feared the most," and it was "important" to remind its users of the potential for abuse. ACADEMICS IS THE OPIATE OF THE MASSES. By the end of the week, the anonymous computer saboteur had figured out a way to program the slogan to appear as the final line of the most complex of problems being worked on by the unsuspecting Wheeze-bag. Through the doorway to the senior lounge, the Keepers of the Get had a bird's eye view of the occasional Wheeze-bag making a beeline for the computer room and then shutting himself in to work fanatically at some problem he had perhaps been contemplating for days. After forty-five minutes of intense, work-filled silence, there would come a scream. "Another Wheezer has faced the truth," Michael Moller would chuckle without looking up from his own work. "ACADEMICS IS THE OPIATE OF THE MASSES."

About then was when Joey showed up with a bagful of goodies which he dramatically emptied onto the conference table in the senior lounge. What rolled out in front of the curious Keepers were a half dozen rubber stamps and ink pads. It only took a moment to verify the observers' instant suspicion as Moller grabbed a rubber stamp, pressed it into an ink pad and then slammed it onto his opened notebook. The words sprang back at the group with the power and indisputable authority of the printed word: ACADEMICS IS THE OPIATE OF THE MASSES.

"Ah, the power of the press," mused Moller a few days later. By then word had spread like wildfire, but the Keepers of the Get were not a greedy lot, being careful not to litter the school with their newfound truth. Instead they chose to implant it neatly onto the readied minds of, first, the Wheeze-bags, and then the rest of the school. Taste and timing were everything, as the Keepers sought to have the words appear only at the most appropriate of moments. On the tops of exams as they were handed out among the needy masses, in the middle of the lecture notes of the most dramatic teachers, on the letter-heads of some of the administrators' stationery, these were some of the choice locations for the critical reminder: ACADEMICS IS THE OPIATE OF THE MASSES.

The campaign climaxed with a daring final exploit pulled off by none other than Joey himself. He had been taking a short-cut through the alumnae reception room on his way to lunch when he noticed a neatly arrayed row of cocktail napkins set out for a meeting that evening for some of the school's top donors. Certain that Providence had ordained this otherwise chance occurrence, he quickly found Allie and Michael Moller and got them to stand guard while he performed his boldest deed in a long time. With the truth imprinted neatly across the corners of each napkin, it was only hoped that its harsh message would that evening be softened for its surprised reader by the gentle anesthesia of a few good belts of expensive whiskey. ACADEMICS IS THE OPIATE OF THE MASSES.

Even in the advance of the following morning's tribunal, it was understood among the Keepers that this bold move would end the now-successful campaign on behalf of academic balance. But the wrath with which their campaign was greeted exceeded even their nervous expectations.

"So much for harmless battles," whispered Michael Moller to Tate, as the Great Stone Face raged in the communal face of the student body.

"Well, we tried to play it cool," said Tate meekly.

"That's what happens when you mess with fund-raising," smiled Allie.

Joey was white with fear. The butterflies in Tate's stomach were only tamed by the reminder that this had all begun as a deterrent to even more volatile campaigns by Allie. There was also the strange security of Father

Miles's place in the scheme, though Michael Moller had often warned about counting too much on the protection of the church.

"History's had too many martyrs to count on having the church save your skin," he would say. "The priests that have been protecting you always figure God can make it up to you in the next world."

As it turns out, Father Miles was himself upset about the final phase of the propaganda campaign. Following morning announcements that day, he rounded up the wayward members of his little flock for an emergency meeting in his office.

"Not good, lads, not good," he fumed. He was pacing about his office stroking his chin and glancing out the window.

"How were we supposed to know they would take it seriously?" asked Joey in a pitiful whine.

"How did you expect them to take it, Joey? Do you think these gentlemen would enjoy having the goal of their donations compared to opium?"

"Come on, Father Miles," said Allie in quick defense of Joey. "Not all of us are as tuned into the pet peeves of big donors as you guys are. I know they've got courses on that stuff in seminary but we—"

"I don't need your wit now Allie," said Father Miles curtly. "Do you realize how hard it would be for me to even keep you lads in this school if they found out?"

"So they won't find out," said Allie undaunted. "Now come on, relax. You're the one who told us the new guys were the real enemy."

"So stay after the real enemy," said Father Miles. "How is it that you keep bringing this all back around to fighting the school itself?"

"Good question," admitted Tate quickly.

Oblivious to Tate's remark, Allie plunged ahead. "Maybe it's getting a little harder to tell the good guys from the bad guys," he said.

"Well, you'd better get good at it quick," warned Father Miles, "or you boys will all be finding yourselves finishing out your senior year in a nice public school. Perhaps that would make it easier for you: all bad guys there, huh lads?"

"Come on Smiles," insisted Allie, "you know God would never let that happen."

"How can you be so sure?" challenged Father Miles.

"Because," said Allie with a smile that conveyed to everyone that he had the situation under control, "who else could you get to be acolytes for you?"

Years of formal training and centuries of stoic tradition melted in a few short moments in the face of Father David Miles. In spite of all the mighty forces working against it, he smiled. "Get out of my office," he yelled, but it was too late. Against his will, he let out a laugh and then yelled at them again. And the hand he raised as a supposed threat became instead a hand of blessing, an inadvertent atonement for the Keepers' recent excesses and an accidental endorsement for their upcoming plans.

All during the Propaganda Campaign so successfully engineered by his comrades, Allie had remained mum on his scheme for dealing with the Barbie Doll trying to take over the feminine side of the Slumberset. No amount of coaxing had been effective in squeezing the tiniest detail from him. "Just wait," he would say emphatically. "It'll be worth the wait." Then he would cast a stern eye at Moller and charge him again, "Just be ready at the North goal post with a Gallery of Angels shot."

The scene at the Somerset home games was decidedly different from their forays on the Highway 12 Tour. First of all, there was the sizable group of old alumnae living out their Ivy League fantasies through the little Country Club school they helped build back home on the range. Insofar as it was too far for them to make the pilgrimage back East for the average afternoon college game, they would instead return to Somerset Stadium, all decked out in their blazers and sweaters, giving it their best rah-rah as they took nips off silver flasks and generally lent any ammunition they could to the intellectual's version of the irresistible belief that We Are the Good Guys.

Into this arena of ideological idolatry a few nights later, Allie quietly led his three friends. Michael Moller had been faithful to bring the 16 millimeter camera and was soon busying himself setting up the tripod with a Gallery of Angels shot of the promised action at the goal posts. By then the pep club was gathering at the north end of the field, and anticipation was building. The game itself had taken on some climactic overtones, as the Somerset Lions had managed a seven-and-one season to date, giving an aura of Pigskin importance to the outcome of their next-to-last game. While Allie had other things on his mind, anything adding to the drama of the evening was nevertheless appreciated.

Soon the infamous banner was hoisted between the goal posts. There was the Somerset old-guard, including Sarah herself, humbly hoisting the banner that was to be the gateway to glory for the social climbing sally-brain of the new Somerset, and it filled Tate and the others with sadness and anger. "You'd think the immigrants would at least do their own heavy lifting," complained Joey.

"Well, now boys," said Allie with a smile, "That might have interfered with the plan a bit . . ."

And with the deep sparkle of his eyes that always preceded his brightest revelations, Allie slowly pulled something out of his coat pocket. It was a thick roll of silver duct tape. Patting the roll of duct tape, he raised one eyebrow and nodded toward the goalposts. "That banner," he explained, "is ego-proof."

Straining their eyes to focus on the banner being strapped to the goalposts, Allie's three friends could see the silver tape running in several long strips across the back of the banner. Nobody was bursting though that configuration.

"If you can't beat 'em," explained Allie, "at least don't let 'em do a victory dance in your stadium."

At precisely that moment, the football team appeared at the north entrance of the stadium. Allie suddenly held an invisible microphone in front of his mouth and began a play-by-play announcement in the voice of an inspired sportscaster: "And there's the Slumberset Lions! In front of the team, ladies and gentlemen, it seems the entire pep squad has ignited into the kind of mindless wiggling and meaningless screaming associated with the lowest forms of pagan ritual. The aspiring high priestess of the cult, dressed as a Barbie Doll for the evening's festivities, is presently standing at the vortex of this male/female fulcrum of idolatrous energy, bouncing uncontrollably on the edge of her narcissistic fantasy."

"And theeeeeeerrrrrree they go," screamed Allie into the invisible mike. "Some sub-conscious signal has set the ritual in motion, and with the whole stadium of Home Team Believers rising to pay homage to this latest idol of their affections, the new high priestess and her following are now running blindly towards the bannered veil of Eternal Pigskin Glory. A massive wall of false enthusiasm and misguided hope is pushing with an unstoppable force towards the white-striped Promised Land. Unstoppable, that is, until it gets to the mystically reinforced banner about to awaken these poor souls from their false dreams. Now you listeners at home are, of course, in on our little secret, but Barbie and her friends, you understand, are completely oblivious to . . . "

On droned Allie as the swarm of players and pep club members pushed forward with what did look like an unstoppable force. Suddenly, panic swept through Tate and the others. Not having had the benefit of thinking through the physics of the situation, it was easy for Tate to envision a real Pigskin Apocalypse, a horrible event caused by the cruelly rejected Barbie Doll being bounced mercilessly back into the stampede of cleated monsters to her death.

Tate, especially, was rocked by this panic. "Allie, wait!" he screamed, but it was too late. He could see that the mob was doomed to whatever fate had been prepared for it. "Please God," said Tate under his breath, "don't let her die."

Whether by God's mercy or in response to Allie's carefully calculated Get, the misguided high-priestess, rather than be knocked flat on her face and trampled, was instead abruptly absorbed by the slack in the banner, the gentle arms of forgiving grace wrapping her safely up in a standing, if completely humiliating, position. The football team came to a ridiculous halt at the banner, not knowing how to deal with this road-block on their own path to Pigskin Glory. With Moller's film camera whirring away, the boldest of the players pulled the struggling priestess out of the banner and then made some vain attempts of his own to burst through the unyielding banner. Ultimately, the delegation from Somerset had to make a humbling detour around the goal posts to make it onto their own playing field. Home Team theology thus debunked, it was little wonder when Somerset eventually lost the game, dropping their record to a less significant six-and-two, while continuing a tenuous undefeated streak of the less-universally accepted group of Good Guys known as the Keepers of the Get.

First, though, there was a vengeful reckoning unfolding at the goal posts. Though Tate was still shaking from the imagined catastrophe, he suddenly noticed the next threat to their existence as the humiliated Barbie Doll had picked herself up from the folds of the banner, spotted the film camera, and bolted towards the only possible suspects in the stadium.

"Run for it," shouted Tate.

Still filming this final detail of the scene, Michael Moller had to be yanked away with his camera and tripod, as Joey grabbed the other camera gear and Allie sprinted ahead to get the car.

By the time Moller and the others made it to the parking lot, their forty yard lead on the enraged Pep Squad president had closed to a few precious feet and only their expertise in piling into a moving car allowed them to escape into the safety of Allie's get away car.

"That's no Barbie Doll!" shrieked Allie in delight, as the last door slammed shut and he sped the car away from the outstretched fingernails of their pursuer. "It's a screaming banshee of mega-death, let's get the hell out of here . . ."

That weekend, spirits were at an all-time high. Tate's momentary panic was swept under the rug in a house filled with laughter and, already, more plans. There was a third group among the new students to whom Allie felt compelled to address himself. "It's the Golden-boys," he announced. He was seated in a leather armchair at one end of the Henry's clubroom. Sarah and Emily were there with a few other girls, along with Tate, Moller, Joey, and a few other guys. "These studs they brought in to beef up our athletic teams and make the school look good in photos," continued Allie, "we need to get them next. I mean, are the Trustees out to start up a super-race or what?"

"So what's it going to be?" asked Moller.

"Well, I've been thinking," said Allie. "They are all so into this pretty-boy thing, you know, body beautiful and the clothes to match, and I was thinking that the best way to show them what clowns they really are would be to trick them out of their pompous outfits somehow, give them a glimpse of their deeper nature you might say."

"So you want me and Joey to jump 'em all," suggested Moller. "Just grab their clothes and not give them back till they say 'uncle', right?"

"Nothing so crass as that, of course," said Allie. "No, it's like this: we've got Halloween coming up in a couple weeks. How about we sucker them into a fake All-School costume day? You know, secretly spread the word among all the new kids that it's some sort of underground Somerset tradition . . . "

"Oh, that's hilarious," laughed Sarah.

"You guys are evil geniuses," agreed Emily.

Before Joey could object to the suggestion of evil in their midst, Moller jumped in. "No, it's righteous to the bone," he said. "It's our little way of letting the administration how inappropriate these kids are for the school."

"Exactly," said Allie. "So here's how it works: first, we spread the word among the Old Guard, we clue the Slumberset in on what we're up to so they can get in on the Get at the grass roots level."

"Yeah," said Tate. "Everybody has to be ready to string the new kids along. And even though it's designed mostly for the Golden-boys, we go ahead and rope in *all* the new kids, just to go along with what father Miles has been telling us about keeping the sheep straight from the goats."

"Right, and when the big day rolls around," continued Allie, "we've got one hundred and twenty new kids standing at Announcements fully decked out in ridiculous costumes...with the Slumberset on hand in their uniformed best—"

"And the administration," laughed Moller, "wanting to know what the hell is going on."

By Wednesday of the following week, the word had been thoroughly circulated among the Slumberset old guard. Slowly, then, the rumors regarding the unveiling of a "great student tradition at Somerset" were released among the unsuspecting immigrants. The following Monday a "Top-Secret Memo" was quietly distributed among the new students, outlining the Halloween prank scheduled to take place the next Friday. Eager to get a foothold on the private school approach to life, the new students were all greatly enthused about the plan. By the middle of the week, the muffled anticipation and whispered costume plans could be heard throughout the school. "This is great," said Allie to Tate and Moller at the lunch table.

"You can just feel the undercurrents all over this place," said Moller.

"It's like a rumbling volcano," agreed Tate.

After a moment of happy reflection, Allie slowly looked at his friends, the long-familiar sparkle beginning to appear in his countenance. "You know," he said quietly. "This is too good an opportunity to miss."

"What do you mean?" asked Tate, his smile dropping from his face.

"I mean," said Allie, "we could turn this whole thing to cut like a double-edged sword. We could score a direct hit on the Great Stone Face without having to lift a finger."

"Allie . . . " sighed Tate. He let out a great breath and his shoulders fell forward as he slumped down into his chair.

"Now just hear me out, Tate," said Allie, leaning forward. "This is still in line with what Father Smiles said about pranking the new kids. All we're doing here, is upping the ante by getting the immigrant to do a little of the dirty work for us?" said Allie.

Tate just shook his head and Joey sat mute, but Michael Moller's curiosity was stirring and it quickly overrode his trepidation. "What's the angle?" asked Moller.

"Moller!" cried Tate and Joey as one.

"It's simple," said Allie as he quickly turned towards Moller. "We get one of the new kids to come dressed as the Great Stone Face himself."

Now all three of Allie's friends were mute.

THE LAST GET

"We pick out the biggest social climber of the lot," explained Allie, "and we play on his greed for instant private school status. We tell him the punch line on the whole costume tradition is that every year one brave soul does the Great Stone Face costumed to the hilt. Who could resist such an easy shot at Slumberset acceptance?"

"I know just the guy," said Moller instantly. "His name is Dale Hoagley and he's a walking target for this Get."

"I know who you're talking about," said Tate. "He's in my chemistry class, and you're right. He's an ego-maniac just looking for his following. But this is incredibly dangerous."

"I know, I know" said Moller, smiling ever so slightly, "but it's so doable. "All you would have to do sort of buddy up to him in lab and let on like nobody's got the guts to do the Great Stone Face this year. He'll go for it like a catfish after stink-bait."

Years of playing the faithful straight man to Allie's punch lines were too strong an elixir for Tate to resist. Against his will, he was picturing in the scene in his mind's eye. "Yeah, I can see it," he heard himself say, "he'd probably go for it."

"Sure he will," said Allie, as he reached over and rested his hand on Tate's shoulder. "He's be crazy not to. After all, it's the opportunity of a lifetime . . . for a sucker."

"But what about Father Miles?" said Tate.

"Well, since the latest heat was on Joey, we'll just leave Joey out of it. If Smiles gets on us we'll just let him know that the three of us were the only ones in on it, and we'll remind him who the big donors in the school are, if you catch my drift. Sanctification by net worth, you know?'

That much Tate did understand, and with the rest of his fears dealt with by Allie in the usual ways, he soon found himself baiting the magnanimous Dale Hoagley for the Great Stone Face caper. By then end of chemistry lab the next day, the overeager immigrant was ready to have plastic surgery, if necessary, to play the part. He had followed Tate out of the lab and made him promise one more time that no one else would try to shoot him out of the job at the last minute.

"I give you my word, man," Tate had said. His blue eyes burned with the sincerity of a fellow revolutionary. "No one will take this honor from you."

The scene in the commons on Halloween morning would always be regarded by the Keepers of the Get as one of the great, panoramic visions of life as they knew it. The bright and ridiculous costumes of the universally suckered new students stood in comic contrast to the never more ordinary-seeming uniforms of the Slumberset. Ghost and goblins skulked across the commons in startling proximity to quietly jacketed lads with neatly fastened neckties. Witches and princesses arrived with great fanfare, only to be quickly found trying to fit in among innocent girls in middy blouses and navy blue skirts. It was a classic chapter in the Keepers' unofficial book of "The Existence of the Absurd in the Life of Everyday." And it was an unequaled demonstration of the Keepers' ability to control the masses.

"This is great," beamed Allie. He strolled among the costumed troupes of his indentured soldiers like a general on a tour of inspection. "How're you doing, Chief?" he said to an uncertain sophomore in full Indian apparel.

Passing another student in a rather impressive rendition of Frankenstein, Moller commented, "Nice forehead, Franky."

Allie tapped a girl in a long, white gown and sparkling crown and asked, "Hey Cinderella, which way to the ball?"

But all this loomed small against the powerful figure entering the commons at the next moment. The teachers and administration were building to a confused uproar with the arrival of each new member of fairyland, when suddenly there appeared at the east end of the commons, the very specter of their anger, the champion of their fury. It was the Great Stone Face.

Filled with as much rage as he had ever expressed, he stormed across the commons and thunderously demanded of every living thing, "What is the meaning of this?"

A mute race of mankind stood before him and shuddered. Evolution at its theoretical best would have taken light years to produce a spokesman for this group. What could they say? But with the silence becoming deafening, Michael Moller suddenly noticed something unnatural about the way the Great Stone Face began to look as he drew closer. The high cheekbones and stiff jaw-line began to appear a bit shiny and too stark. The thick, arching eyebrows grew darker and a bit cartoon-like. The drab suit hung a little awkwardly on a frame of not quite the right stature, and the waxed crew-cut that was the icon of the Somerset student's submission to unquestioned authority seemed strangely stiff and almost crooked. "It's Hoagley!" gasped Moller suddenly.

As the fake Great Stone Face marched close, his paralyzing stare pivoting in every direction, Allie and the others saw it too. "That disguise is a masterpiece," rasped Allie.

But before they had the time to enjoy the work of their shanghaied disciple, a still greater cataclysm appeared. At the west end of the commons an infinitely more real version of the dreaded school disciplinarian appeared.

On a cloud of deeply rumbling rage, the real Great Stone Face stormed across the commons towards the outrageous impostor at the other end of the floor. Charging obliviously through the ranks of costumed onlookers, the Great Stone Face met his adversary with a merciless grip to the throat and began throttling him furiously before the entire student body. Before any sane member of the faculty could stop him, he had dragged the flailing Hoagley back across the commons to his office. Once safe in his lair, there was no telling what form of retaliation and torture the Great Stone Face would inflict on his victim.

While Allie and Moller chuckled beneath their breaths at the overwhelming success of the Get and Joey stared in bewilderment at the scene, Tate shook his head quietly.

"That was intense," he whispered to Allie. Putting his arm around his increasingly shaky friend, Allie shrugged it off with a bolstering bit of Get rhetoric and then the usual diversion.

"Hey, buddy, this is war," he said, "And check out the Headmouster trying to organize this costume party." The veteran Headmaster was surprisingly calm as he assessed the situation. Quickly deciding that the costume epidemic was too widespread to deal with confrontationally, he announced that, despite the "unscheduled Free Dress Day," classes would be held as usual, inadvertently promising the perfect kind of day for Allie and company. The possibilities were too exciting to allow Tate to dwell on his doubts.

"Come on, Tate Head," encouraged Allie. "We've got western Civ with a bunch of costumed morons. What a slice of life that should be." Feeling numb, Tate allowed himself to be pulled along and was soon lost in the many hilarious situations called into being by the great Costume Get. He was truly amazed at the way Allie's plan had captured the imagination of the entire school, and yet he felt strangely adrift. By the end of the afternoon, Tate found himself floating in some kind of cartoon boat, bouncing gently above the dark waves below him, wondering how far he was floating from the safety of the shore.

CHAPTER EIGHT

THE POWER OF THE ROSE

The Five-Star Auto Hotel towered above the decimated streets around it like a lighthouse on a barren shore. On most nights, its fourteen stories were topped by a shinning crown of light, made possible by the late hour activities of four unlikely artists. Around its lower stories, the dark ghosts of business past wandered aimlessly through the shadows of deserted buildings, sadly unaware of the hope being worked out in the skyline roost above them by the engineers of the Eighth Wonder of the World Music and Light Review.

It was a cool November evening, and the strong chill in the air warned of winter's approach. In the vaulted room of the Light Show studio, however, the familiar warmth of the place denied the power of the weather, even as the embattled architects of the Light Show endeavored to explore the depths of life.

"It's way too heavy," complained Allie. "Nobody's gonna buy this stuff."

Tate sighed and put his head down on the keys of the piano. After an agonized pause he raised his head and looked to Michael Moller for help.

"Too soon to tell, Allie," said Moller. "I say we can lighten up the song enough with the right images."

"You never know till you try," agreed Joey weakly. He shot an empathetic glance at Tate and then looked up at Allie.

"Thanks for sharing that thought, Joey," said Allie sarcastically. "Is that from Proverbs or did the Tooth Fairy tell you that one last night?"

"Funny," said Joey. "You're a real killer."

"The point is we've got two weeks to get this show ready," insisted Allie. He was speaking more gently, however, as if aware after all of Tate's tender condition. The pressures brought on by their careless campaign of Gets had taken their toll on Tate as had the ongoing doubts about his father's health. In response, Allie had at least agreed to lay off the Get campaigns for a time, as they put all their efforts into the Light Show. "Look Tate," he said softly, "it's just that, if we keep working on this new stuff, we may never get the rest of the show back together."

"He's probably right," said Tate quickly. He folded up his notes from his new song and opened a worn spiral notebook on top of the piano. "So let's nail this old stuff."

"Is that alright, man?" asked Allie gently.

"Sure, Allie," said Tate. "It's fine, really."

"You're not just saying that to make me think I'm not a jerk?"

"No, we all know you're a jerk," smiled Tate, "I wouldn't want to take that away from you. It's just that we probably should make sure we have the old stuff down . . ."

"Okay, great," beamed Allie, "so let's get on with it. How about we polish up the 'Aloha' sequence?"

"Yeah," agreed Moller. He knew Tate had given in gracefully and it was just as well to go off in another direction. "We need to tighten up the soundtrack in that one part for sure."

"Alright, boys," said Allie. "So how about we run it from the top?"

After a few minutes of work at the 16 millimeter projector, Moller gave Joey a signal for the lights, and the room fell silent but for the whirring of the projector. The momentary darkness was broken by a burst of light on one end of the room followed by the appearance of a grainy screen image of a Rolls Royce sedan navigating a wide turn out of a driveway onto a street. Tate laid out a beautiful chord on the piano, and the film was off and rolling.

Up on the screen, the Rolls Royce wheeled down a boulevard lined on both sides by majestic homes. Then the film cut to a shot of the car rolling to a stop at an intersection and making a turn onto a more commercial street as the music shifted to a more rhythmic passage accentuating the sense of motion on the screen. The car rolled past small shopping centers and office buildings then gas stations and hotels, as it made its way towards the outskirts of the cinematic town. As the last images of commercial civilization gave way to scenes of fields and farms, a view of the sun sitting low on the horizon accounted for the diffuse light present. Longer camera angles and a heightening sense of drama in Tate's music hinted of some important destination drawing near.

For a moment, the point of view of the camera's eye switched to the inside of the car, searching the highway ahead for the end of the unspecified rainbow. A climaxing passage in the music built to a crescendo until the camera caught a glimpse of something towering ahead beside the highway. The shimmering monolith came into focus just as the music announced the arrival of car, film, and viewer to their promised destination. The neon markings on the side of the man-made cliff read: "The Aloha Drive-In."

Inside the studio, the Keepers of the Get burst into applause. "Bravo," shouted Allie.

"Thar she blows," laughed Michael Moller. Joey clapped happily and even Tate—feelings healed for the moment by the music and images—smiled broadly. This was great stuff.

The Aloha Drive-in had a long and happy history in all the boys' lives, taking each of them back to times when their families would load up at dusk in their automobiles and head through the twilight for the mystically lit land of giant movies. With the car filled to capacity with kids, cokes, and popcorn, Dad would confidently take the helm and launch out for points unknown, as Mom assumed her role as British heroine on an African river boat adventure. Memory's strongest image saw the sun dropping behind the horizon just as the realm of fields and farms was made other-worldly by the mysterious appearance of a grove of huge, neon palm trees dancing along the highway ahead. Waving in a breeze of optical effect, the trees announced the presence of a magical outpost of Hollywood itself set on the rolling hills of an Oklahoma evening. This was the Aloha Drive-in.

On the screen in their workshop, the black sedan rolled into the long entrance drive, easing between the rows of plastic-covered lamps and up to the ticket booth where the boys' memories took over again and the image of Chan Aloha appeared in their minds' eyes. A tall and quiet Asian man, the owner of the Aloha drive-in had been unceremoniously named Chan Aloha by the Mayor one evening long ago as a car carrying Tate, Allie and the Mayor had approached the ticket boot. With the car still a good two hundred feet form the ticket booth, the Mayor had begun an imaginary conversation with the owner of the Aloha Drive-in along the lines of "Good evening, Chan, and how's Mrs. Aloha?" From this impromptu outburst had grown a tradition of imaginary dialogue with the unsuspecting drive-in owner, which from that day forth was enacted in any of the Keeper's cars as they entered the Aloha. The trick was to continue the conversation—"So tell me, Chan, what did you think of the film . . . yeah, they just don't make 'em like they used to . . . "—right up until the last possible moment before the alleged Mr. Aloha could actually hear the gag taking place. Then it was a complete switch to a courteous exchange with the real owner of the drive-in, known only as "Sir" in reality, so as not to offend the kind-looking gentleman at work at his business.

It was an unwritten law that no one ever make fun of Chan Aloha to his face. This rule was at least partially due to the influence of the Mayor and the other fathers involved, an unyielding insistence that a practical joke ceased to by funny if it hurt an innocent bystander. This type of consideration, the young Keepers were told, was what separated the life-giving humor of a gentleman from the destructive gags of the less principled classes. "A little thoughtfulness," the Mayor would say, "is not too much to ask of a gentleman on his way to a good laugh."

This line of thought had forged its way firmly into the aristocratic doctrines of the Get, as well, though the difficulty of adherence to it was often relieved by the fabrication of some more specific reasons for self-restraint, as was the case at the Aloha, where an entire life-story of Chan Aloha had been created to aid in the administering of respect to the man. Over the years it had been decided that Mr. Aloha had once been a highly successful film director. It was determined that he had soon found himself a prisoner of a corrupt studio system, however, and had ultimately freed himself from its somehow immoral demands by taking self-exile in the most humble station available in the field of his calling: he had become the owner of an obscure drive-in movie theater on the proverbial back side of the desert, there to live out his life many light years away from his true dream. For the Keepers, it was easy to have respect for that kind of guy. So at the ticket-booth, it was nothing but courtesy for the great Chan Aloha.

Meanwhile, in the current film version of the Aloha, the Rolls Royce was pulling away from the ticket booth and making its way through the curved wooden screens leading into the drive-in. The camera was now stationed out in front of the car, giving an initial view of the interior of the sedan. A uniformed chauffeur was clearly visible at the wheel, while behind him two figures could vaguely be seen leaning comfortably against the back seat. As the car rolled past, the camera caught a better view of the passengers, a young man and woman of handsome features and attire. The young man turned casually toward the camera and raised a gracious hand of acknowledgment.

THE POWER OF THE ROSE

"Moller, you're such an aristocrat," chided Allie as they watched.

"Comes with the territory," smiled Michael. "And, hey—when you're escorting a queen . . . "

The other passenger was indeed the Queen of Arts, and the little drama unfolding had been Moller's clever way of winning a bona fide "date" with the object of his nearly out-of-control affection, Jane Quinn. The premise of the film was to explore another side of the Aloha: apart from its importance in the family life of the community, the Aloha held and even more hallowed place in the romantic lives of the region's teenagers. For those between the ages of twelve and twenty, the Aloha was all about romance.

"It's the make-out capital of the world," Michael Moller had explained to Jane Quinn a few weeks earlier. "You've got this entire city packed full of teenagers, hormones hopping like cans of Mexican jumping beans, and the release valve on the whole system is the Aloha Drive-in."

Jane Quinn had smiled and tilted her head, a mannerism Moller had learned to interpret as interest. "So in ancient cultures maybe they took their sex drive out to the Fertility Rites or whatever, but this is the twentieth century so what are you going to but try to coax some little cutie into the confines of your car and deliver her to the altar of the celluloid god of romance?"

"And I suppose you're above all that, Mr. Moller?" baited the Queen.

"Of course, I am!" insisted a convincingly aghast Michael Moller. "I mean, I assume you know I am talking about the masses, Miss Quinn . . . the Publics . . . those poor imprisoned slaves of the middle class culture whose economic position does not afford them the luxury of a lake cabin weekend without the parentos—if you know what I mean—or a simple stay in town while said parental supervision is away on a business trip. Surely you realize, Miss Quinn that the member in good standing of the Slumberset does not have to stoop so low to fulfill his romantic inclinations—"

"Romantic?" questioned Jane Queen.

"Well, that's what I mean," said Moller. "It's really more of a carnal thing if you ask me, so this whole romance thing is a big charade—at least at the high school level. Do you know what I mean?"

"Yes, I do," said Miss Quinn, her tone surprising Moller with a hint of past pain.

"So that's what me and the boys have been talking about," continued Moller. "With the teenage situation at the Aloha and all, it just seems like we need a nice Get on the whole deal. You know, shine a little spotlight right through the candlelight and see what gets exposed."

"So what's your plan?" asked Miss Quinn.

"Well, it's still a bit sketchy at this point, but we've got this idea for contrasting the reality of the Aloha situation with some of the grandiose fantasies involved. I mean, if we could play the actual starkness of that old gravel drive-in against the ridiculously sublime beauty of the average 'fantasy date'...well, it could be great."

"Go on," said his young teacher.

"Well, picture this: you've got all these couples out in their cheap hot-rods and pick-up trucks and the guy is trying real hard to make it feel like Casa Blanca simply because he's convinced that the romantic deal is what really gets a chick going. The girl, meanwhile, is riding on a fantasy cloud fueled by her own hidden hormones and the inner knowledge that she can justify any amount of illicit sex if only it's a 'magic' enough night. So what can we do but..." and here Michael Moller spread out his arms and crooned out his best Robert Goulet voice as he sang, "Bring on the romance..."

Jane Quinn laughed as Michael Moller spelled out a few more details. A chauffeur-driven Rolls. A couple dressed for the French Riviera. A candle-light dinner set up on the back of a flat-bed truck. This was visual stuff and visualizing was one thing Jane Quinn was good at.

"So what do you say," said Michael Moller at the peak of his presentation. "Will you be my fake dream-date?"

"Moi?" said the not completely surprised Queen of Arts.

"Oui, mademoiselle," said Moller suavely.

Jane Quinn looked at Michael Moller for a moment then unleashed an unexpected flood of hormonal savir-fair in the direction of her suddenly naive student. "Je't le tout al fris," she purred in phony French. "I would be delighted."

On the appointed night, Joey had assumed Michael Moller's usual camera duties. With his father out of town, Allie was able to come up with the family Rolls, and he had enlisted the notorious Griffin Ragsdale, the Reed's handyman and occasional chauffeur, for "a handful of silver and a fifth of Jack Daniels," as Allie put it. Tate had come up with a stunning waiter's outfit, and with a second camera being operated by an aspiring young member of the Slumberset, the entire affair had been captured perfectly on film, edited down, and put to music. Only a few finishing touches, presently being worked out in the studio, stood between the great event and its lasting place in the fall program of the Light Show.

"Check out that shot of the Rolls," exclaimed Allie. The second camera had captured a magnificent long shot of the sleek sedan moving across the rolling gravel lot, gracefully making its way through the maze of aisles to its destination beside a large, flat-bed truck waiting near the center of the drive-in. Joey, meanwhile, had scampered diagonally across the same area with the first camera, and was soon ready to capture the action unfolding at the cars.

"Man, was Griffin ever primed for the performance," said Moller. On screen, the front door of the Rolls had swung open and the aging black man rose up from his seat with a profound air of importance. He stepped to the rear door and, checking inside first, pulled it open carefully. Michael Moller, dressed in tuxedo complete with tails, stood up — "What a prince!" shouted Allie in the studio — placed a top hat on his head, tapped the ground with his cane, and walked with Griffin around the back of the car to the other door. The studio filled with "ooh" 's and "aaahhh" 's as the never-so-stunning Queen of Arts appeared from the back seat in a low cut gown of near-speechless elegance. On screen, Moller offered the Queen an arm — graciously accepted — and escorted her to a small set of make shift stairs behind the flatbed truck.

The second cameraman had by then set up his camera on the front of the truck-bed, so the film cut to a front view of Moller and Jane Quinn ascending the stairs towards a beautifully-lit table set in fine silver and china. "Nice touch there," said Allie as the camera caught a reflection off one of the plates and Moller seated the Queen of Arts on one side of the table and himself on the other. About then a violinist wandered into the scene—a friend of Tate's recruited for the evening and dressed in a gypsy outfit—and Tate appeared at the table handing out menu's and offering cordial welcomes. He disappeared for a moment as Moller and the Queen engaged in genteel conversations; then he re-appeared cradling a bottle of wine, which he poured for his guests.

Meanwhile, a small crowd had begun to gather around the back of the truck, as revealed by Joey's camera, now set in its final position atop the concession stand nearby. Even in the less than ideal light, the quizzical looks could be made out on the faces of the drive-in crowd. In the studio, Tate's musical accompaniment took a humorous turn, as the camera panned through the collection of curious onlookers and then cut away to the dashing Michael Moller and his Lady Drive-in.

The violinist on screen was in full swing as Tate-the-waiter appeared with a lavish tray covered with the dishes of the main course. As he swept in close to Lady Drive-in and lifted the cover off a steaming plate, the camera zoomed in for a close-up of the cheeseburger-under-glass, five-star cuisine for the realm of the fantasy date. As the camera pulled back, Lord Moller was caught gleaming with a sense of aristocratic satisfaction. Ah, this was the life.

It was at this point in the film, however, that the music took a turn back towards the serious, and the song was given words. "You only see what you want to see," sang Tate, "What are the terms of this fantasy?" The film cut to a sweeping panoramic shot of the drive-in itself, taken by Joey atop the concession stand. The sheer grittiness of the dirty gravel expanse appeared in grotesque contrast to the warmly lit scene at the table. Wandering souls and garish automobiles swept throughout the frame like so many demons of life as it really is. And when the film returned to the lovely glow around the fantasy date, the music began a forewarning of the fate of the high school romantic. "Happily ever after," went the song, "is a fantasy hard to maintain."

At precisely that point, just when the action of the screen should otherwise have been culminating in a passionate kiss, Michael Moller suddenly stood up and tore off his tuxedo jacket to reveal a grossly undersized tee shirt smeared about with grease and other evidence of the workingman's life. Tate appeared wearing the jump-suit of an appliance repairman, knocked everything off the top of the table clean with one sweep of his arm, and threw a soiled bathrobe over the shoulders of Jane Quinn. Then he whirled around and quickly propped up a stage-set version of a domestic kitchen behind the newly defined characters. With Moller suddenly ranting and raving, the misty glow of "Casa Blanca" had been suddenly transformed into the stark conflict of "Streetcar Named Desire."

"That's chilling," said Allie as Michael Moller stormed back and forth across the tiny stage, giving his best rendition of a bullying and ignorant Marlon Brando. Jane Quinn cowered in the dreamy desolation of the immortal Blanche, completing the cruel contrast to the scene of the beautiful fantasy date a few moments earlier. The long postlude of the song slowly trailed off and the film ended with a shot of the baffled on-lookers wandering away in dismay. Tate held his breath as the last chord faded, wondering if Allie was about to cast the crushing judgment of "Too

Serious" on this piece too. Instead Allie only smiled and shook his head. "It's perfect."

Moller and Joey agreed and Tate looked up relieved. "Yeah," he said. "I think it works."

With the song ended and the projector off it was peaceful and quiet in the studio. The wind blew against the glass occasionally, and the building had a way of creaking and popping for no particular reason, but the studio's position so far above the streets that were largely deserted anyway accounted for a sense of solitude that was hard to find in the middle of even a small city. Though the quiet was largely taken for granted, there was no mistaking the slightest intrusion into the silence, as was the case that night. For just as the boys were turning their thoughts towards packing up and heading for home, a distant rumbling appeared from the very depths of the building.

"What the hell is that?" said Allie as the sound grew. Everyone fell silent to study the sound until Michael Moller spoke out, "It sounds like a car."

"And it sounds like its heading up here," said Tate. In their use of the studio, the Keepers had been instructed to park on the lowest level of the parking garage and use the huge elevator for transporting themselves and their equipment to the top floor. Though the ramp leading up through all fourteen floors to the top had never been officially closed down, it was always assumed to be in a state unsafe for passage. So to suddenly hear a car obviously navigating its way steadily up the winding ramp was an eerie experience indeed.

"Who the hell could it be?" said Allie and Tate together. As the car continued to climb, strange fears began to appear.

"I was sure I locked the door," said Tate.

"Maybe we should hide," suggested Joey. "It could be some kind of burglars."

"Yeah, even if it's just some hoods," said Allie. "We better lay low so as to get the drop on them."

"Yeah, let's hide out in the elevator," suggested Moller. "That way we can beat them back out of here if there's too many of them."

"Great idea," said Tate. By then the sound of the car, amplified by the concrete acoustics of the cavernous building, was as loud as a division of German tanks. Adrenaline was at an all-time high. And though their lack of experience in any kind of real danger made them feel more excited than anything, there were brief flashes of terror, particularly in Joey, that had to be contained.

The top half of the elevator was open screen mesh so the boys, after piling into the elevator, had to stoop down behind the lower half of the elevator to hide. With Joey shaking like a rabbit, the others vacillated between fear and an almost delighted excitement.

"This is great," exclaimed Moller.

"Very funny," snapped Tate at Moller. "There's ten thousand dollars worth of equipment out there and you're experiencing existential bliss." Joey, meanwhile, was muttering prayers and trying to keep himself from shaking so noticeably.

A flash of headlights against the top of the far wall announced the arrival of the car at the bottom of the final ramp. "Here it comes," squealed Joey. The entire studio erupted with the sound of an engine gunning as the car strained its way up the last ramp.

"Get ready, boys," said Allie. He was clutching a small crowbar he had picked up on his way to their hiding place. With Tate and Joey tucked firmly behind the bottom wall of the elevator, Allie and Michael Moller bobbed up and down in curiosity and fear, until the headlights of the car appeared over the crest of the ramp and the car lunged into the room and lurched to a stop. Squinting their eyes to see past the headlights, Allie and Moller could soon make out the familiar grill and body: it was a black Cadillac.

"Holy shit," breathed Allie in relief and complete surprise. "It's the Mayor!"

Tate bolted up and Joey was soon to follow. Allie was right. The engine coughed and then rumbled to a deathly silence. It was the Henry's Cadillac, alright, and the slouching silhouette behind the windshield could only be the Mayor himself.

There was a pop of metal and then a loud creaking as the driver's door swung open. "Tate?!" shouted the Mayor's voice. "Boys, where are you?"

Allie tripped the handle on the elevator door, sending their own metallic signal across the expanse of the room. "Over here, your Mayorness," shouted Allie. "We're over here." The Mayor turned around as the boys piled out of the elevator, relieved and astonished. Sheer curiosity rode the last wave of their adrenaline, as they bounded across the room toward the Mayor. "What the heck are you up to, your Mayorness?" asked Allie.

"Juss payin' a lttle vsit," slurred the Mayor. He was having some difficulty pulling himself out of the car and when he did he swooned slightly past the fully upright position he intended. The boys slowed down as they realized something was off. Tate stopped dead in his tracks. His stomach knotted and his face flushed warm. His father was drunk.

Moller figured it out quickly, too, and put a hand out to slow Allie down. They all came to a stop some thirty or forty feet from the car and stared silently as the Mayor, who was steadying himself on the car door and looking glassy-eyed at his four stunned friends.

"Tha's correck, lads, the ol' Mayor thought it wasss time to pay you a vsit."

"Great," said Allie, before the gaps of silence grew too noticeable. "We're glad you could make it."

Tate was numb. While the sight of the Mayor with a glass of bourbon in his hand was a familiar sight to Tate and his friends, the late-evening stages of his fathers' drinking had never been witnessed by any of them except Tate. This tragic and humiliating side of their beloved Mayor was one of the secrets Tate had tried to bury beneath the surface of his life. "Dad—" he began, but he could not find a sentence to say.

"Tate, my fine sssson," said the Mayor, and his affection as loosened by the alcohol caused him to let go of the car door and walk towards Tate. Any doubts of the Mayor's condition and any hopes of overlooking the drunkenness were shattered by the Mayor's staggered effort to come to his son. Tate bolted forward to cut short the pitiful scene, but it was too late. The Mayor's impeccable image had been destroyed. The Keeper's beloved icon of aristocracy stood in an obvious stupor on the cold concrete floor of their studio.

"I wannnted you to play mee that song about the ennnd of an era," said the Mayor to his son. Tate was holding his father up by the forearms in the middle of the room. "You know, the onnnne about the roses."

"Sure dad, let's sit down first," said Tate.

Allie and Moller were too embarrassed to move yet, but Joey stepped over to take one side of the Mayor. "Come on your Mayorness," he said with a firm tone that surprised his friends. "Let's get you over here to the best seats in the house."

"Thanks, lads," said the Mayor, glad to play one of their charades. "The besst seats in thugh house, itis."

Tate and Joey walked the Mayor over to an overstuffed sofa facing the wall of projection screens at one end of the room. The grand piano was nearby, being Tate's usual spot for working the music and visual images into one another. "There's your piano, Tate," said the Mayor as he sat down. "Now play me that new one about the end of an era."

"Well, pop, we were kind of shutting down," said Tate softly.

"Nonsense, boy," said his father, taking out his handkerchief to wipe the corners of his mouth. "This is the old Mayor you're talking to. Haven't you ever huurrd of a command performance?"

"Well, right dad, but it's just that . . .well . . . well, for one thing we're not even going to be using that song in the Light Show just yet—"

"What!" exclaimed the Mayor sitting upright. "Not using it? Why that song's a classic."

"Well . . . maybe . . . but like Allie was saying, it's maybe a bit too serious—"

"Too serious! ?" interrupted the Mayor again. "Allie says it'ssss too serious? Where isss that joker?" The Mayor spun around in his chair and began wagging a finger at Allie, who with Moller had been slowly moving across the room towards the others. "Come here Allmand Harrison Reed and tell the Mayor that song is too serious. You think life is one big punch line, do you? Well, I'll tell you—as your own father would—you better get ready for a few you can't laugh offf. Now come here boy."

The mayor had been pulling Allie toward him by the force of his will and was soon able to grab Allie by the wrist and pull him firmly down onto the sofa beside him. Grabbing Allie by the nape of the neck, he shook him playfully back and forth as he continued his speech. "Too serious, indeed. I'll tell you how it really is. The end of an era, that's what that song is about, am I right? And you're thinking you lads are seeing the end of some kkind of era in you own life and it'ssss probably true and there's no escaping it if it iss and you may as well face it because you'll hate yourself later if you feel like you could have ssseen it coming and didn't. Not that that changes anything really because you can't stop it coming, but at least you feel lessss the fool if you at least savored the last bit of the golden light instead of closing your . . . your . . . your . . . eyes until it was too dark to sssee at all . . . "

By now the Keepers were completely silent. Tate had slumped down onto a corner of the piano bench and put his head quietly in his hands. Joey and Moller had let themselves down onto chairs nearby and Allie, though no longer clutched by the Mayor, was stranded on the sofa next to him.

"The end of an era, lads, let'sss talk about the Golden Era of America's petroleum industry, let's talk about the Oil Capital of the World . . . let's talk about a handffful of men, your grandfathers, our fathers, who learned the secret of releasing the treasures of darkness, the ssssecret wealth of

THE POWER OF THE ROSE

hidden places, from the depths of the earth...men who fashioned a new type of aristocracy in the image of the great European aristocracy modifffied only by the great spirit of American ingen . . . ingenuey . . . ingenuity and individ . . . ualism. And imagine their sons, your fathersss, born into the royalty of petroleum, turned loose on their various fiefffdoms to further milk the earth of her precious jewels, to further establish the names of their fathers in the neon sssigns of a million roadside colonies to whom their oil was delivered and sold. Sinclair, Phillips, Skelly, even Getty himself was counted among us. Imagine the splen . . .dor of Solomon and the grand . . . eur of Rome. Then, lads," and with this the Mayor suddenly slumped as if the life had been knocked out of him, "imagine it all gone. Picture the bankers: one day they are tttreating you like Babe Ruth, the next day you are ssssuddenly a stranger. Picture the hottest young geologists in the world: one day they are lined up at your door begging for a shshshot at the bigtime, the next day they are gone, forwarding address: some post office box in Ssssaudi Arabia. This was it lads, this was the end of an era, just like Tate's song says. Only for us it was too late for a new life. Sssso what could we do? Nothing left to do but maybe play Mayor for a fffew years and what's that all about? Playing head kangaroo in a court that has no power but to announce the next social event of faded glory, the next luncheon of regret for a city passsst its prime."

The more the Mayor spoke, the clearer his speech became. The presence of such earnest listeners in the room seemed to sharpen his senses just a bit, and—with or without the stutters and slurs—his words were unmistakably accurate.

"And when there's nothing left to put you heart into," he continued, "you go for the next nearest organ, which is the stomach, and you start living for that. You pump it full of food and liquor until the byproductssss of beef and whisky are drifting though your veins so fffast that your heart mistakes it for life. But these vagabonds of the body go looking for a place to congregate and if you're lucky they end up in your legs in varicose veins that leave you looking like a two-legged road-atlas and ifff you're not so lucky they end up in your heart which leaves you looking like me, namely a silver-haired guy on his back in a hospital gown. And if they can't get Roto-rooter to come out and make a hosssspital call, well then they set up little detour signs in your heart and start bypassing three-fourths of your life past your best organ, which is only a cruel, medical parody of what'sss already happened to you so many years ago.

THE LAST GET

"And if you can buy a ffew more years that way, you suddenly notice your liver feels like one of those specimens they set out in biology class, except instead of floating in formaldehyde in a mayonnaise jar, this sss-specimen is fffloating in bourbon in a body that was once so 'fearfully and wonderfully made' by God."

Tate's eyes burned uncontrollably and his throat began to quiver. The embarrassment over his father's drunkenness had been swept away by the Mayor's eloquence and unbearable honesty, but it was all too much. "Don't, pop," he said quietly.

"It's alright, son," said the Mayor. "These boyssss are your ffriends and they are a fine bunch of lads. But I believe you are right about the end of your era and that makes me sadder than my own sssituation. You're terribly young to be riding on the last waves of whatever good things this decade must have meant to you. We at leasssst basked in the afternoon light for the better part of our years, but for you, I don't know. Seems a sh-shame to be shipping out so soon after raising the flag."

"We'll be alright, Mayor," said Allie, but his usual spunk rang a little flat beneath the high ceilings of the room. Tate looked at his friend and suddenly wondered how Allie kept going sometimes. Moller and Joey remained mute as the Mayor patted Allie on the knee.

"Perhaps so, son," said the Mayor. But it was clear he was humoring Allie rather than agreeing with him. "Perhaps so . . . now let's have that song, Tate."

Tate gazed at his father and Allie seated on the sofa. Allie's narrow features looked strangely youthful beside the full frame of Tate's father, and Allie's earlier assessment of Tate's song, so convincing before, seemed without authority. Tate realized that he wanted to play the song.

"Sure, pop," was all he said. Then he spun around on the piano bench, reopened the notebook he had earlier closed, and put his hands on the keyboard. When he began to play, he felt a power and purpose in the music that was quite rare. Though he could not see his father or the others behind him, he could feel his song going out to each of them in its own way. To the Mayor the song went out as comfort and confirmation, to Moller it was more valuable information. To Joey the song was sent as some kind of translation of concepts Joey could only voice in doctrine and abstractions. Most powerfully of all, though, was the force of the music in Allie's direction: to him it went out as a warning.

The song was called "The Power of the Rose," and the beautiful cascade of lyrics atop melody rained on conscious and subconscious mind alike, speaking gently and wisely of flowers among thorns, beauty in the midst of difficulty. But this was the sub-theme. In the final verses and the chorus there emerged this idea that the Mayor had called the end of an era, though in the song it was actually spoken of as the change of season. The Mayor sat with regal posture beside Allie as Tate played the chorus a final, piercing time.

> "Never knowing whether winter will forever end their reign,
> The petals of the flower slowly close,
> When it awakes once more to spring skies blue but never quite the same
> There's a sadness in the Power of the Rose."

When he had finished the song, Tate got up from the piano bench and walked over past Allie to where his father was seated. "Come on, pop," he said, "Let's go home."

Weary but satisfied, the Mayor took his son's arm and rose quietly, offering simple farewells to the other lads, and walked with Tate to the car. After starting to open the front passenger door for his father, Tate closed it and opened instead the back door. "Your car, sir," he said gently, and he bowed slightly.

The Mayor straightened a bit at Tate's words and took a deep breath to fill his frame to its fullest. He tugged the tails of his dinner jacket and straightened his tie. "Very well then, Tate," he said clearly. "You know the way home son, let's go."

Then, turning to Allie and the others, the Mayor smiled his charming smile and spoke his standard farewell. "Gentlemen," he said, and raising an open hand to them all, he ducked into the back of his limousine for the chauffeured ride home.

CHAPTER NINE

THE QUAIGMIRE

Senior Philosophy: Dr. Lester McQuaig
Monday, Wednesday, Friday, 1:00 p.m.
Room 201

To the knowing member of the Slumberset, the heading on the class schedule read like a harsh prison sentence with no hope for parole: Senior Philosophy was as much a rite of passage at Somerset as football was for the male students of Odell, Oklahoma.

It was said among past students of Senior Philosophy that the reading requirement alone would qualify you for a lifelong need for psychotherapy. But even the difficult reading list might have been manageable if not for the cruel intellectual antics of the teacher of the class, the notorious Dr. Lester McQuaig, whose style of lecturing had been compared to that of a Zen master suffering from caffeine withdrawal. The viscous challenges spewed out of Dr. McQuaig in unpredictable outbursts were made all the worse by the scheduling of the class at 1:00 p.m., when all the stout-hearted soldiers of the bloodstream have left their normal posts in the brain to fight the battle of digestion on another front. All things considered, Senior Philosophy was a matter of pure survival.

Through the first part of their senior year, Allie and the others had kept themselves in tact through Dr. McQuaig's class by the usual method: after the third class of the semester, the Keepers had found themselves assembled in the Senior lounge, the small conference room of executive privilege that was to become their counsel of war room, and had begun to spin the type of allegorical images that would help them maintain their sanity through the ordeal of Senior Philosophy.

"It's the OK Corral of Somerset school," Allie had declared. "You've got all these hot, young gunslingers riding into town with their bright ideas and fancy rhetoric, and there's old McQuaig, sitting in the saloon playing five card stud with some other burned out members of the faculty. He's laying low, like he's never fired a hand-gun in his life, you know, but then some young gunfighter starts shooting off his mouth a little too much and next thing you know he's squared off on Main Street with the fastest gun in the territory: Lester McQuaig."

"That's it," agreed Michael Moller, as the others laughed. "And he gets you out there on Main Street, but he's already tricked you into facing off with the sun in your eyes, as if you're not outclassed enough as it is. No, he wants to make it easy on himself so he can pump a couple bullets into your belly instead of one clean one to the heart, 'cause he knows that it takes you longer to die that way, and he's the kind of guy who likes to watch 'em squirm."

Joey shuddered with the image as the others laughed harder.

"Or maybe," continued Allie, "it's more like one of those Tarzan movies. You know, like we're some kind of great white hunters coming carefully through the jungle, cartoon sweat-beads on our foreheads, and no matter how horrible the wild beasts can be, there's nothing like the scariest threat of them all: quicksand!"

Everyone had grasped the image immediately and laughed again. With the timing that was his trademark, Allie nailed the scene down, "Yeah," he laughed, "it's the Quaigmire!"

"Exactly," said Tate, as the others cracked up. "You're walking though this jungle filled with philosophical pit vipers and blood-sucking leeches, and just when you think the coast is clear the floor of the jungle gives way and you're floundering in . . . in . . . in—"

"THE QUAGMIRE!!!" shouted everyone on cue.

"Aaaargggh, help!" screamed Tate, clutching his throat and flailing his arms.

"Wait, hold still," warned Allie, as if to help Tate, "you've got to stay still!"

Allie's point was taken from rule number one of jungle movie law, and the quicksand wisdom of the Tarzan movies held true for the Quaigmire as well: the more you struggled the deeper you went. It was a terrible trap from which only the carefully tossed rope of a friend could save you—at great peril to the rescuer as well.

"We'll get you out of there," shouted Moller and he reached his hand out to his friend. But when Tate grabbed hold, Moller lurched forward with a blood-curdling scream of his own. Now they were both stuck in . . . THE QUAIGMIRE.

Thus had humor come to the aid of the Keepers in fighting their worst fears of Senior Philosophy. But it had indeed proved to be a struggle. Serious attention in class could not be neglected for too long, lest the terrible trump card of a failing grade be played on their lives by the sadistic Dr. McQuaig. "He'll fail you in a second," warned Allie a few weeks after classes began, when Joey had decided to mentally boycott the class. "You better listen up."

The content of Senior Philosophy was particularly offensive to Joey, a fact which seemed to be instantly recognized and then capitalized upon by the wily Dr. McQuaig. He had long been known to single out a few students for special harassment and this year it seemed he had decided to dedicate all his efforts towards attacking and destroying the vulnerable views of the school's only blatant Christian fanatic.

By the middle of the semester, the conflict had grown from subtle innuendo to outright abuse. Joey had responded to earlier stages with his usual brand of cryptic remarks about hell and Armageddon. Increasingly, though, he had been forced to support his remarks with sound logic and specific philosophical formulas, as the cruel doctor closed in on his prey.

Though always an easy target, it was soon obvious that Joey would be no easy kill. His genius level IQ, once dedicated to the task of supporting his beliefs intellectually, was soon successful in coming up with some rather complex systems of thought to defend his faith. For McQuaig, however, this was like the smell of healthy blood to a shark. The presence of a worthy opponent only served to bring out a still more vicious side of the man. By the week before Thanksgiving, hardly a class went by without some direct and demeaning challenge to Joey.

The toll being taken on their sensitive friend was obvious to his friends, but they could be of little help. For Tate and Allie, the arguments had long ago surpassed their ill-defined ideas about their own faith, and Michael Moller, though glad to help Joey get a better understanding of his adversary's point of view, could find little that was inconsistent in Dr. McQuaig's logical progressions.

"Within the context of what he's saying," Moller would tell Joey, "the guy is bullet-proof." His advice to Joey had been to "go after his starting assumptions—don't let him get away with that bullshit about 'a priori' knowledge—or else to after the meaninglessness of his ultimate conclusions . . . but stay away from everything in between, because his logic will chew you up like bite-size bits of gray matter."

Like a bantam-weight prizefighter revitalized in his corner, Joey would storm back into the fray, his head ringing with Moller's advice, only to forget his strategy in the first exchange of blows: he could not resist the temptation to get sucked into Dr. McQuaig's digressions. Joey's friends could only look on in anguish as he walked out onto the deceptive cloak laid out over the latest quadrant of the Quagmire, falling full-force into the suffocating slop of Dr. Quagmire's philosophical soup. They found themselves barely able to pull their increasingly exasperated young friend from the nasty bowels of the earth, coated as he was with a humiliating film of Quagmirish muck.

After several weeks of such abuse, and perhaps motivated by the need to rally the troops after the unsettling scene with the Mayor, Allie had called the Keepers to their counsel-of-war room at school and announced the need for a direct Get against the "twisted and perverse Dr. McQuaig." With the annual premier of the Light Show at the Harvest Ball only a few nights away, Allie spoke about the need to unify themselves for the sake of the show coming up that Saturday night, as well as to stand up for their young friend being so ruthlessly mistreated.

Though Joey tried to downplay the pains of his conflicts with Dr. McQuaig, he offered no resistance to the idea of a Get in that direction. "He gets my vote for being demon possessed," he said.

"Twisted, at least," agreed Tate. If the events in the studio a few nights before had widened the gap between his own beliefs and those of Allie's generally accepted Get ideology, Tate was not ready to admit it. "I guess we should go after that werewolf parading as a teacher of Philosophy," he said.

Casting his vote in the affirmative, Moller simply asked, "So, what's the plan?"

"Well," said Allie in response. "It's not going to be easy."

"The man is no slouch," agreed Tate.

"Maybe we need some advice," suggested Joey, and it was understood that he meant going to Father Miles.

"You might be right," nodded Allie. He rubbed his face thoughtfully. "But I'm thinking Father Smiles might be a little gun shy just yet and maybe—yeah, definitely—we need a word from someone else on this one." The others looked at Allie as he paused for dramatic effect. ". . . A *Final* Word."

"The Magnificent Bolo," said Moller.

"Exactly," said Allie.

"Perfect," said Tate. "Let's go."

Mr. Don Bolin looked up from behind the wall of papers and magazines on his desk and grunted a greeting to the four visitors squeezed into his office. "Mmmmfffg, what can I do for you gentlemen?"

"We need your help, Mr. Bolin," said Allie briskly. "We're having a hell of a time with this existentialism stuff in Dr. McQuaig's class."

"Can't make heads or tails of it, eh?" said the Magnificent Bolo with a welcomed sense of empathy.

"Exactly," said Allie. "It's like trying to hold onto a fistful of sand underwater."

Don Bolin's head twitched and he looked slightly bug-eyed at Allie. "Well said," he smiled. "So what's the rub?"

"We want to know where it's all leading," said Allie. "Moller?"

Michael Moller nodded at Allie and then turned towards their teacher to begin his Full Report. "It's like this, Mr. Bolin," he began. "I mean, McQuaig starts off innocently enough: Descartes and John Locke and those boys—a little empiricism, a bit of rational skepticism, nothing too threatening, you know, just a little 'what you see is what you get.' But then he slips on into Hegel and Nietzsche—and it starts getting just a little weird with all those Germans thinking they're God's gift to the world, but even that's cool since we kicked their ideological butts in a couple of world wars, and it's kind of funny really, that nowadays just about all that Germany makes us think about are sausages and beer—kind of history's hot dogs—but then . . ." and here Michael Moller paused a moment for dramatic impact, "all of the sudden it's Kierkegaard and all the dark powers of Lester McQuaig start coming to life. The man is an angst hound, you understand, a junkie for despair. He uses Kierkegaard to paint this incredibly bleak picture of middle class hopes and virtue, kind of destroys Disneyland for us, if you know what I mean, and just when you think the black hole is all that's left, McQuaig dangles this stuff about Kierkegaard's concept of a Leap of Faith out in front of you like a canteen in front of a man dying of thirst, only to cruelly pour the water out onto the hot sand in the name of, you guessed it, Sartre and Camus. And from there, it's *No Exit*, to say the least."

THE LAST GET

The Magnificent Bolo stared silently at Michael Moller. The Full Report indeed, he seemed to be thinking. The trace of a smile softened his face for a moment. Knowing the Bolo to be an impatient man, however, Allie seized the moment and got right to the point.

"So what's the Final Word on all that stuff?" asked Allie bluntly. "Sartre, Camus, Kierkegaard, what do you think of those guys? Should we be putting up with all this stuff?"

"Well, they're not such a bad lot," said the Bolo slowly. He rubbed his bald head like a crystal ball holding all the secrets of humanity. "You certainly couldn't fault them for intellectual honesty," he said between pauses. "But you couldn't say they ever found the Fountain of Youth, now could you? At least not Sartre and Camus. Now Kierkegaard, there's a puzzler for you. Leap of Faith and all that. Who knows, maybe he landed on the other side of the rainbow. But as for those other guys, it was a pretty grim scene."

As expected, the Magnificent Bolo was by then reveling in a state of mind so similar to personal recall that an outside observer would have assumed the man had spent many a steamy night, carousing through the summer streets of Paris with the philosophers in question, drinking and talking the night away.

"Define 'grim scene'," insisted Moller. "Where did all this existentialism thing lead them?"

"Well, for the most part," answered their teacher quickly, to suicide." The Magnificent Bolo pressed his lips shut to emphasize his point. "Suicide was the logical conclusion of their philosophical system, as they themselves eventually pointed out. For them, the only courageous way out was suicide." Then their teacher chuckled. "So, consequently, most of them lived out their lives as cowards."

"But not Kierkegaard?" asked Allie. It was clear to his friends that an idea was forming itself in Allie's mind.

"No," said Mr. Bolin thoughtfully. "Kierkegaard talked about making a leap of faith, of somehow stepping beyond the limitations of the rational world, in hope of finding . . . well, another dimension of life."

"So how come McQuaig skipped over all that?" mused Allie.

"Because he'd rather torture us with the dark side," interjected Joey, "than even let on there might be some way out."

"I think you're right," said Allie, and Mr. Bolin did not disagree. Turning to his friends, Allie continued, "And what would we do to undermine such a scheme?"

"Force him to face the music," said Tate with a faraway smile. "Make him admit there is hope."

"But how?" asked Joey.

"Well, I don't know," said Allie with a smile that indicated that he probably did know. "But I suppose it would take some kind of 'leap of faith' on his part." He eyed his friends to let them know that he had found what they had come for.

"Well, thanks, Mr. Bolin," said Moller. "It seems we've got an idea."

"Very well, gentlemen," said the Magnificent Bolo. His mind had already wandered back towards an open magazine on his desk. "Good luck, then."

"Thank you, sir."

The next day was the Wednesday before Thanksgiving. Despite the pressure of final preparations for Saturday night's show, the Keepers had agreed that it was time to make their move on the Quagmire. "The tension between Joey and McQuaig is too great," Allie had insisted. "That bastard won't let a class go by without trying to take a shot at Joey." Then Allie smiled, "So what better time to strike?"

At the outset, Allie's timing proved to be impeccable. From the moment the 1:30 lecture began, Dr. McQuaig was blatantly engaged in spinning his web of darkness around Joey. His thick hands pressed down on his notes as if they were on Joey's chest. The deeply set eyes beneath his heavily lined forehead and coarse black hair stared directly at this one student. As promised, the lecture was a continuation of the exploration of existentialism, specifically as it was expressed in the writings of Jean Paul Sartre and Albert Camus. With Kierkegaard out of the picture, the final scenario was bleak indeed. But this was just what the Keepers had planned for. With Dr. McQuaig bearing down relentlessly on the case for hopelessness and despair, Joey began making noticeable twitches in feigned response to Dr. McQuaig's words. Believing that his words were at last having their intended impact on his young adversary, Dr. McQuaig became almost shameless in the directness of his attack on Joey.

"Hopelessness, despair," he raved into Joey's face, "the dark night of a soul who has realized that the universe is silent to his existence. God has fallen asleep, has died, has never existed in the first place. This is the resting place for the true seeker —" on the word 'true' he literally sneered at Joey, whose twitches had turned into melodramatic convulsions, too obvious for the other Keepers' tastes but convincing to everyone else--"the dark bed of nothingness upon which the seeker lays his head to ponder the further meaninglessness of his being. What way out is there, but death?"

With perfect timing Joey jolted upright and screamed, "You're right! What way out indeed? Only death! Suicide! The way of the courageous man is suicide." With a clumsy effort he pulled a large handgun out of his jacket, sending shrieks through the classroom as everyone dove to the floor, including the suddenly shocked Keepers. The plan had called for a bottle of sleeping pills.

"You've been right all along, Dr. McQuaig," said Joey coolly. "You have made your case for despair, and with your help, I'm prepared to take the courageous way."

Dr. McQuaig's face flushed as pale as his soiled white shirt. "Just a minute, young man," he rasped. Holding out his hands to Joey he fumbled for words. "That's not what I meant at all. These are just Philosophers. These are just ideas."

"Ideas with power, Dr. McQuaig," blurted Joey. "Ideas with the power to motivate people!"

By then Allie had found his voice too, and he crawled over beside Joey. "Hey Joey, settle down," he whispered, but Joey did not acknowledge him.

"Now how about walking me through that hopelessness and despair thing again?" raved Joey to Dr. McQuaig.

"Joey, this is not what I meant, repeated Dr. McQuaig. "Now put down that gun and let's talk this over."

"What's to talk over?" insisted Joey. "The way I heard it, it seemed to pretty absolute. 'No Exit', I thought. Unless"—and here Joey kicked Allie to signal that the plan was still on--"unless there's any hope for that leap of faith thing."

Allie and the others breathed a deep sigh of relief. The gun had been a crazy idea of Joey's, but at least he was still with them.

"Leap of Faith?" asked Dr. McQuaig.

"Yeah," said Joey. "You were telling us about Kierkegaard's deal on the Leap of Faith. Sounded like a feasible alternative to me."

"Oh, absolutely," said Dr. McQuaig, seeing his chance for talking Joey down. The humble earnestness in his voice was almost as shocking to the class as Joey's gun had been. "Kierkegaard's leap of faith, that is certainly an alternative to suicide."

"Well . . . ???" said Joey and this was Allie's cue.

"Sir," said Allie, peering up bashfully from the floor. "I think he would like to, well, actually *see* a Leap of Faith. Perhaps you could humor him, you know, demonstrate." Allie had a special gift for sounding reasonable in the face of crazy events. After a long, quizzical look, Dr. McQuaig addressed Allie as if Joey were behind a soundproof window in an institution, "You mean, you think it would help if I . . . jumped or something."

"Yes, sir," said Allie with the authority of a practicing psychiatrist. "I've seen that sort of thing work with him before."

Joey convulsed again and began raving, "Oh, it's hopeless, after all, never mind then, just lead me to the darkness." He began to raise the gun to his head, but Allie grabbed his hand and held it down.

"Do something!" shrieked Allie to Dr. McQuaig, suddenly not sure himself if Joey was acting or not.

"Hold on Joey, shouted Dr. McQuaig. "And listen to this. It's like we're here, on this side of the line . . ." The teacher held out his foot and drew an imaginary line across the floor. "And it's as if there is a thick curtain separating us from the spiritual world on the other side of the black line—" The teacher held out his foot and drew and imaginary line across the floor. "This side is the world of our rational perceptions. On that side is—" and here Dr. McQuaig paused as if he had never had to find words for this other dimension—"on the other side is . . . well, to use a phrase I think you can relate to, on the other side is 'God- knows-what'."

At this Joey had to smile, before quickly returning to his glazed stare. "God knows what," he murmured, "that doesn't sound like much! How about, 'God knows something?!? No, how about, God knows everything?!! "

"Right, that does sound good," continued Dr. McQuaig, desperately trying to placate Joey. "And in Keirkegaard's view, the Knight, as he calls his true seeker, must be willing to leap through this veil in hopes of some sort of salvation."

Joey continues to stare blankly into Dr. McQuaig's hopeful expression. "Some sort of salvation," he whispered. "Some sort of salvation . . . "

"I think he needs to see it," suggested Allie again. "You know, sir, visualization and all that."

With a final look at Joey still clutching the gun and straining against Allie's grip, Dr. Lester McQuaig backed up from his imaginary line, and, with a desperate sigh, gathered himself into one amazing bundle of intellectual abandon and ran headlong toward the invisible curtain. "Like this!" he shouted as he left the floor and sailed airborne through the former barrier of his accepted universe.

"Oh," said Joey as his teachers slid to an embarrassed stop. Dropping the gun limply to his side, Joey smiled shyly. "Yeah, I see what you mean." Then he glared intensely at Dr. McQuaig to let him know the whole thing had been a set-up. "Yes sir," he smiled, "I think I GET it now."

"GOOD EVENING LADIES AND GENTLEMEN..."

Allie Reed stood in a tight circle of white light and slowly lifted a microphone to his mouth. Dressed in long tuxedo tails over blue jeans and red high-top sneakers, he rocked gracefully to a lilting drum beat and bass guitar. "On behalf of the Eighth Wonder of the World Music and Light Company," he announced, "we would like to welcome you to the Thirty-Sixth Annual Harvest Ball. We invite you tonight to put your lips to the Cornucopia of American life and . . . BLOW. . . THAT . . . HORN."

A sonic blast from a saxophone was immediately followed by a burst of bright stage lights, and the Eighth Wonder of the World appeared. Allie gracefully bowed out as the fully lit stage came alive with Tate and his band.

Behind the band, giant swatches of color washed across a huge screen. With the song kicking in, images began to appear and then fade in point and counterpoint to the music. A cascading guitar riff filled the air as the bass and drums shook the floor. Somewhere in between was the warm sound of Tate's grand piano, electronically amplified and somehow engineered to gather all the sounds into a wave of deep and rich music. On the edge of this wave was Tate's clear voice, gently sending its whimsical message across the hearts of his listeners.

"This is it," shouted Allie to Michael Moller and Joey. It was Saturday night and the auditorium was packed. Allie had bolted from the edge of the stage to the back of the auditorium and joined his friends on the projector scaffolds. His cameo as MC complete for the time, Allie was now free to operate behind the scenes.

"Opaque number 2," reminded Moller from the center of the scaffold. Joey operated the stage lights from Moller's right and side and it was Allie's job to man the opaque projectors. Allie nodded to Moller and, eyes straight ahead, focused the initial image onto the screen behind the stage. The changing sea of smaller still photos was slowly over-shadowed by the luminous red cloud of Allie's "strawberry" gel. Joey took the cue and faded all the stage lights except his bank of reds and oranges, igniting the entire room in a reddish-orange glow that seemed to be heated up by the music itself.

"Okay," smiled Moller. "Now take it all to blue." With the verse changing into a brighter chorus, Allie shifted to opaque number three and Joey brought his red bank down and pulled up the blues. "Beautiful," smiled Moller, and the Eighth Wonder of the World was up and running.

Out in the crowd the adrenaline was pumping hard. For those accustomed to the Light Shows, the Harvest Ball was a welcomed return to one of the brightest parts of their lives. And for those experiencing the Light Show for the first time, the power of the medium was always overwhelming. As Tate hit the climaxing bridge of the first song, the crowd broke out into a spontaneous scream with Allie and the others joining in. When the song ended, the room filled with a great swell of applause and shouts. Tate and the rest of the band reeled beneath the flood of appreciation. "Thank you very much," shouted Tate, and before the crowd noise had time to let up, the click track in the drummer's head phones signaled the start of the second song. "Hang on for the ride," shouted Tate, and then a searing guitar sound put the show in motion again.

From the lyrics and images of the second song, the main themes of the current Light Show began to emerge:

> "Take a vacation from life at the school,
>   Take a slim chance on the run,
> They have a repairman for mending the rules
>   You break on the way to having some fun . . ."

Images of fences and walls appeared and faded in a gentle kaleidoscope of color and shadow, filling the room with a feeling of entrapment. Then, as the music broke away from the lyrics, images of gates and doorways filled the screen and the effect was liberating as the chorus advised,

> "You don't have to take my word for it,
>   You can go and find out for yourself;
> But if ever it all seems too hard for you,
>   I'll try to be there to help . . . "

This was heartfelt stuff and the crowd could tell. Sincerity of this kind was a welcomed elixir, as was the happy notion of stepping outside society's boundaries to chase the dream of childlike freedom. The commercial music of the times was filled with the desire for such liberation on a grand scale; Tate's boyish treatments of the same hope were all the more alluring for their innocence and humble size.

"How about a short journey," he invited between songs, "to a little place called 'Victrolian Gardens'?" The ensuing piece was a delightful fantasy about a quasi-British mansion alive with animated techno-gadgetry and living musical instruments. Here the visuals of the Light Show became decidedly surrealistic and much brighter, as the music hopped along beneath the sweet harmonies of Tate and his other vocalist. As hoped, the crowd seemed happily transported.

From here the engineers of the Light Show took their audience through a changing maze of human experience and artistic visions. The music was intricate but completely accessible. New melodies that instantly seemed somehow familiar swept out across the room atop rhythms that were impossible not to dance to. The visuals were equally irresistible in their simple power of identification. By intermission, no one had been left untouched. The crowd was ready to go anywhere.

"We'll be back in a few minutes," announce Tate. "Don't get lost out there."

Backstage, Tate waited on a cloud until Allie and the others found him.

"The best, Tate," beamed Michael Moller, slapping his friend on a shoulder wet with sweat.

"It was great," agreed Allie.

"Yeah, perfect," said Joey.

Tate nodded his agreement, a smile filled with both excitement and relief brightening his face. For Tate, especially, the Light Show was by now a critical stronghold against life's ever-encroaching threats. To be able to control completely the world around oneself for even a little while, to be able to steer one's life through realms of brighter possibilities and happier potentials, this was the hope offered by the Light Show's assault on the sensibilities. With life on the outside closing in on Tate, he was placing high hopes on the Eight Wonder of the World.

"This place is ours," said Allie. Michael Moller was positively animated and Joey was fidgety with excitement. Tate was glowing too, alive in a way that never failed to take him beyond his deepest fears. This was what he was best at, and he knew it. The others talked excitedly about little things to remember in the second half of the show, interspersing these nervous reminders with exclamations about how well the first half had gone. Tate listened without hearing, completely happy to be resting but, at the same time, ready to go back on-stage right away. When the time came, Tate took the stage like a man pardoned for a crime. The others had to run back to the scaffolds to get ready in time to bring up the volume on the first microphone.

"We're ready," announced Tate, "we certainly hope you are."

The drummer hit a downbeat and the show was off again. The second half of the show had mostly been re-programmed from the previous year's material, with only a few small changes. It opened with a day-in-the-life film sequence of a rich young lad, played by Allie, braving the various "hardships" of the privileged class. Breakfast with oblivious parents was followed by a series of rich-boy chores—cleaning the swimming pool, trimming a giant hedge, sweeping an endless driveway—and then lunch at the country club. Allie's character was some sort of reverse image of Charlie Chaplin's Little Tramp figure, a happy-go-lucky character in a world of melancholic wealth. Tate's music was convincingly poignant, and the lyrics made their usual waltz across the heart of the matter:

> "In the morning your life has gone away,
> > But you come down for breakfast anyway . . ."

The tone was subdued to say the least, and, as always, it brought a different mood to the audience. The rollicking joy of the first set gave way to a deeper sense of appreciation for the things being said. The opening song was followed by an authentic Delta-blues style tune that Tate called "The Trust Fund Blues." Most of these kids understood:

> "You've got your father's reputation, your grandfather's too,
> Your mother's expectations going right through the roof;
> They all plan for your future, and nobody thinks to ask you;
> Somebody said, 'Son, you' got a bad case of the Trust Fund Blues' . . ."

But most of these kids also wanted to forget, a fact well appreciated by the engineers of the Eight Wonder of the World Music and Light Review. To that end, the climaxing finish of the show was dedicated to a rock and roll celebration of youth's titanic hopes. A song called "High School Immortality," though written as a scorching parody on teenage optimism, was always received as an anthem of just that kind of innocent belief in the power of youth. Tonight the song was played with a fierce irony in every line, as Tate gave utterance to his newly defined respect for the end of every era. Paradoxically, though, the response of the crowd was all the more enthusiastic. The greater the odds, it seemed, the greater the energy required to pretend it wasn't so. The show ended with a thunderous ovation that cleansed away all the contradictions. Never mind the paradox, the applause seemed to say, we're just grateful to be alive with a year or two to go. At least, that's the way Tate and the others heard it, and it gave them great hope for their last year together.

When the demand for a second encore forced the Light Show beyond the limits of their prepared material, there was no doubt in Tate's mind what to play. "The band is gonna have to sit this one out, because we haven't' exactly worked up this song just yet. But it should be a good one to go home by. It's called 'The Power of the Rose,' and somebody told me it's all about the end of an era . . . whatever that means."

CHAPTER TEN

HOAGLEY'S REVENGE

The Monday following Thanksgiving weekend dawned wet and gloomy. Tate and Allie rode out to school together in silence mostly, staring through the blurred windows of a drizzling rain, weighing the sadness of the Mayor's condition against the hopefulness of the Light Show. It was too early in the morning for much hope, however, and the radio offered little help.

"Turn that sucker off," said Allie finally. "I hate that song. And rap that heater again, man. It's freezing in here."

"Sure," said Tate from far away.

Once at school, the threat of impending tests and term papers hung over the commons in clouds as thick as the ones outside. Moller wandered over to the spot where Allie and Tate were already leaning against their usual section of wall, waiting for morning announcements.

"Hey, boys," he said. "Nice weather, don't ya think?"

As announcements began, Allie embellished their grim moods with sarcastic remarks and sighs of disgust. "French club, my ass."

About then, Moller spotted a familiar figure slouching his way around the back of the listless crowd. 'Hey, what's with Joey?" he asked, elbowing Allie.

Tate and Allie picked out their friend between the heads and shoulders of the other students. Joey was slumped over his books more than usual and seemed almost to be staggering in his walk.

"What's the deal?" said Allie.

Michael Moller slipped away from his spot and walked toward Joey with Allie and Tate right behind him. When they met up with their friend near the door of a conference room, Joey practically bumped right into them. Moller grabbed him gently, and, when Joey looked up, Moller's stomach tightened. There was blood all over Joey's face and shirt. "What the hell?" said Moller.

In the next moment, Allie and Tate had got a glimpse of Joey. "Get him in here," said Allie pointing to the conference room. Tate laid hold of Joey's arm opposite Moller and they eased their shivering friend through the door.

"Shut the door, Tate," said Allie. "Joey what happened?"

Joey stood shaking like a wounded rabbit, unable to speak.

His face was streaked with rain and tears mixed through the blood streaming down the side of his head. With great effort, he finally managed to push a message through his quivering lips. "Hoagley . . . " he blubbered. "Hoagley."

"Holy shit!" whispered Tate.

"That son of a bitch," said Allie. Tate just sat down. This was all getting to be too much. Moller jumped right into pulling the details from Joey, however, as if some facts would make it all less horrible. Unfortunately, the details were pretty simple: Dale Hoagley and two of his friends had waited for Joey in the parking lot before school. Whatever civilized wrath the Great Stone Face had unleashed on Dale Hoagley the previous week was passed on to Joey in the most barbaric and humiliating of forms. They had surrounded him as he got out of his car, punching him in the face and slapping his head with schoolbooks.

Joey blurted out the strangest detail. "Hoagley just kept knocking me in the face with a history book and saying, 'Let's make sure history doesn't repeat itself, little wise-ass.' "

"Oh, very clever!" said Allie. "Those bastards. Those psychopathic mafia bastards. We'll get their asses kicked out of here. Man, I'll go straight to the Great Stone Face, straight to Martin if I have to. This isn't gangland, here, it's a fuckin' school! Come on, what is this?"

With Allie's tirade out of control, Tate was speechless. He just kept looking up at his little friend and picturing Hoagley and the others beating him, and it was more than he could take. Joey hadn't done anything to them. What was going on?

It was Moller who made the connection. "Hold on, you guys," he said. "Don't you see what these assholes have done? They must be shrewder than we think. They're figuring us out. They could've just as easily have jumped Tate, who was really the guy who tricked them, or Allie, who they probably knew was behind the whole thing, but they somehow figured out that getting Joey would be the best way to get us."

"That's a low blow," said Tate. He knew Moller was right and it filled him with still more dread. "What is this, some kind of conspiracy?"

The door to the conference room snapped open. It was Father David Miles. Easing the door shut again, he took a quick look at Joey and bolted upright at the sight. "Lord of Mercy," was all he said.

"It was Hoagley, Fr. Miles," stated Allie. "Hoagley and some of his fuc—some of his Golden Boy friends. You were right. They are the enemy. And this is war, now."

"Slow down, Allie," said Fr. Miles, with a calm power that surprised everyone in the room. "This is starting to get out of hand."

"Out of hand is right," said Allie. "It's not enough that they invade our school, but they've got to start trying to take over the place—like that stupid Barbie Doll bitch—and now they're starting this Mafia stuff, like they can get some new territory by strong-arming us . . . if we don't do something quick they'll have the Headmouster on their Mafia payroll, and then they'll start working on the Board of Trustees—"

"Settle down, Allie," insisted Father Miles. "You've made your point." Then he paused and looked over his four old friends, as if surveying his own past. "I'm afraid," he said with a sight, "that it's time you lads face up to some things."

Allie fell silent, and Tate and Moller were already mute.

"I was hoping," continued Father Miles, "that you bright boys would begin to see this for yourself, but if Joey's present condition isn't enough of a testimony to you, then I suppose nothing experiential will do—at least not before it's too late."

An ominous, almost ecclesiastical tone rang through the last of Father Miles' words. "What do you mean, 'too late'"? asked Tate.

"Yeah," said Allie with a tone of challenge in his voice. "And what are these 'things' we're supposed to face up to?"

In a gracious but increasingly unyielding way, Father Miles squared off with Allie and smiled. "You need to realize for one thing," he said calmly, "that things change."

"Yeah, we know that," said Allie quickly. "So tell us some news."

"No," said Father Miles, "I mean it's time to face the real implications of the fact that things cannot stay the same. The time had passed, my young friend, for living your lives in this American aristocratic version of Never-Never Land. The time has arrived to begin living life with an understanding of its transitory nature."

"No fair," protested Moller suddenly with a laugh that showed he knew exactly what Father Miles was getting at. "I know what you're saying, and I disagree. I say a kid ought to at least get to live out his high school years in exactly the kind of Never-Never Land you're talking about—as long as he can afford to, I mean. From where I'm sitting it's one of the few worthwhile things our parents' money can buy. Keep the clothes and cars. Just give me a few years to figure it out before you toss me to the dogs."

"Amen, Moller," shouted Allie, slapping his friend a little too hard on the back. Whirling back around, he glared wide-eyed at Father Miles. "There's some gospel truth for you, Smiles. This other stuff you're saying—well, it sounds like high treason to me, Padre. I mean, I thought you were on our side. Now it sounds like you've been setting us up just to send us down the river of adulthood."

"Oh, please, Allie," said Father Miles impatiently. "This 'Get' business was fine for elementary and junior high school, and I would say what Mr. Moller has to say is acceptable at that level. But enough is enough, lads. It's no good for you to be heading off into the real world thinking you'll be able to hoodwink them into treating you as princes. It's come to the point where I'm almost glad to see your world being disrupted by the changes around here."

"Yea, like this," interrupted Allie pointing at Joey. "Does this look like a great life lesson for you, then?"

"No, Allie," said Father Miles quietly. "It hurts me more than you will know for some years, more than you may ever know, actually. But this is exactly my point. The world is full of characters much worse than Dale Hoagley and they're not going to bow down to this princely station you seem to think is yours for life. In fact, they'll be just waiting for a chance to bring you down. And, as harsh as Mr. Hoagley's methods may seem, I have to warn you that they are not out of keeping with the rest of the world."

"Ah, the 'cold, cruel world' routine," said Allie sarcastically.

"Shut up, Allie," said Tate suddenly. There was a fierce tone in his voice and tears at the rims of his eyes. "Can't you just shut up for a second and hear what he's trying to say? You know what he's talking about. We both know it—shit, we've all known it for quite a while—how much longer did you think we could keep it up? Father Miles is right. It's time we remembered that we were the guys who made up the game, and we'll be a lot better off if we're the ones to call it off."

"Says who?" said Allie sharply. "Who says we have to call it off at all? And if we do, who says we can't just change the rules a bit for the next go around? Who says?"

"Reality," said Moller coolly.

"What?!" said Allie. "What do you know about reality, Moller?

"Just enough to know that it shows up in a big way from time to time," said Moller with a narrow gaze at Allie. "Which is apparently about 10 percent more than you know about it."

"Very funny," snapped Allie. "Mr. History turns philosopher . . . and just in time for graduation into the world of suckered-in adults. What a deal . . . "

"Stop it, Allie," whispered Joey. He had been absorbing his friends' words like more punches to his body until he could not take any more. Wiping his nose with the palm of his hand, he looked up at Allie and took a deep breath. "Please stop it."

Allie looked at their little friend and felt the others watching him. Joey wiped his nose again and then he took a step toward Allie but stumbled. Tate jumped forward and caught Joey with one arm. Joey leaned against Tate and buried his face in his hands again. His head shook as if he were crying again, and the conflict in the room quickly melted away.

"It's okay, Joey, I'll shut up," said Allie quietly. Then he turned to the others and said, "we gotta get him out of here."

"Let's take the back stairs to the gym," said Michael Moller.

"Father Miles," said Allie with a sudden humility, "can you cover for us?"

There was no hesitation in their sponsor's reply.

"Right, lads," he said. "I'll tell your teachers we have an emergency rehearsal for chapel."

"Thanks, Father Miles," said Tate, lifting Joey's other arm. "Let's get him out of here."

Once in the locker room, the humor that had so long sustained the Keepers of the Get returned. For the time, the serious tone of the conversation in the conference room a few moments earlier would be buried again.

"So, it looks like you worked them over pretty good with your nose," began Allie.

"Yeah, agreed Moller, "you should have seen their knuckles when Joey got though with them."

"Lucky for them they were wearing gloves," smiled Tate.

"Yeah," said Joey weakly. "I mostly tried to make an example of that history book. I kept slamming it with my head as hard as I could until I was pretty sure it was wasted. I figured they would realize that next time around their fists could end up like that." A deep, if broken, laugh erupted out of Joey and instantly spread though the others. "I think they got the point," he blurted between bursts of laughter.

"Good man," laughed Allie. "It's always nice to give those kind of guys a fair warning . . . now, come one, let's get that shirt off and get you cleaned up."

In truth, Joey had been greatly relieved to find out that he had been beaten up for the sake of his friends. As he was taking the flurry of blows from Hoagley and his accomplices, Joey's mind was flooded with accusations from his own mind about the reason for this attack. He had been instantly convinced that he somehow deserved what he was getting. Confused theology twisted around his lifelong insecurity gave him these thoughts, and only Moller's insight into Hoagley's more perverse motives released Joey from a pain far deeper than the physical abuse he had suffered.

"Hey, take it easy on me," he said happily to Allie and Tate as they pulled off his shirt. "Or maybe you guys want a taste of the old Nose Karate—"

"No, man!" shrieked Allie as he jumped back from Joey. "Not the Nose Karate, Anything but that, buddy . . . "

Tate, meanwhile, had found an extra dress shirt in his gym locker. "Here, Joey, put this on. It's only seven sizes too large for you. You'll look like a real stud."

Joey smiled again as his friends surrounded him with their jokes and their gentle attention. They sat together in the locker room laughing and laying phony plans for blowing up Dale Hoagley's car and the like until first hour was over. Then Joey and Moller had a second hour class together, so Michael was entrusted with escorting Joey to his class.

On the way, Joey, faraway but still smiling, asked Moller, "So, do you think I saved you guys from getting beat up?"

Moller though a moment and then said, "Yeah, I think that's what the deal was."

"That's really great," smiled Joey. Moller watched Joey carefully as they headed up the stairs to their class. He was puzzled by the pure joy on Joey's face, at the peace that had descended on him. "Well, let's not overdo it," Moller said finally. "We wouldn't want you to get into some sort of martyrdom trip."

"Oh, I know," said Joey quickly, and then he was drifting away. "But there are worse things that could happen to a guy," he muttered, "than taking a bullet for his friends."

Moller started to rebut Joey but he knew the conversation was over. "Come on, man," he said gently, "let's get you to your next class."

Given the magnitude of the recent events, the Keepers of the Get had never been so glad to bury themselves in the relative trivialities of Finals Week. There were two weeks of classes after Thanksgiving and then a week to finish term papers and prepare for exams. Finals gave way to the Christmas rush, and it was usually not until the week between Christmas and New Year's Eve that the Keepers began regrouping. Then it was a rush of another kind, to get the final touches on the Eighth Wonder's infamous New Years Eve Extravaganza, a three-year-old tradition held in the upstairs ballroom of one of Tulsa's old downtown hotels. This year's show had long been heralded as a nearly cosmic event: the year was 1969 turning to 1970, and it signaled the end of what appeared to many of its admittedly affected constituents as the single most important decade in modern history.

While the Keepers of the Get had never bought in completely to the political ideology of the Sixties, they were nevertheless delighted to cash in on its bright offerings of new ways of looking at life. As the decade drew to a close, there was something in its passing that made a bittersweet backdrop for the end of their youth. These were a part of the unspoken truths, which recent events and the Lights Show itself seem to be conspiring to reveal. The Keepers had been working on this show for nearly a year, holding out much of their best new material until the fateful night of the New Year's Eve show. By the time the evening rolled around, it had become apparent that much of what they had been working on foreshadowed the developments that had lately appeared in their lives.

It was Jane Quinn who gave the Keepers insight into this phenomenon. Since giving the boys access to her arsenal of slides, the Queen of Arts had been given an open invitation to check in on their school workshop. She accepted this invitation on a regular basis and seemed to enjoy seeing the objects of her study brought to light in new ways. Once, at Michael Moller's eager bidding, she had even made a late-night appearance at the downtown studio. It had been a cold December night and the boys had looked up from the end of a song to see the Queen of Arts appearing from the dark cage of the freight elevator. She had swept gracefully across the floor of their studio, as if spreading paper flower petals of blessing in her wake. Greeting them with her indescribable smile, she had given some sort of validation to their years of effort in a simple heartfelt phrase. "So this is where all your genius work is born," she had said.

Sitting in the overstuffed chair that was the perfect observation spot for the watching the fusion of music and image being forged by her young protégés, the Queen of Arts had quietly watched as the Keepers went though their material with heightened intent. Finally, after the now completed version of the "Power of the Rose" that would be shown for the first time on New Year's Eve, she spoke. With a subtle sense of timing hinting these words might be the only clue to her reason for coming she had said, "Art imitates life." It was a modern catch phrase she had introduced to her class as they considered various theories of art, but this night she had spoken the words more authoritatively, and in that poetic way that denied immediate criticism. "And some say," she added with still more unchallengeable endorsement of her radiant smile, "that life imitates art."

Michael Moller had acted as if he understood her, and the others pretended not to hear, but it was not until the night of the New Year's Eve show that the meaning of her words began to emerge in their midst. In the middle of the first set, during the song singled out by both the Queen of Arts and the Mayor, the Keepers of the Get began to understand what was happening to them. This time the verses of the "Power of the Rose" unfolded like the pages of a current events magazine of their lives. Tate's lyrics drew a simple comparison between the twilight of the Sixties and childhood's end, forecasting a Seventies' adulthood that was lackluster indeed, as he lyrically mourned the "death of the child" in one verse and the closing of the rose's petals in the chorus. From their distant stations on the stage and scaffolds of the Light Show, the Keepers were united in a view of their lives that brought everything into focus. The auditorium was filled with others completely tuned into the band's message. It was live performance at its very best and a moment the Keepers would one day realize was what every artist hoped for. At the time it was just the greatest feeling they had ever had.

Looking out from their various outposts around the room, the Keepers saw their world transformed. The young and reckless crowd of their peers had been temporarily slowed by Tate's song and could suddenly be seen standing on a floating plateau, bodies gently rocking to the deep rhythms on the piano. The stage lights cast a gentle glow across the room, igniting in jeweled brilliance each pair of eager eyes. Despite the plaintive tone of Tate's music, these hearts were interested. If he had something to say, they wanted to hear it. But, right on cue, Tate's chorus came around:

> "Don't look to me for answers—
>   You can read a calendar as well as I;
> You can count the years on your own fingers,
>   From the day you were born till the day you die."

It was up to them. With the song loping towards its sweet instrumental end, Tate was holding out a poetic mirror to the audience. It was up to them, and time was ticking away. As the song ended and a grateful flood of applause began to ripple through the audience, Tate smiled. "That's all I can tell you, folks," said his gently amplified voice. "But it's probably worth looking into."

Ironically, the next song was the "Day-In-The-Life" sequence, making for a poignant sense that, despite man's deepest yearning, life goes on pretty much as usual. Tate caught the irony and threw in a quick, "Don't let this happen to you," as the song took off. Never had these scenes appeared so jaded, and the music came across with message that was caustic and clear: without the kind of awareness urged by the previous song, life was a chilling proposition. Before anyone had time to run for a coat, however, the program took off for the newly charted waters of the night's main feature. It was time for the Eighth Wonder of the World's "Tribute to the Decade."

From the first blasting guitar riff, the Tribute was an impressive display of speed-of-light journalism and state-of-the-art observation. Covering all the political, cultural, and even spiritual implications of the times, it was mind-boggling and enlightening, frustrating and entertaining, catastrophic and euphoric. It was the Sixties.

> "Was it just another time,
>   Or has it found a place forever in your mind?"

The question crept out of Tate's lyrics like a pop quiz on the era. Before anyone had time to study the barrage of event over the last ten years, it was already being asked: was it really so significant? Did the Sixties really stand apart from other decades in lasting impact? Did anything really change within? A Beatle-esque melody posed the challenge playfully but with unexpected power. If the audience had not been couched comfortably between the two coasts, the question would have been downright threatening.

As it turns out, by the time the Sixties got to the middle of America they were practically over anyway. This fact, plus the simple truth that most of the decade had taken place just a bit before the Keepers' prime meant that the boys just didn't have as much invested emotionally as the adherents of hippiedom just a few years their senior. Instead the Keepers and their peers remained, for the most part, armchair enthusiasts of the era presently being "extolled and patrolled" in their Light show handiwork. They were fortunate enough to sense that their salvation did not depend upon the dawning of the Age of Aquarius. At one level at least, it was all just part of the show.

Which did nothing, of course, to dilute the intensity of their Tribute, and the audience, regardless, was enthralled. Literally hundreds of images poured by on the screen as the music pressed on in double-time and faster. Tate plastered the room with lyrical content as vivid and rapid-fire as the visuals. The band had never sounded better. With the precisely timed climax of the show approaching its rendezvous with the midnight changing of the guard, Allie leaned out over edge of the scaffolding and screamed a melodramatic warning to his peers, "Look out," he bellowed beneath the roar of the music, "here come the Seventies!"

"I don't think they heard you," shouted Michael Moller to Allie. Joey just smiled. With the seconds until midnight ticking off now on the center of the main screen of the Light Show, they knew their point was about to be made. The rich and happy music of the band filled the auditorium with an exuberant sense of well-being. The pleasant images surrounding the descending numerals added beautiful embellishments to the celebration of the passing decade. "Ten . . . nine . . . eight"—the music swelled as the crowd began the final countdown—"seven . . . six . . . five"—images of a fountain of fireworks filled the screens—"four . . . three . . ."—the crowd was estatic—"one . . . ZERO!!!"

A blaring bullhorn split the room wide open. Behind it pushed a wall of discordant music and a flash of strange red lights. "NINETEEN SEVENTY!!!" It was a garish voice of carnival barker become television announcer. "THE NINETEEN SEVENTIES ARE UPON US . . . "

The music played chaotic descending scales that prophesied a great letdown to come. The audience was quickly and completely deflated. This was certainly not the kind of unconditional hope traditionally offered up on New Year's Eve, but as the engineers of the Eight Wonder of the World would argue, tradition would be among the first things to go in this brave new era of cut-throat competition unto unbridled materialism. And, as always, it was the policy of the Light Show directors to "call 'em as we see 'em," even at the expense of an audience's approval.

And so the auditorium was filled with a taste of the things to come. Moller and Joey had not had to venture far with their cameras to capture overwhelming evidence of the superficiality and crass commercialism making its assault on their world: the rapidly emerging outposts of the franchise food specter were projected against a montage of alluring ads for cigarettes and consumer-crazed products such as disposable diapers and plastic trash can liners. Tate had no trouble finding the words and fitting melodies for his observations of the same frightening trend. A song called, "America in Search of a Bargain," was a searing indictment of the growing masses of Americans "living in a land of waste and want."

By the end of a humorous but terribly morbid song entitled, "The Plexiglass Blues," the crowd had become practically mute. Luckily, the Show had been planned for such a reaction. It was expected that by then the point would have been well-made, allowing the Show to proceed into whatever brighter horizons could possibly be foreseen. The final song of the night began in the murky fields of the previous series, but slowly climbed to a finale of guarded but strongly held hope.

"Don't worry, friends, everything good must come to an end," the song began. The first part of the song was a loving eulogy to happier times coming to a close. By the end of the song, however, Tate was giving voice to the belief in the full cycle of all those things. "Don't worry, friends, some fine things live on past the end . . . "

They were comforting words atop a comforting melody, a hopeful lullaby for the child-like crowd becoming suddenly sleepy with the weight of the hour. The song ended on a gentle major chord, and Tate signed off for the night.

"Don't worry, friends," said his amplified voice. Reverberating off the many walls of the huge room, the clear voice made its long-distance journey back to his own listening ears. "It'll probably get weird," said this echoing voice of Tate, "but it's all going to turn out for the best in the end. Happy New Year and goodnight."

CHAPTER ELEVEN

FOR THE MOMENT

On the afternoon of January 3rd, in the year 1970, a great snowstorm rose up over the middle of America. From Colorado to Kentucky, a massive cloud formation hovered in apparent indecision over the heart of the continent, and then slowly and silently began to release immeasurable amounts of snow onto the earth. In most sections it was wet and heavy, as if specifically created for conspicuous application to every line, angle and surface in the architecture of both nature and man. The storm lasted for three days, leaving no exterior surface of the American heartland uncovered by inches or even feet of pure white adornment. The visual beauty of this newly-created realm was only overshadowed by the awesome silence of its aural landscape. The silence, it was said for years afterwards, was almost mythical.

Somewhere near the center of this great snowstorm, buried in the sprawling old neighborhoods of a middle-sized city, Allie Reed studied the initial flurries from a large den window for nearly two hours. Then he picked up the phone and dialed his friend. "Tate," he said quietly, "this is big."

Having been similarly stationed at his own observation post, Tate was in tune with Allie's perception. "I think it's the end of the world," he calmly replied.

Allie paused to absorb the undercurrents of Tate's wry remark, then he responded with a simple, "Come on, let's get Moller and Joey and go for an adventure."

"Well, alright," said Tate. "I'll be by in the Safari Wagon."

"Perfect," said Allie, "I'll call the boys."

THE LAST GET

Thirty minutes later a rumbling heap of metal and rubber came barreling up the long driveway to Allie's house. The vehicle affectionately know as "The Safari Wagon" was an early model Travelall originally purchased by Tate's family for use at their "gentleman's farm" just outside town. Its title came from its resemblance to the high-roofed station wagons likely to be seen in current movie tales of Africa. Somehow, the car had ended up in dry-dock behind the Henry's garage in town, making it available for occasional use by the Keepers of the Get, as called for by the demands of their more unusual driving assignments.

A blast of the horn pulled a ready-and-waiting Allie out of the house into the thick of what was by then a full-scale blizzard. He made a staggering dash for a car door, which was magically opening in the blur of wind and snow. Grabbing the door as a burst of wind knocked him back, he pulled himself into the car and slammed the door shut. Tate had already picked up Joey and Moller, and Allie acknowledged them all with a warm rush of excitement. "Gentlemen," he said, "this is big."

Tate signaled his agreement by shoving the Safari Wagon into gear as Joey and Moller let out a chorus of screaming laughter to indicate their unbridled support.

"All engines full ahead," announced Allie. Tate revved the engine again and then let out gently on the clutch. With the tires spinning to grab a foothold, the car took off as slowly and smoothly as an ocean liner. Michael Moller gave the sound effect of a steam ship's whistle and the sensation was complete. Another round of laughter sealed the unspoken understanding, and the ship was soon out of the harbor.

There was no discussion necessary for deciding on a destination. "Dead Man's Hill," stated Allie, and Tate just nodded. There was a gigantic hill on the edge of the neighborhoods that was the universal rendezvous-point for daredevils of any season, but particularly so for snowstorms. It was here at Dead Man's Hill that the wintering clans gathered. The sledders and the snowball fighters, the winter trekkers and the snowman builders, everyone with a winter-hearty soul seemed to show up at Dead Man's Hill at the first sign of a good snow.

The streets above Dead Man's Hill converged from three directions at the crest of the hill. Joining in a huge intersection there, they funneled into a single, very wide road which plunged some one hundred and fifty feet downward into another wide intersection at the foot of the hill. It was on one of these winding roads at the top of the hill that the Safari Wagon made its approach on the first day of the new decade. It was nearly dark, and the heavy overcast and late afternoon hour surrounded the warm interior of the car with a sense of foreboding.

"Steady as she goes," said Allie quietly. The engine purred gently along as the heavy vehicle plowed its way through the fresh snow. Occasionally the rear wheels would break loose in the snow and the rear end of the car would slide out slowly, raising spirits in the car as the sense of danger increased.

"Here it comes," reported Moller. He had his face pressed to the windshield and was the first to spot the crest of the hill. "It's wide open, let's take it at full throttle."

"No," said Joey, sliding to the edge of the back seat. "Slow down."

"Have a little faith, Joey," said Allie, their voices getting louder. "Full speed ahead."

Tate was quiet and focused. A barely noticeable smile appeared on his face as he slowly pressed his foot down on the accelerator. He gave his horn several long blasts to warn anyone on the hill to clear the way. "We're taking it over the top, Mates," he announced.

"Tate!" screamed Joey, but even he was smiling as he gripped the back of the front seat. There was a unanimous scream as the road disappeared beneath the crest of the hill and then instantly reappeared when the front end of the car began its plunge. The bottom of the hill was barely visible through the blizzard, and, as always, much further away than memory had indicated. The sweet, youthful elixir of mild panic welled up from within them as the car sailed headlong down the steepest part of the hill. A hypodermic needle the size of a lunar rocket began dumping its payload of pure adrenaline into the communal bloodstream of the four friends, now joined at the jugular vein, and a chorus of crazed joy rose up from all of them at once: "Whooooaaaaaa—"

At the peak of their euphoria, a terrible thing began to happen. A car appeared out of nowhere at the bottom of the hill, barreling up the steep slope at full force. The huge object was destined, of course, to be slowed by gravity and the slick surface, causing it to slip sideways on its course and sending a piercing fear though the driver and passengers of the Safari Wagon.

"Look out, Tate," screamed Allie. All playfulness in his voice was gone. Tate's face went dead as his stomach wrenched into a knot. In spite of knowing better, he put a panicked foot on the brake pedal, instantly sending the Safari Wagon into an uncontrollable spin and hurtling them sideways at full speed towards the car stalling out halfway up the hill.

At that instant Tate's perception of his friends in the car suddenly snapped. A sound resembling music filled the space around him and the awful feeling of being trapped in the chaotically spinning car was silently replaced by a peaceful sense of distance from first the danger and then the entire situation. Tate calmly realized his center of being was not in the car at all. For a timeless moment, he felt himself to be very far removed from his life on earth.

Before Tate knew what was happening, the mundane image of four boys spinning in a motorized vehicle lay on the back of his consciousness like an old comic book on a dusty shelf. In his mind's eye, there now stood a vastly more wonderful realm of infinite possibilities in a land unbounded by human limitations. "Am I in heaven or what?" he heard himself asking, but the clumsiness of words seemed comic as well, and he agreed to be silent, as requested, it seemed, by the universe around him. Instantly the sense of music renewed itself like the second striking of the same chord that had unveiled this encounter with the ineffable. By now, Tate could see himself and his friends alive in a world where joy and laughter held sway over all else. In that moment they are perhaps laughing still—at a car that should have killed them and a world that eventually would. In that moment, Tate saw himself seated with his friends in a version of Joey's Balcony of Angels, watching together as they slid through the rest of their lives on a blanket of forgiving snow.

Eventually, from somewhere far beneath that balcony cradling Tate in its loving perspective, the sound of a human voice rang out. With the Moment still stretching like a kite-string spinning forever out from the hand-held spool of his life, Tate found himself leaning against the inside of the door of his car.

"Tate . . . hey man," said the voice of Michael Moller, "we made it. This thing is sitting on a sandbar."

The silent music that had surrounded Tate in his ethereal moment closed gently in around him until the known universe was again no larger than the wintery scene just outside the car. Eternity disappeared without a trace, other than the vague sense of loss in Tate's heart. He was back.

"Hey Tate, snap out of it," said Allie. "We're alright. We made it."

"Made what?" was all Tate could say. And then he was flooded with a bitter taste of irony. "Made what,?" he repeated. "Made the football team? Made the grade? Made it in the shade?" The sounds of the words made him laugh at what he expected to be private jokes. But at once there was the sound of someone else laughing, too. It was Joey.

"No, man," snickered his friend from the back seat. "Made a mistake: we didn't make it out of here while we had the chance!"

Tate's heart connected with Joey's in waves of laughter. "Exactly," sputtered Tate. "Exactly."

Allie and Moller looked at each other in complete puzzlement. "Did we miss something?" asked Allie sarcastically. "Or have our two frail friends finally gone completely over the edge?"

"We saw it coming," said Moller half-seriously, half-joking. "But it's worse than we thought."

"Yeah," laughed Tate. "It's much worse than we thought, too."

"Much worse," agreed Joey with a final laugh let out through a sigh.

Allie was aggravated by this strange understanding between Joey and Tate. "Yeah, well . . . whatever, boys," he said. "I thought it was kind of a nice miracle that we weren't smashed to bits, but if you guys know something we don't, maybe we should try it again."

"Not a bad idea," said Tate with a sincerity that irritated Allie even more. By then, however, the ever-observant Michael Moller was beginning to realize that something had happened to Tate. Given Allie's presence, however, he quickly tabled the idea of investigating it just then and instead played the role of ambassador. "Perhaps not," he said to Tate lightly. "But it is a bit late in the evening for any serious death runs. Maybe we should try to make it home instead . . . you know, get a fresh start on things in the morning?"

"I suppose so," said Tate sadly. He paused for a long while until Allie jumped on him again.

"Come on, man, Moller's right. Let's get this wagon rolling."

"Sure, Allie," said Tate, and he pulled himself up a little and fumbled for the ignition. The car had died as they were spinning off the road, but it started right up— "what a great car," said Allie—and had no trouble bouncing its way back onto the street.

Once headed for home, the boys fell silent. Tate was still in a daze, and Moller abandoned Allie to begin pondering what was happening with Tate. Actually a bit shaken by the near miss himself, Allie made no objection to the silence. Most distant of all was Joey. He remained pressed comfortably against the back seat, a peaceful smile covering his face. His eyes were wide open but seemed to gaze beyond the world in front of him. The sound of the car moving steadily through the snow united the friends in one world, while their journeys of thought took them far away from each other. After a time, Joey began speaking quietly, as much to himself as to any of the others, though his words reached Tate's ears with their strange shades of meaning and were observed by Michael Moller as well. Joey was reciting obscure passages from the Bible as if he were humming an old, familiar song with mysterious meaning: "I know a man, who in the body or out of the body, only God knows, was caught up into the Third Heaven, and he saw things no man is permitted to speak . . ."

The blizzard in front of them poured against the windshield in a most hypnotic way, making the world seem as unreal as it ever had. " . . . You are seated with Christ in heavenly places," Joey continued, "if then you have been raised up with Christ, keep seeking the things above where Christ is, seated at the right hand of God . . . " Joey's voice had found a rhythm not unlike a Jewish Rabbi, and his tone lilted up and down as if he were reciting the most beautiful of Hebrew psalms. "Set your mind on the things above, not on the things that are on earth . . . For I have died and my life is hidden in Christ . . . To live is Christ and to die is gain . . . "

The others listened quietly to Joey's gentle bantering as the Safari Wagon made its way through the mesmerizing snowfall heading home. Joey's words played like a litany between two worlds, making little sense for the prisoners of the snow-covered earth even as a certain reality was conveyed beneath it all. When they arrived at Joey's house, however, the smile left his face and he echoed Tate's earlier sigh. "Can't we go back to the Hill for one more try?" he sadly joked. "I know there must have been some mistake."

Tate nodded his pained agreement, and Michael Moller raised and eyebrow of understanding. Something in the communiqués between Tate and Joey struck a familiar chord with Moller, but there was not enough in their words to let him make out the whole story. Solemnly watching his friends, himself touched by the mystery of it all, Moller nevertheless felt compelled to break the news to the others.

"Sorry, boys," he said gently. "I'm afraid we're gonna have to stick this one out."

In the weeks and months following, the harshness of Michael Moller's prophetic sentence became increasingly evident to the four friends. Beginning on the first day of Second Term Classes, the remaining bastions of hope in their already suspect world began to crumble. Headmaster Martin climaxed his yearly "half-time pep talk" with the shocking announcement that, "In the long-term interest of academic pursuit, the recently escalated wars of practical jokes will have to come to an end."

It was an idle and impotent threat, of course, but the mere fact that Somerset official policy would position itself in such direct opposition to the Get was a development that brought sadness and ill feelings to the hearts of all the Somerset lifers.

"It's the beginning of the end," moaned Tate after announcements, and, for once, the others had nothing to offer in the way of consolation. Things did not look good.

A few weeks later, Dale Hoagley and a few of his friends managed to steal two of the launchers out of the trunk of Allie's car and then used them to toss eggs and grapefruits into the stands of a school soccer match. By the time Allie discovered the launchers were missing, he was sitting in front of the Great Stone Face being accused of this devious stunt. The obvious stupidity of such a dangerous twist on the Keepers' more sane use of the launchers should have been proof enough of Allie's innocence. In all the years of Gets large and small, there had never been a malicious or violent prank pulled. Whether the Great Stone Face had actually never noticed this fact, or whether the corroding effects of forgotten tradition had already begun to show, it ultimately took a diplomatic appearance by Allie's father to convince the administration of the theft. Needless to say, the pressure to abstain from anything resembling a Get was overwhelming.

"This must be what it's like living under a fascist regime," said Allie one bleak February day. He was talking things over with Michael Moller on a cold, gray Saturday afternoon at Moller's house.

"No kidding," agreed Michael Moller. "And it makes it tough. We move too soon and we're in deep trouble; we move too late and we lose Tate to complete depression."

"Or Joey to uncontrolled fanaticism," said Allie. "We can't just sit here."

Moller nodded a tentative agreement. Tate's mystical experience on Dead Man's Hill had at first renewed their friend to a hopefulness that had been missing from his life. Before long, however, Tate's inability to explain his new feelings to his friends—or to recapture them for himself for that matter—had left him more down than ever. And the ongoing pressure of the Mayor's condition was almost more than he could bear.

Joey, meanwhile, was becoming more intense by the day. His brief victory over Dr. McQuaig had been more than obliterated by the terrible vengeance with which the cruel doctor renewed his humiliation of Joey. At the same time, the Czar had responded to Joey's "insolent attitude" the previous summer by placing him under a ban of silence. There had been no letter, no phone calls, no presents over the holidays, only the brief word through his mother that the upcoming summer "will be different if Joey values his father's place in his life." Joey had shared this information with Michael Moller some weeks before, helping to explain the intensity of his behavior, but making the prospects of helping Joey find any real happiness all the more remote.

Allie paced the floor of Moller's bedroom, becoming more and more irritated. "You'd think people would just lighten up on each other," he said. "What is it about life that makes people so fucking serious?"

Moller answered with a heartfelt shrug. He was about to say something in the way of a theory he'd been working on, when the phone rang. "It was Tate," he said after a brief exchange of words. "The Mayor's back in the hospital."

Out behind the stately white mansion of the Henry Estate, Tate sailed a stone across the surface of their private lake. The stone hit the smooth and silent water with rapid smacks and then dropped beneath the surface. Behind him, Michael Moller stood with his hands in his front pockets and watched as the ripples moves away from each other on the surface of the lake.

"So?" asked Moller finally.

"So . . . " answered Tate slowly. "So, I guess he's gonna be alright."

"That's good," said Moller. "We were sure sweating it."

Tate smiled vaguely and stared straight ahead. "Yeah."

Moller and Allie had rushed to the hospital on the first news of the Mayor's latest stroke, but things had been too unsettled for them to do much for Tate at the time. The Mayor had not fully stabilized until the next day, and the Intensive Care Unit at the hospital did not seem like much of a place for cheering anyone up. After thirty-six hours at the hospital, Tate had come home and slept for fourteen hours straight. Allie and Moller had kept in touch through Beuleah, the Henry's main servant, and when Tate finally began to get around, Allie had been tied up at a family function, so Moller headed for Tate's on his own. When he spotted Tate down by the lake, Moller was suddenly glad he had come alone. He had walked down to the lake and then stood by Tate for some ten minutes before venturing to speak—an occurrence not likely to happen with Allie regardless of the circumstances. When they did begin speaking, there was a candor Moller was sure would not have happened with Allie there.

"Nobody told me it would all get so scary so fast," said Tate still staring straight ahead.

"It was a close one," said Michael Moller.

"Man, when I first spotted him in the Intensive Care Unit I thought he was . . . I mean, I didn't think he was gonna make it. All I could think about was all the times I'd been mad at him for monopolizing my life. All the petty times I'd been so pissed off that he wasn't letting me show off instead of him. That stuff just dropped away, and I started making deals with God. Man, I told Him I'd never get frustrated with the Mayor again as long as he . . . " Tate choked on the warm tears running down his throat, "as long as he was alive."

Michael Moller looked at his friend and spoke softly. "Well, he's alive now, so you better get ready to keep your promise."

Tate brightened slightly at his friend's point. He watched as Moller picked up a handful of stones and began tossing them at a group of the Henry's ducks huddled by the shore.

"Lazy pissant ducks," said Moller with a grimace over a grin. "They bitch worse than we do." He was quoting the Mayor's standard comment on his ducks, recalling the way the Mayoral disdain for his own pets had given rise to the Keepers' tradition of lightly pelting the ducks with stones--"to really give them something to complain about."

Tate smiled at the memory. He was glad Moller was there. Allie and the Mayor were the ones to have around when he felt like being entertained, but only Moller could be counted on to listen. Tate had wanted to talk to Moller about his experience on Dead Man's Hill ever since it happened, but this was the first time it had seemed right to discuss it.

"So what was it like?" asked Moller on cue. "The thing on Dead Man's Hill?"

Tate smiled as the sense of the moment on Dead Man's hill returned to him like an aroma. "It was like I was gone," he said quietly. "It was like I was somewhere else, and I wasn't coming back."

"Yeah," said Moller with an instant sense of understanding. "I thought so." He paused for a moment as if remembering something from his own experience and then continued. "It's like you're above or beyond your mortal life—but not like you've died or anything . . . "

"Exactly," said Tate. He was surprised and thrilled to hear Moller describe so perfectly his own vague feelings. "That's it. I felt like my life as Tate Henry was a kind of play, some sort of ongoing enactment of really unimportant events based on purely arbitrary circumstances. And—for that moment—even the possibility of the Mayor dying seemed powerless, because there was this overwhelming sense of something more important going on."

"Yeah," said Moller, nodding. "Death for once takes a back seat."

"Exactly," said Tate again. "Unlike around here—"

"Where Death is in the driver's seat all the time," said Moller. Sensing Tate's intuitive understanding, Michael Moller suddenly had an audience for some of his deepest thoughts. These were the unspoken theories that clothed Michael Moller in a slight sense of mystery to his friends, the silent calculations and observations that seemed always to be taking place behind his hidden eyes. "That's the whole deal," he said. "I've wondered for a long time if this entire seriousness of life thing is actually just about the seriousness of death. I think maybe everyone's just trying to stave off their fear of death."

Tate tilted his head slightly to let Moller know he was all ears and in so doing opened up the floodgates inside his already animated friend. "The way I'm beginning to see it," Moller continued, "all of our feeble lives on earth are a response to this impending threat of death at the end of the line. Think about it. Either we're busy chalking up all sorts of good deeds to wear on our chest at judgment day—whatever that is—or we're totally consumed with some meaningless diversion geared towards helping us forget that there will ever be an end to this life. Most of the time it's some weird blend of these two, but—think about it, man—what else do we spend our time doing? Good deeds and diversions. That's the way I see it."

A slow and peaceful shiver ran through Tate's body as the meaning of Michael Moller's words sank in. "Man, that's true," he said quietly. As he stared out across the lake, scores of life situations played themselves out in his mind, and each one of them dropped neatly into one of Moller's categories or the other—or bounced crazily between the two. "Good deeds and diversions," repeated Tate thoughtfully. Then he laughed. "Sounds like a great line for a country and western song," he said. "And that means it must be true."

Moller laughed, "Hell yes. And it's about that obvious."

Tate smiled and picked up a handful of stones to toss at the ducks. "So," he began slowly, tossing a stone in the direction of the still-complaining ducks, ". . . so where does that leave us? I mean, if death is the big issue, how do you get around that? If there is some eternal dimension, then where's the door? How do you get there to stay?"

"Ah," said Moller smiling wistfully. "Now there's the rub!" Moller ruffled up his hair and tossed it briefly out of his face. "That one, I haven't quite figured out."

Tate studied his friend's quizzical look and was about to press him with a further question when a voice rang out from up the hill.

"KEEPERS OF THE GET!" shouted Allie, and Tate and Moller turned to see their friend bounding down the hill towards them.

"End of discussion for now, I think," said Tate to Michael Moller.

"Yeah," agreed Moller, and then he smiled at his friend as he got up to greet Allie. "End of discussion . . . for the moment."

CHAPTER TWELVE

JOEY'S DREAM

Joey sat up in his bed, clenching the sheets and gasping for breath. It was only a dream, he told himself finally, but it would take some time for the great sense of relief to overcome the images still tormenting him. He had been struggling for what seemed like hours against a long series of terrifying scenes quite out of control. Already the specifics of all but the paralyzing climax were slipping away from him, but those last few scenes were enough to send him reeling through the bowels of his beliefs looking for the strength to handle it all.

At the end of his nightmare journey, Joey had been standing on the foyer stairs of a huge American mansion, vaguely intending to ascend those stairs for some nondescript reward awaiting him in the upstairs rooms. Suddenly, the massive crystal chandelier had broken loose from its place in the ceiling and come crashing to the marble floor with a cataclysmic impact. Gripped by the fear that the house was about to fall down on top of him, Joey had rushed out the front door, only to be greeted by a great heat, the smell of smoke, and the terrified whinnying of horses. He looked across the darkened lawn and saw the estate's stable complex being consumed by fire.

Frozen on the steps of the mansion, Joey watched as the roof of the main stables collapsed into the flames. At the last possible moment, a sole surviving horse appeared out of the smoke, running at break-neck speed away from the holocaust. Riding the still-smoldering horse was Allie.

Somehow Joey managed to intercept the horse and rider in the field in front of the mansion. Allie was objecting somewhat but with less authority than he would normally have. Ignoring Allie's comments, Joey was able to grab the horse's bridle and began pulling it towards a calm body of water which was soon recognized as the Henry's pond. Though there was a slight sense of relief as Joey succeeded in pulling the suffering animal into the cool waters of the pond, he woke up tormented by the uncertainty of whether Allie had still been on the horse by the time he made it to the water.

When Joey was finally able to fall back asleep, he continued to fight against vague images and feelings of urgency until he at last awoke in the morning. He was unable to eat any breakfast, and his drive to school and morning classes were saturated with haunting flashbacks of the dream the night before. By noon, he was in the office of Father Miles, trying to explain what was so terrifying from the night before.

"The smells were awful," he was saying, "like burning hair and something worse . . . and the way the horses were crying . . . and the fire burning so out of control. . . but mostly it was just the fear, this feeling like the whole world was on the edge of a cliff and losing its balance with us right in the middle of it. Have you ever felt like that, Father Miles? I mean, is it normal? Is life that awful, and do we just cover it up, or am I not supposed to not that way?"

Father Miles was gazing intently at Joey and gently rubbing his own forehead. A man of many dreams and nightmares himself, he knew well the feelings Joey was experiencing, but he also knew that, for all his years and training in such matters, he rarely felt the authority to give specific advice to others struggling with their own dark nights of the soul. Still, he told himself, it was his job and, theoretically, his calling. He took a long breath, hoping that some wise answer would come through. "You cannot deny the power of these things," he began. "I think it's a safe to say that there is some reality behind our more vivid dreams. And yet we also have our daytime consciousness by which we can deal rationally with these things as well."

"But where do you draw the line between being rational and just plain rationalizing?" asked Joey.

"Where indeed?" mused Father Miles. "I guess that's the big question, and I don't think I can answer that one for you. I do know that we've been given minds that work both rationally and subconsciously, and I don't think it's advisable to rule out either one, but where each of us draws the lines, now there's a life-long project for you."

"But it's so hard," objected Joey. "How's my rational mind supposed to deal with last night? Allie riding on a smoldering horse, that mansion about to crash on my head, all those other things I can't remember. What do they all mean?"

"First of all," said Father Miles, "try bearing in mind that dreams have a language all their own. Some of the images are symbols in their own right, others you can follow in the more usual narrative sense. It would probably help you to write down everything that you can recall right away. That may help you to sort things out, may even bring up a few more of the scenes you can't remember. At the very least, you won't lose any more of the important ones."

Joey was listening and agreeing and making up his mind to do what Father Miles was suggesting. But he also had deeper thoughts on his mind. "Father Miles," he said suddenly. "Do you think dreams come from God?"

"Well," smiled Father Miles, "we're certainly asking all the big ones today, now aren't we?"

"Well, yeah," said Joey. "But what do you think? I mean, there's all these major events in the Bible that involve dreams, so many important people connecting up with angelic beings and being given some pretty important information, that sort of thing. So what's the deal? Is there really a hotline to God in our subconscious minds or not? I mean, is God trying to tell me something or do I just need to lay off the midnight grazing?"

Following an easy laugh, Father Miles narrowed his gaze and pressed his hands together. "What do you think, Joey?"

"I think it means something," said Joey immediately.

"Well, so do I," said Father Miles.

"It's the death of the American aristocracy," said Joey with a sudden clarity. "We're on the edge of a cliff. Our world's caving in on us, burning to the ground."

"Perhaps so," said Father Miles wistfully.

"So what am I supposed to do about it?" asked Joey.

"What were you doing about it in the dream?" responded Father Miles.

"Freaking out mostly," said Joey, breaking into his wheezy laugh. "I mean, it was killing me just watching it."

"And what about the end of the dream?"

"That's true," said Joey quickly. "I did forget about my fear for a second and grabbed the horse and—yeah, now I remember—I forgot all about myself actually and all I cared about was helping Allie and that horse. I mean, it felt pretty good getting that poor, smokin' animal down to Tate's pond. It felt really good, like he was going to be okay, you know?"

"Yes," said Father Miles.

"But what about Allie?" asked Joey, the anguish from the night before returning to him. "I can't remember if he was still on the horse . . . you know, he was burned pretty badly too, and I can't remember if I made it down to the pond with him or not."

"Maybe that part was not your responsibility," suggested Father Miles.

"No . . . it felt like it was," recalled Joey. "It felt like it was, and one reason I woke up feeling so bad was I just couldn't remember if he was still on the horse. Why can't I remember? I mean, do you think he was still on the horse? Do you think he made it to the water?"

"I couldn't say, Joey," said Father Miles slowly. Then his expression grew deeper, and he looked off into the distance. "I wish I knew, but I'm afraid I don't."

Michael Moller and Tate rode in silence on the hospital elevator, staring straight ahead, feeling no awkwardness. It felt good to be able to be silent. They were going to visit the Mayor.

At the door of the Mayor's hospital room, Tate looked at his friend and, breaking the silence with a gentle warning, reminded him, "Remember, there's a lot of tubes, and he doesn't look so great, just don't let it weird you out," he said. And then, with a deep breath, he pushed open the door and walked in. Following behind, Michael Moller took a breath himself and got his first look at the Mayor since his latest stroke. Though he had tried to prepare himself, it was still a shock.

The Mayor lay in a deathly stillness, sheets pulled tightly up to his neck, his face pale and sallow and covered with a thin stubble of facial hair. Clear plastic tubes ran out of his nostrils and from a single arm laid atop the bed sheet. At the chest, the sheet rose and fell in barely perceivable signs of life.

Tate walked over to the bed and gently touched the exposed hand. "Pop, it's me," he said quietly. "And, hey, I brought Moller." Glancing at his friend, he signaled Moller with a nod. The Mayor had been semi-conscious for eight days, able to listen it seemed, but unable to respond, except by the simplest of movements. Tate had made up his mind from the start to keep talking to his father in all the usual ways, and he had grown used to interpreting the slightest movements or expressions. This day, Moller had agreed to come with Tate to visit the Mayor, gently joking, "This way, we get to monopolize the conversation for a change."

Here was Moller's cue, however, and he found it harder than he had anticipated. "Hey, your Mayorness," he said as naturally as he could. "It's . . . it's good to see you."

Tate smiled and rested his hand against his father's side. "We came to fill you in on the latest, Pop," he said. Though it had been equally hard for Tate at first, he had overcome the strangeness of just talking to his father. Eventually, he had actually come to somehow enjoy his one-way conversations with his otherwise gregarious father. Though he felt guilty for feeling this way, it was nice not to be interrupted. "It's getting really crazy out there at school," continued Tate, "and I figured we better keep you informed. You need to be on top of it for the next board meeting and all. Not that there may be any hope for the place really, cause I think it's all over."

"He may be right, your Mayorness," chimed in Michael Moller. "The administration is caving in like a sand castle at high tide, sir." Moller's reflexive need to clarify and embellish had suddenly and completely done away with the awkwardness of the moment: it was time for a Full Report. "They're falling for the lure of this academic greatness stuff," he continued. "I never knew the phrase 'progressive education' could take on such a religious aura. Who would have thought you could fashion a golden calf out of such hype?"

"We've been fighting back pretty hard, Pop," chimed in Tate, "but I'm not sure it's going so well. They're still pretty hacked off about that 'Academics is the Opiate of the Masses' Get, and then there was all the confusion about the stupid stunt that some Golden Boy pulled with the stolen launcher, that sort of thing."

"Right," agreed Moller. "So get this: at announcements this week Headmouster Martin tries to tell us that this, and I quote, 'practical joke stuff' is going to have to end. Can you get a whiff of that? He didn't even have the presence of mind to distinguish between our Gets and these new kids' brainless attempts to jump on our bandwagon. It's like he was throwing ten years of Get tradition in a toilet bowl with every stupid practical joke ever tried—"

"And he's reaching for the flusher, Pop," interjected Tate. "He really is."

All along, the Mayor lay gazing straight at the ceiling, chest rising and falling slowly beneath the bed sheet. His face twitched occasionally and, when the boys paused in their report, his eyes seemed to narrow a bit as if to indicate that he was hearing them. Tate shot a glance at Michael Moller and his friend nodded back.

"So it's like this, you Mayorness," continued Moller. "We feel like there's something at stake here. It feels like there is something worth defending. It just doesn't seem like a whole way of life should go down the tubes just because some out-of-touch suckers fall for some new sales pitch. It's just like what happened to you and our dads: so they find some big oil fields in the Middle East? Does that mean everyone has to jump ship on fifty years of friendships and start making like Lawrence of Arabia? Same deal here: are they just going to cancel everyone's memberships to their country-club schools and turn the golf courses over to motocross bikers just because they found out that some Golden Boys and Wheeze-bags can learn calculus, too? It's crazy, your Mayorness. I mean, what about tradition? How about a little respect for the home team, fellas? It's like these guys are crashing a formal party and then complaining that there's not enough food. Where do they get off with this stuff?"

By now, Tate was smiling. Moller was in rare form and Tate was convinced the Mayor could hear them. The room itself seemed filled with a warmth that had not been there when they arrived. Had the sun broken through the clouds outside, or did it just seem to lighter in the room?

"So that's the deal, Pop," continued Tate after the short pause. "The administration almost seems out to get us, as if we are somehow standing in the way of their big plans for the future. It's like, 'move out the dinosaurs, folks, we've got some new tenants here, and they're paying top dollar.' And maybe we should bow out gracefully, but maybe not. Maybe we should make a stand instead, which is certainly what Allie wants to do. Moller and I aren't sure. What if this is just part of growing up? What if it's just part of moving on? We don't know. Allie wants to dig in, and we can't exactly disagree. I mean, it is our school, and it is our senior year. You'd think they could at least humor us for a few more months, but I don't know. Then there's all those younger guys from the old guard too. It seems so sad that they may miss out on the whole deal now, and that makes us want to go for it even more. You know, like we should leave them something they can get their bearings on and maybe carry on with after we're gone."

"So what do you think, Mayor?" asked Michael Moller without thinking. In the past, of course, the Full Reports to the Mayor had always ended with an opinion from the silver-haired patriarch, some bit of advice or word of wisdom that was usually received by the boys with a reverence even deeper than that given a Final Word by the Magnificent Bolo or a sermonized statement by Father Miles. Given the circumstances, it was understandable that Michael Moller would request a word from the Mayor. He had just forgotten that the Mayor was not talking.

Before the moment had time to grow awkward, however, something strange and marvelous began to happen. The Mayor moved.

The hand on top of the sheet first twitched, then twitched again, then began ever so slowly to turn over on the sheet. After a short pause, it began to rise off the bed. Tate and Moller looked quickly at each other and then stared back at the hand. Still just a few inches off the bed, the fingers lightly pawed the air in the direction of Tate. The Mayor was reaching for Tate.

Instantly Tate moved his hand over to his father's. The Mayor's fingers touched lightly on the top of Tate's hand and then found their way around it into a grasp. He squeezed the hand for a long moment as the tears welled up in his son's eyes. "Pop, you're there," he blurted. The Mayor's eyes narrowed as they had before and he squeezed his son's hand again.

"He heard every word, Tate," said Moller with tears in his own eyes. "He's there, buddy."

Again the Mayor narrowed his eyes and then his hand began to move around on Tate's wrist as if on a mission. Fumbling for a moment at the cuff of Tate's white shirt, his fingers grabbed a firm hold of the shirt and then rested for a moment. Then the entire hand united in a weak but definite tug at the sleeve. Tate and Moller watched as the Mayor slowly repeated the movement. Having come straight from school to the hospital, Tate was wearing a corduroy sports jacket over his shirt, and by the time the Mayor pulled for the third time on his shirt cuff, the movement was unmistakable: from the time Tate could first remember being dressed by his father as a young boy, the familiar tug on the cuff of each sleeve was the final touch on the ritual of dressing up. The pleasant feeling of the shirt sleeve being freed and neatly arranged beneath the jacket was the signal that father and son were now ready to face the world together—as gentlemen. Now, from his place on his back on what many feared would be his death bed, the Mayor was preparing his son once more, this time to face the world without his father—but as a gentleman still. Tate burst into tears as he understood his father's loving offer. Warm shivers riddled his body with the memory of the first time his father had shown him how the shirt cuff's proper length was to break on the middle of the muscle beneath the thumb, advice that even then was meant to be remembered for life. Tate smiled as the cuff of his shirt moved with the tug of his father's hand to its appointed station. "Perfect length, Pop," said Tate, and his father's hand relaxed as his body sank gently back into the bed. The Mayor's face, too, seemed to relax gently in the direction of a smile. He let go of his son's hand and rested his hand back on the bed. The Mayor's face, too, seemed to relax in the direction of a smile.

"It doesn't matter what we do," said Tate quietly to Michael Moller, "but we gotta do it as gentlemen. That's what he was telling me, Michael, we gotta keep our integrity through whatever happens."

Moller nodded his head and, without thinking, reached for his own shirtsleeve. He gave it a gentle tug and repeated the motion on the other sleeve as he stood up to leave. "You're right, Tate," he said. Memories of his own father welled up from within him, and he choked back the warm tears in his throat.

The Mayor let out a deep breath and his face relaxed further into what seemed even more like a smile. Tate squeezed his hand one more time and then put his head down to his father's chest. "Get some rest, Pop, we'll be in touch."

"Thanks, Mayor Henry," added Moller. "We won't let you down."

Nobody knew exactly which night of the weekend the vandals had struck. According to Sherman, the head of school maintenance, everything had seemed fine on Saturday. No one had made any rounds through the main part of the school until Monday morning, when all the damage was discovered. As far as any other clues, there were only the motives to be deciphered behind the graffiti written with soap bars on all the blackboards, and a certain pair of gym shorts hung over the bronze head of the bust of the school founder in the main foyer. The name written in black ink on the label of the gym shorts read, "Hoagley."

"I say they should string him up," exclaimed Allie to his friends. It was the middle of the morning on Monday, and the Keepers were making their usual third hour rendezvous in the senior conference room. Allie had walked in with the air of the Great Stone Face about him, made his announcement, and then laughed. "What kind of dumb shit Public would try a stunt like that on the Slumberset?"

Joey, Tate, and Moller had been just been bantering about the same topic themselves. "No kidding," agreed Moller. "And can you believe someone would be so stupid as to use their own gym shorts?"

"It is hard to fathom," smiled Allie. "Maybe this will allow the administration to see just how far these guys are willing to go—and how stupid they are to boot."

Tate eyed his friend slowly and, by the tone of his voice, seemed to agree, "How about that graffiti, though?" he said. " 'Down with the divine rights of kings'...'survival of the fittest' . . . 'make way for the new regime'—not bad copy for a bunch of illiterates."

"Well, I gotta give 'em that much," grinned Allie. "They're at least getting an education around here. Beyond that, however, it's clear they're still a bunch of barbarians."

"Heathens," agreed Joey. "Pagans, public school pagans."

"Amen, Joey," said Allie. "So what do you say we give 'em the stake? They've probably got Salem witches filling up their family tree like hoot owls. What do you say we get up a nice bonfire on the football field and just end this thing right here."

"Allie, the Grand Inquisitor," proclaimed Michael Moller sarcastically. "From whence floweth this outburst of self-righteous militancy?"

"Just trying to protect the Holy Realm, old boy," smiled Allie.

"Protect, indeed," said Tate, suddenly disgusted. He stared at Allie with cold eyes for a long moment and then told him. "We know, Allie," he said flatly. "Sarah told us."

"That traitor," said Allie melodramatically. "Never trust a woman . . . " He tossed his books down on the conference table and flopped down into a chair. Leaning back, he put his feet up on the table and smiled. "Oh well, I was gonna make a formal announcement today anyway. You know I couldn't keep a great Get like that to myself."

"Get?!!!" exclaimed Tate. "Since when do we classify third-rate vandalism as a Get?"

"Tate, my boy," explained Allie slowly, "as an outright prank by Hoagley it would have been vandalism . . . but as a frame job it's pure genius. It's a Get, and you can't deny it."

"Sounds more like an excuse to vent some pretty barbarian feelings under the guise of a Get," said Moller.

"Oh thank you, Dr. Freud," sneered Allie. "I so appreciate your pop psychology. I suppose next you'll be figuring out that it's my latent homosexual tendencies that make me want to be friends with guys like you. Very deep."

Joey meanwhile had been speechless. Tate and Moller had not told him the news before Allie walked in, and the revelation that Allie had broken into the school sent his head spinning like a top through the meaning of it all. Though the prank did not seem like much of a Get to him, Joey usually defined Gets mostly by Allie's own assessments anyway, so this was confusing. When all his frustration finally boiled over into the conversation, all he could manage was an exasperated, "Alllllllie???!!", sung in a pitiful tone somewhere between an accusation and a request for an explanation.

"It's war, Joey," said Allie. "Spiritual warfare. Powers, principalities, demons, Joey, public school, mass marketing demons, and they're trying to take over control of our country. Can you get a handle on that? We need to stop them right here—"

"Come off it, Allie," interrupted Tate. "Who's taking himself too seriously now? We're talking about of bunch of high school kids who are trying to make it at a new school. Period."

Allie sat up as if he had been slapped. "What?! Are you joking, or have you completely lost it? Look, Tate, I know you've been under a lot of pressure lately, but let's not lose touch, son. I was waxing a little poetic there for Joey's sake, but let's not kid ourselves—these guys are out for our turf, and if we don't stop them, nobody will."

"And who says anybody should," said Michael Moller. "Why not let them have what they can? What if there's plenty to spread around?"

"And what if there isn't?" interjected Allie. "Go ahead and give them your spot at MIT, Moller. You'll look great at junior college! Hey, maybe you could meet a swell girl there with a great future in dental hygiene. Why, figuring in your income as a professional key-punch operator, you guys could probably own your own motorboat by the time you're fifty. Hey, no thanks, pal. You can roll over and play dead if you want, but I know what's at stake here."

"What are you saying, Allie?" said Tate quietly. "That the masses are going to rise up and take control of your trust fund. I mean, really, what *is* at stake here?"

"How about, for openers, respect?" said Allie, a little quieter himself. "How about dignity and class and the ability to lead with integrity? Think about it, Tate. Can you really picture Hoagley as Mayor someday, or one of his little pals as head of my father's corporation? Do you see what I'm saying? And I don't mean that they might not do a great job . . . it's just the way they would do it. We're talking about style here, boys, class. We were born for this stuff, and we need to take care of it."

"By vandalizing our own school?" pressed Moller.

"By making our school *appear* like it had been vandalized," said Allie. He paused a took a breath. "Look," he continued more calmly, "think about what I really did: soap-writing on the blackboard, a bunch of desks turned over but not broken. Some long streamers of toilet paper down the halls. All highly visual stuff, but nothing really destructive. No permanent damage. Now if Hoagley and his boys had really done the job, they would have used spray paint, and broken a bunch of glass and stuff—hey, I've seen the handiwork of guys like that on the warpath. We'd be lucky if they didn't take hostages. So it was just a warning. What I did was more of a dramatic renditions, a kind of prophetic forewarning—right Joey?—and a potentially fruitful frame job, although I have to admit that using Hoagley's gym short may have been a bit too obvious."

"No kidding, Sherlock, " said Moller.

"Plus I already heard that he has a perfect alibi," added Tate.

"Oh, really?" asked Allie.

"Yeah, genius, "said Moller with a sardonic smile, "he was out of town for the entire weekend . . . *with his parents!*"

"Oops," smiled Allie, and then he waved the thought away like a fly. "Oh, well," he said, "that wasn't really the point. He and his buddies will still be guilty by public opinion, which is what we're up to here."

"Don't you think they'll suspect us?" whined Joey.

"No way," said Allie, "what kind of member in good standing of the Slumberset would vandalize his own school?"

"What kind indeed?" said Tate curtly. He picked up his books quietly and got up from his chair. "I'll catch you guys later, I've got some stuff to do in the library."

As Tate turned around to reach for the door knob, however, the door suddenly swung open to reveal the dark specter of their worst fears. It was the Great Stone Face.

"Mr. Reed," he said in his gravelly voice, "I need to see you in my office."

CHAPTER THIRTEEN

CLASS DISMISSED

Michael Moller held the carousel projector a few inches off the table top and shook it with calculated anger. "Work, you bastard, or you're headed for the spare parts department." He dropped the projector to the table for a final jolt and laughed when the lamp suddenly came on. "That's better, you coward. Now, no more trouble from you." Then Moller looked up and announced, "Okay, number twelve's ready, we're ready, let's take it through the first verse again, Tate."

Seated at a grand piano near the center of the studio, Tate nodded, laid out a couple introductory chords, and then sang into a microphone as he played:

"Three businessmen in the back of a Lincoln,
    Stuck between the leather and glass;
You can see it in their eyes, you know what they're thinking,
    As they watch the limousine pass;
        He was friend of theirs and now he's gone,
        He gave at the office, he seemed so strong,
        All of his friends say, life goes on,
        But all of them wonder just how long;
            Cause this is . . . this is what's called Death,
            As the rest of us take . . . another precious breath . . ."

Tate leaned back from the microphone and let the music trail off.

"Great," exclaimed Michael Moller. He had been manually projecting a series of photographic images and was now satisfied with his series. "Just give me a second to program these in."

At the back of the room, Allie sat with Joey and pondered the new material. "Pretty heavy stuff, heh, Joey?"

"I guess so," said Joey noncommittally. Tate and Moller had explained their recent musings about death to Joey, who listened intently and then blurted out a disjointed version of his dream about Allie. Ultimately, the three agreed that their strategy with Allie was to use the Light Show as the only meeting ground for deeper topics. Allie had survived his interrogation by the Great Stone Face without a confession, but it was made clear he was treading on thin ice, regardless of the important position his parents held in the community. Still, he remained unrepentant around his closest friends and had even succeeded in winning back some of the confidence of his larger circle by continuing to pontificate on the subtleties of his latest *statement*.

As for their own research on the death topic, however, Tate and Moller had agreed to leave Allie out of it for the time. "Otherwise, he'll wise crack us to pieces," Tate had said. It was easy enough to get Joey to agree to such and arrangement, so in this case, he let Allie's comment ride.

"Okay, the first verse is programmed in," announced Moller. "Let's try it again."

The sound of the piano filled the room again, and the images on the screen now dropped perfectly into the lyrical spaces of the song. Tate could feel the power as he ended the verse abruptly. "That's great, Moller!" he exclaimed into the microphone.

"Yeah," said Moller, "this is gonna work out just fine. Great song, Tate."

Joey beamed his agreement as Allie leaned back against the couch. "Pretty heavy stuff," was all he said.

Tate and Moller had only told Allie that they had some new material for the Light Show. "We're gonna take on a few heavy-weight topics," they had explained. They were now fairly clear in the notion that death itself was their true adversary, but they had backed off trying to explain that to Allie. "It will be better if Allie comes up with that idea himself," advised Tate, and Moller had agreed. The Light Show was enlisted then in helping their friend—and hopefully their audience—in identifying what Moller had dubbed the "True Enemy."

On this particular evening, Moller and Joey were putting together the visuals for the last of Tate's new songs, in preparation for a concert on the night of Good Friday. "The most important death in history is celebrated on Good Friday," Moller had said. "We lay this new stuff out against that kind of historical backdrop, and we're gonna see some goosebumps, I guarantee. And surely Allie will begin to see it all then." Tate had written a half-dozen new songs in a few short weeks, and the visuals had come together almost as rapidly. With two weeks left to go before Easter Weekend, the show was almost ready.

"Okay," said Michael Moller at the end of the second take. "That's close enough on the first verse; let's go ahead with the rest of the song."

Tate readily agreed and began the second verse of his ode to the American Everyman facing death. Moller and Joey had been speechless the first time they heard the song. As they worked on the song and developed the visuals, the imagery seemed only to grow more powerful. On this night, while Moller and Joey were preoccupied with their technical responsibilities, Tate suddenly began to wake up to the power and meaning of some of his own words. By the time his friends had worked through each of the verses and were ready for a run-through of the final product, Tate was feeling almost trance-like, as he stared up from his seat at the piano into the brightly illuminated screens.

When the music started up again, Tate felt himself moved by the images in ways he would later find difficult to describe. It was as if his bluff had suddenly been called—somehow the reality of their topic found its way through his previously academic interest into a heart that was far more desperate than he had realized. Questions crying out for answers could suddenly be heard above the constant laughter of his masked personality. His heart flushed warm with the overwhelming awareness of his need to know about these things. In that instant, Tate gave up control of his life for the length of one song. "Okay," he said beneath his breath. From the piano bench set on the concrete floor of his favorite observation post, Tate suddenly found himself quietly addressing the closest thing to God he could imagine. "If You've got any answers," he said, "I'm listening."

Somewhere between the spiritual cloud of Tate's hoped-for answer and the bright images on the screen, the pieces of a puzzle came back into focus. First to appear was the Death of the American Aristocracy. As poetically portrayed by his own lyrics and the visuals provided by Michael Moller and Joey, the realm of their forefathers was shown to be in a state of slow, cataclysmic decay. The images from Joey's dream suddenly made perfect sense to Tate, as he watched the symbols of a way of life meet their destruction. In his mind's eye, the crystal chandelier crashed again to the marble floor of the mansion, while outside, the beautiful stables went up in flames as scores of champion thoroughbreds screamed for mercy from their stalls in a rich man's hell. Finally, with his music playing somewhere in the distance, Tate's head was filled with the sound of his father's weary footsteps in the hallways of their house—in cruel counterpoint to the amplified rasp of the Mayor's troubled breathing in his hospital bed.

"This is . . . this is what's called Death..."

The words of Tate's song came back to him from the walls and ceilings of the room. They beckoned him to follow. Despite the grim message of the lyrics, the gentle bidding of the music was too sweet to resist. "I've got to know," thought Tate to himself, and he turned the frame of his soul to let the music envelope him until he was completely isolated in its world. Then it was only he, safe inside a stereo bubble, hovering somewhere well above the floor of his life, just as he had that night on Dead Man's Hill. This time his connection to the earth was kept alive by clear notes on a piano.

Soon, Tate was at peace. This was his true place, this brightly lit station of contemplation and insight. Watching as the specifics of his life fell away to reveal the larger forces they represented, Tate realized that this was the realm of myth and archetype, of gods and eternal heroes, of angels and demons. This was the dimension of the aesthetic, a single and infinite universe from which all outer reality emanated like so many shadows of a single sun, and it was only attached to the world of everyday by the thinnest of metaphors. The times Tate had spent here before returned to consciousness from the deep recesses of his mind. The countless dreams, the fleeting insights, the brief reveries: were these forgotten experiences the foundation for the life of laughter he had shared with his friends? Was this where they received the inspiration for all their crazy efforts to bring a sense of hope to their confused world? Did this realm of the supernatural exist for all time behind his own world, allowing the hand of God to move invisibly and at will through the most mundane events?

Slowly, Tate could look back over the many times this ethereal otherworld had collided with his own world of everyday, silently knocking some sense into it, one way or another. He grieved, though, with the memory of how quickly such glorious moments faded and how long between visitations he had sometimes waited.

"How to stay here?" he asked. How was it that a man might gain entrance in to the realm of angels and still live as a man? Slowly, the role of death was called into question in a new light. Was death, in some sense, the doorway into a less restricted life? Was physical existence the stronghold for pride, for selfish action, for self-preservation? Perhaps the threat of eminent death twisted and corrupted the noblest of sentiments. Maybe to be alive on the other side of death was the key. Maybe walking bravely through death would end its power. But what, then, of the realm of life? What good is a dead man, however free, to the welfare of his fellow human? How, then, to die completely and yet live?

So this was the quandary. To die to Self and yet live as a whole person. Could this be possible? In his mind, Tate ran through every conclusion he could stir up. "Not suicide, not suicide," warned some trustable voice, and Tate could see why. A murderous self was no savior for a frustrated self. The murderer would escape and all would be lost. "Not asceticism, either." A self-righteous self was the worst kind of self. So how to die, how to die and yet live?

The question was so clear that, for now, it was almost as good as an answer. The urgency was sure to return, but, in the meantime, there was so much peace in perceiving clearly the problem that Tate was happy to return to his friends. The last set of images froze on the screen, and the voices of his friends brought Tate back. Vowing to hold steady to his new-found course, Tate decided against trying to verbalize his thoughts for the present and instead returned to the company of his friends only to join in the more general excitement overt the power of the new Light Show material. When he bid his friends good night, however, and he found himself back in the solitude of his bedroom at home, his thoughts returned faithfully to the puzzling question he had discovered. How to die and yet live? How to exist on the other side of death and yet maintain contact with the land of the living? The question formed gentle arcs in the rooms of his heart, playing gracefully against the walls of his soul like shadows that were evidence of a light somewhere nearby. These were questions that had an answer.

Tate fell asleep with the questions of the shadow-dancers humming gently around him. He awoke the next morning with a sense of impending resolution that was soon exhilarating. Once at school, the place seemed alive in a way he had never noticed before. There was knowledge here. As diluted and misdirected as it normally was, there was true knowledge in this place. The teachers passing through the Commons suddenly seemed worthy of respect. To some extent, at least, these individuals were giving their lives to the hope of imparting knowledge to another generation of questioners. The thought filled Tate with a sense of gratitude he had before only felt for the few teachers he liked. Encountering the infamous Dr. Lester McQuaig in the middle of this revelation, Tate happily slapped him on the back and wished him the most sincere of greetings. Then, he headed for his first class, feeling as excited as an aspiring pilot on his first day of flight training.

At the door to the classroom, Tate paused for a moment, as if he were crossing a threshold into yet another dimension. This time, however, the world of his deep yearnings seemed casually expressed in the simple furnishings of a modern classroom. And yet, in some unexplainable way, Tate expected a direct encounter with the truth as it was known. As he slowly entered the room and took his seat, he realized whose class he was in and instantly felt another rush of excitement. This was the domain of Bolo the Magnificent, the Hall of the Final Word.

The grand view of life presented by Mr. Don Bolin returned to Tate's mind in colorful segments of past orations. The shotgun sprays of pure truth and sheer speculation spattered against the shiny lens of Tate's suddenly clear perception in newly understandable patterns. Bolo the Magnificent was a genius after all. His moments of utter brilliance now shined from the midst of his comic exaggerations like priceless diamonds set in the gaudiest of costume jewelry.

On this morning, however, Tate had eyes only for the diamonds, and his expectations greeted the unpredictable Mr. Bolin with an enthusiasm perhaps powerful enough to bring forth the best from his teacher. Whether owing to this unusually inspired listener, or whether this day's lectures just happened to be one of his personal favorites, there was no denying that Bolo the Magnificent was in rare form that day.

As was his style, the Bolo opened up the lecture with another hilarious tirade on the state of modern society. Gathering steam from everything from the latest dog food commercial to the previous week's congressional record, he built his case for the utter depravity of modern society. Leaving no stone unturned, Bolo the Magnificent exposed the hypocrisies and petty concerns of twentieth century culture in terms too caustic to be discharged completely by the laughter that was the listener's first reaction. Just when the tension between hilarity and overwhelming disgust peaked at its frenetic summit, the Magnificent Bolo released the class into the calmer waters of objective academic inquiry with his classic refrain: "Can someone please tell me . . . what causes such behavior?!"

The answer to the comically screamed question traditionally signaled the beginning of the meaty part of Mr. Bolin's lectures. On this morning, Tate had found the introductory part of the lecture almost too hilarious to bear. Every one-liner and every observation seemed to hit directly upon one of Tate's own thoughts from the last few days. As the Bolo bellowed out his refrain a second time, Tate felt like he was walking into a set-up. "WHAT causes such behavior?"

"This morning class, what do you say we cut right to the chase? Let's leave out the middleman, forget the small talk, and call a spade a spade. May I then simply suggest that the single motivating factor behind all this foolish behavior is plain and simple: the FEAR OF DEATH."

Tate sat up straight in his seat. Across the room, Moller's head jerked around, and his eyes connected with Tate's in a line a tightrope walker could have bicycled across. The Magnificent Bolo, sensing his audience's intense interest, just smiled. "That's right, folks, you don't have to go too far in any neighborhood to realize that everybody is afraid of dying."

Tate's heart was beating out of control while his mind raced. This had to be planned. But his lip-synched interrogation of Moller, "Did you???", was answered with an emphatic, "No!!!", by his friend across the room, and Tate was left in a state of bewilderment. Certainly, the Magnificent Bolo had many times spoken to the immediate situation of his students, but this was too much. It was if Don Bolin had been reading the script of Tate's life and was about to write the climax.

There was a strange optimism in the voice of the Magnificent Bolo, and somehow his tone resonated with the unexplained hope inside Tate. After continuing to build an undeniable case for the role of society in masking its members' fear of death, the impish Bolo again paused, as if ten months pregnant with glee. "But, hey," he blurted finally. "We're not going to wallow in this stuff. We're gonna talk about the loopholes; we're gonna talk about the various ways society has overruled itself on this deal. We're going to talk about overcoming the fear of death as an individual or as a civilization. We're gonna talk about madmen and artists, prophets and pinheads, poets and priests. We're gonna talk about the real heroes of the human race."

By now Tate was welded to his chair. The entire room could have emptied, and he would not have noticed. He had no idea how his other friends were reacting, and it did not matter. This performance, it seemed, was especially for him.

"Due to the shortness of the hour," continued the Magnificent Bolo, "and the greater shortness of even your most fear-gripped attention span, I'm gonna skip over the particulars and get right to the essence. There is one great underlying principle that even makes possible any kind of victory over death. Strip away its many outer manifestations, and this one universal principle stands smiling in its confident help to the mortal man. Every great prophet, political leader, and charlatan throughout time has tapped into this principle, and this morning, dear students, your humble teacher—at no additional charge to your parents or the Board of Trustees—is going to let you in on this mysterious key to life. Get out your pens, boys and girls, and take this one down. It's the one-word answer to the only question on the real Final Exam."

Turning to the black-board behind him, the Magnificent Bolo reached as high as his short frame would extend and wrote out a single word in crooked capital letters: "IDENTIFICATION".

Though Tate's mind drew a complete blank as he read the word to himself, something in its sound again struck a familiar chord within him. As the Magnificent Bolo began to explain, Tate's thoughts fell into league with his heart. This was it.

"Identification with some entity outside oneself is the single most important aspect of human life," said his teacher. It was a grandly sweeping generalization, but this was the Magnificent Bolo speaking. "I am here to suggest," he continued, "that who or what we choose to identify with will ultimately determine the outcome of our battle with death."

Here Bolo the Magnificent paused, slapping the chalk from his thick hands. "So what are out choices?" he continued. "Romantic love is certainly an option. One can easily transfer his hope in life to a thrilling member of the opposite sex. So, we got any Romeo and Juliet types in here? Let's see now, how did that one turn out? I think even in the movie version they came up a little short in their little bout with death. So let's write that one off."

Pausing briefly to let the point settle in, he then went on. "How about identifying with a great statesman?" he suggested. "Anyone here get any vibes off the name Caesar Augustus? I didn't think so. So where's the fairy dust of all those Roman suckers who transferred their mortality to his? I don't think you could even find any of it in your vacuum cleaners."

"So what other options we got? How about great political movements? Any Third Reichers around here?" At this point, Dale Hoagley made a lame attempt at being funny by giving Mr. Don Bolin a "Heil Hitler" from his seat.

"Okay Mr. Hoagley," responded the Magnificent Bolo instantly. "So you're carrying the torch for the Reich. Anyone care to place the fate of their eternal souls with Mr. Hoagley this morning?" Pausing to let the silence and then laughter speak for itself, the Bolo then continued.

"So what are we left with then? Ah, yes, the artists. The poets and the painters, the composers and writers. Now we are getting into an interesting area. Haven't we even heard them called 'the immortals'? And perhaps something could be said for living on in the folds of one's own works, I don't know. My problem with that is the same one I have with chain letters. It seems to me that the success of the concept depends upon a type of perpetuation that just doesn't quite flesh out. One dying person slipping a copy of *Gone With the Wind* to another guy who's gonna die a few years later—I mean, ultimately, what's the point?"

"But in each of these cases, you can see the intent. And you can see how the principle works. A mere mortal like me literally transfers his faith in his own life, as it were, to a person, ideology, or what have you, in hopes of investing his soul in an eternal purpose. And the identification part is a snap. We all know someone who has mastered the technique so well that he can effectively transfer his life blood three times a year every year to identify with some great new thing: from his favorite pro football team to his favorite pro basketball team to his favorite pro baseball team. Identification. It's a real breeze. But the catch, boys and girls, is in landing on the right square for getting past Death. If you're gonna hop a ride on a freight train, you better hope it's going all the way."

At this point Tate was completely focused. He knew the Magnificent Bolo had given him an inside track on his quandary. Identification was easy enough, and the potential for pole-vaulting oneself over death seemed plausible indeed. The mechanics of the operations were now clear. All that remained was to find the right target for his hope. Looking squarely at Mr. Don Bolin, Tate's eyes suddenly met with the still-pregnant smile of Bolo the Magnificent. "Come on," urged Tate through his silent stare. "Spill the beans, Bolo . . ."

For a moment, Mr. Don Bolin looked directly at Tate with a smile that hinted at an inside track on the answer. But then, as if on some incredible cosmic cue, the bell rang, causing the suddenly impudent teacher to laugh out loud. "Wouldn't you know it," announced the Magnificent Bolo. "Class dismissed."

CHAPTER FOURTEEN

REVELATIONS

"Sorry, Tater-head," said Allie. "I'm afraid I'll have to pass on the whole concept. It's getting a bit too mental for me."

The Keepers had left school after the Bolo's lecture and headed for their usual lunch rendezvous at Tolstoy's. Seated in a favorite back booth behind the towering magazine racks, Tate had taken up where the Magnificent Bolo had left them hanging, pondering out loud the strange message as Allie, Moller, and Joey had listened in various states of interest themselves. When Allie finally voiced his cool reservations, Tate became even more animated.

"Too mental!?" objected Tate. "What else have we got to work with here?"

"Feelings, Tate, feelings," replied Allie at once. "You remember: intuitions, the unspoken understanding, that sort of thing. I mean, it's beginning to sound like we're trying to explain the punch line of a joke. Let's remember boys, you either Get it or you don't, and that goes for life as much as for a joke. You either Get it or you don't."

Tate smiled in spite of himself, and Joey and Moller laughed out loud. Despite the increasing sense that Allie was beginning to spin out of control, he continued to win the confidence of his friends.

"May we assume, then," said Moller playfully, "that you Get it?"

"Yeah," said Allie quickly. "You can assume that. You don't see me slitting my wrists, do you? I mean, how hard can it be?"

"Hard enough," said Tate with a sudden intensity. Joey wheezed a tiny, "Amen," as Tate took up his monologue again. "Maybe you're not slitting your wrists, but plenty of people are. It's plenty hard for the average guy to figure it out, and I'm feeling more like the average guy all the time. What if Smiles it right? What if we can't laugh our way through the next three-fourths of our lives? What if nobody does give a shit about how rich and clever we are? I mean, what if we pulled a Get and nobody Got it? Then what, Allie?"

"Then we'd be down to just the four of us," said Allie. "Which is probably where it's all happening anyway. What do we care if the stupid masses get it or not? We were just trying to help them along, you know, but if they're not into it, then so be it. That's not going to change my worldview. Hey, funny is funny, whether the whole world gets it or not."

"Sure, fine, swell," said Tate. "So we've got these four rich, genius kids riding through life together on the wings of an inside joke, and everything is great because they can see how screwed up the world is but they're okay because they can see the humor in it, only pretty soon they're not kids anymore, they're grown-ups and everyone around them has grown-up jobs and grown-up problems, but that's okay because the Fantastic Four have this bullet-proof outlook on life that says everything is ultimately funny, and they happen to have the money to prove it, if only to themselves. Sure, I can see that," said Tate sarcastically, "And even if I could live with that, what about this other deal? Can we buy our way around death? Sure we can laugh all the way to the graveyard, but my big question is, can we laugh all the way *through* it? Joey says yes, but he has a hard enough time making it through life, and Allie says yes, but we wonder if he's just kidding himself about that, too. Me and Moller, we're not so sure. We'd like to think that somewhere in the midst of all this million-dollar knowledge is some two-bit wisdom. We'd like to think that somewhere in the folds of Smiles's sermons, or Bolo's lectures, or Queenie's slide shows, there is a ticket out of here."

"That's right, boys," said Michael Moller. He had been listening with his usual reserve and was now ready to help clarify his friend's stream of thoughts. "We're approaching the Boundaries of the Ineffable, here, and it may be time to jettison all the extra baggage, gain a little altitude, you know, try to make it over that last mountain range."

"Alright, then," quipped Allie. "That's exactly my point. Let's start the jettison process with all this headgear, gentlemen. Let's lose two-hundred years of ugly fat by throwing our Slumberset rational/scientific mindset overboard. That's my only point, Tater-head. Let's just not be so mental about the whole thing. Let's streamline and pay attention, sure, but let's keep cruising. It's easier to steer with a little forward motion on the deal, so let's keep cruising."

Tate took a deep breath and let it out. He looked at Michael Moller, who shrugged back. Allie looked at Tate with fifteen years of friendship coming though his crooked smile. He studied his friend's uncertainty and then shifted in his seat. "Okay, man," Allie said finally, "I'll tell you what we'll do. We'll go up against this death thing together."

Tate looked at Moller again; this time his friend looked back at Allie. "Yeah, that's what we should do," continued Allie. "I mean, you guys have already been taking some nice stabs at this thing with the Light Show, so maybe it is time I got with the program. Joey, what do you say you and I work out the visuals for a couple of the new songs?" Joey's eagerness spilled out in an earnest nodding of his head.

"We'll chime in on the new Light Show material and see what else we can come up with there," said Allie. Then he leaned back in his chair and, as the air above the booth at Tolstoy's slowly filled with the faint sound of the wheels spinning in his head, Allie announced, "And then, lads, we'll put a Get on Death himself."

Jane Quinn stood at the entrance to her cubicle in the teacher's lounge, books and legal pads propped on her hip, sandy blonde hair pulled back in a clip. "Come in, Mr. Moller," she smiled.

"Thanks, Miss Quinn," answered Michael Moller. He slouched a bit lower as he swerved past the Queen of Arts into her lair. The wooden partitions serving as moveable walls in the teacher's lounge formed a twelve by fifteen sanctuary insulated by rows and rows of books. There were slide files and prints covering every inch of shelf and wall space. On the floor was a worn Persian rug, and the Queen's desk was a small antique table piled higher than its spindly legs should have allowed. In one corner was an ancient easy chair covered over by a quilt. "Have a seat, Mr. Moller," said Miss Quinn, motioning towards the chair.

"Thanks," said Moller. Easing himself down into the deep chair, Michael Moller pushed his hair back from his face and waited for his teacher to put down her things. Somehow she managed to slide her load onto the table while pulling a certain legal pad out of the middle of the pack.

"Here we are," she said cheerfully. "The Moller File."

Michael Moller beamed with gentle surprise. A week earlier, he had approached his teacher after class with a shy request for help. Finding a gracious audience with the Queen, he had ended up giving her a Full Report far beyond what he had expected to divulge. A number of quizzical looks notwithstanding, his teacher had seemed to sympathize deeply with his quest, and to somehow understand at least some of his direction, as he explained in detail the latest problems and theories of his friends. By midway through their conversation, Michael Moller had been surprised by his own bluntness. "It's death, Ms. Quinn," he had said. "We're trying to get around death."

Michael Moller had gone on to explain their plans to assail the topic by way of the Light Show and some 'Get of epic proportions', and had ended by asking his teacher to provide whatever ammunition she could from the arsenals of Western art. Though he had left that first meeting full of the hope that his teacher would try to help him, he was nevertheless relieved and then honored when she produced a legal pad filled with notes on her research in his behalf. "The Moller File," he repeated quietly. His eyes shined from behind the hair dangling in his face. "I like the sound of that."

By then, Jane Quinn had seated herself and was rifling through the pages of notes and little sketches filling her yellow legal pad. "Well, Mr. Moller," she began, "I would hope you already know from your classwork that, as far as dealing with death by way of Western art, it's going to pretty well come down to Christ imagery. There's not a lot of treatment of the topic by the classicists—Zeus and his ilk, it seems, tended to sort of skate around the issue, you know."

"Yeah, those whimps," cracked Moller. "So what have you got?"

"What I've got is several hundred years of painting and sculpture that purports to stare death in the face: graphic crucifixions, martyrdoms, apocalypses . . . it's all there for those, I suppose, with eyes to see." Here the Queen waxed, if not quite sarcastic, perhaps a bit wistful. Of Jewish persuasion herself, she handled Christian themes in art with an arms-length sense of detachment that passed for academic objectivity but hinted at something deeper and perhaps colder. On this morning, however, her interest in Michael Moller's search betrayed an inspired curiosity of her own. In any event, she seemed eager to toss him the ball and let him run with it.

"So without taking you through a complete review of the subject—putting you at an unfair advantage on the final," she joked—"let's just say that there is little question that the key to overcoming death for this traditions of artists seems to revolve around the image of the cross."

"The cross . . . " repeated Moller. In his mind, the images from the Queen's earlier tours of the centuries flashed through his mind. The muscle-bound Christ of Rubens being lifted up to the cross gave way to the shadowy Savior of Rembrandt being lowered after His death. Then there were the dead Christs of the various *Pietas*, pitifully rendered corpses convincingly mourned by the Virgin Mother or Christ's followers, until the gloom of these scenes was triumphantly replaced by the spectacular risen Christ of Grunewald and the intensely realistic scenes by Rembrandt of Christ at Emmaus, casually dining with his friends after His resurrection. Nameless paintings of Jesus taking off into the clouds completed Moller's mental journey and returned him to his meeting with the Queen. "Right," he nodded, "the cross. It's a pretty major deal."

Jane Quinn eyed her student carefully. "And for a shameless gentile like yourself," she smiled, "it could be the key."

"I don't know, Miss Quinn," said Moller, shifting in his seat. "That's just the point. I guess I should get it, but I don't. I've stared at crosses and crucifixes all my life, sat through *Ben Hur* and *The Greatest Story Ever Told* a dozen times each. I've been to a zillion different churches and heard TV and radio preachers till I could tell you their next line every time, but I still don't get it. Jesus died for my sins? I mean, how does that work?"

"You're asking the wrong person here," said Jane Quinn with a laugh. "You might want to talk to Father Miles about that one."

"Oh, we've been through it with him a hundred times already," said Moller. "And he lays it out pretty well, he really does, and I always end up not disagreeing with him, but still not having a hold of it like, say, physics or something. It's just never quite tangible or real, at least for me."

"I understand," said Jane Quinn with a gentle smile. "I certainly understand."

"It's then that Smiles always falls back on his revelation thing," continued Moller. "He says that even the comprehension itself—of these things deeper kinds of things—comes from God. As if you could have all the pieces to the puzzle laid out on the table, but you can't quite get them to fit together without some burst of insight or grace or something that gets it all to click. You know, a revelation."

"I see," said Miss Queen, and for a moment her thoughts wandered to some faraway point that Michael Moller could not even guess about. "Well, in any case," she said finally, "I did find one intriguing element that I somehow thought might mean something to you. For some reason I did not happen to mention it in class this year, although it's always been a curious enough little tidbit for me to point out." Reaching over to the pile of books she had dumped on her desk, she pulled one out and opened it to a marker. "Here," she said, "have a look at this."

She handed the open book to Michael Moller who eagerly looked on to find a full-color reproduction of a realistic interior scene featuring Mary, Joseph, and the angel Gabriel informing her of the birth of Christ. "It's the Merode Altarpiece," explained Miss Queen. "By the Master of Flemalle."

"Yeah, I remember it from class," said Moller.

"Good lad," said his teacher playfully. "But what I think I failed to mention this year is a very interesting element in the right panel. Remember how we talked about the significance of this piece being its use of everyday reality in conveying supernatural events, how for the first time in history the artist used what we called disguised symbolism to make his point?"

"Yeah, I do," said Moller as he listened.

"So, in the center panel," continued his teacher, "the flowers each represents a different aspect of the Virgin, and the water bowl represents 'the well of living water,' that sort of thing? Well look closely at the panel on the right. See? Joseph is at work in his carpentry shop. But do you see what he is making? It's right there on the table."

"Yeah," said Michael Moller squinting at the page. "What is that little deal?"

"It's a mousetrap," said his teacher with a smile.

"A mousetrap?" said Moller blankly.

"Yes." Pausing for dramatic effect, the Queen of Arts then lowered her voice almost to a whisper. "You see, the idea was that the cross was a mousetrap for Satan: Jesus Christ was the bait, and Satan fell for it, crucifying the Messiah so that God's plan of atonement could be realized."

With the smile rising on Michael Moller's face, Jane Queen knew the words that were about to erupt from behind his droopy locks, and she could not resist chiming in.

"It was a Get," they said together, and then they looked at each other wide-eyed and laughed.

"Exactly", said Moller and then his years of chapel attendance began to pay off. "Christ had to die to create this doorway through death, but he couldn't commit suicide because that's murder so he just went around telling the truth and loving people you weren't supposed to love, and sooner or later the political and religious leaders couldn't stand it so they killed him."

"Maybe so," said his teacher. "And if you choose to believe the paintings of the likes of Grunewald and Rembrandt, he made it through death, just like you were hoping."

After a long, charged moment during which Moller could feel the final piece of the puzzle beginning to move into place on the table, he looked still wider-eyed at his teacher and friend and quietly said, "Now that . . . is a revelation."

When Moller met up with Tate, his news was at first diffused by Tate's preoccupation with other matters. He was sitting alone in the Senior Lounge, his books spread out on the library table at one end of the room but his mind had been somewhere else. Still, Tate had listened with a faint smile that grew momentarily bright when his friend had reached the punch line on his story. For a brief instant, Tate latched onto the cosmic proportions of Moller's mousetrap idea, but then he was forced to file away the information for the present, as a deep sigh signaled his need to discuss something more immediately pressing. "It's Allie," he said. "I think he's really going off the deep end."

"What's the deal now?" asked Michael Moller.

"Well," began Tate, "I was just talking with Sarah and Emily and they were filling me in on things from their perspective. He's always kind of confided in them in a way he really doesn't around us, and they think he really is changing. Sarah was doing this frightening imitation of the way he gets lost in his monologues these days, and that's always been part of Allie's deal, of course, but this was scary. I mean, we've seen enough of it to know what she's talking about, but I guess it's worse than we thought."

"What do you mean?" pressed Moller. "What did they say that we don't already know?"

"Well," said Tate slowly, "For one thing, Emily was telling me about a couple stunts Allie's pulled while they were together: this one deal where he got really weird with some girl behind the counter of a fast-food joint. He asked this poor overweight girl if her ancestors were Anglos or Saxons or just fat. Not too funny to say the least. And then he became convinced that he should slash the tires of the school guard's car—as if that poor old geezer has ever done anything to hurt anyone—but it's this symbol of authority thing, and it took everything Emily could do just to talk him out of it. At the last minute she made up some story that she had heard that the guy's wife was in the Daughters of the American Revolution, and that fictional aristocratic connection was all that saved the poor guy's tires. I'm telling you, Moller, he may be losing it."

"So, what's the good news?" said Moller glibly.

"Well, since you asked," said Tate, "the other not-so-good news is that Joey seems to be ramping up in direct proportion to Allie, only along more religiously fanatical lines. He called me last night and was reading me all these out-of-context things from the Bible: that 'living sacrifice', 'dying to this world' kind of stuff and it really spooked me out. I don't know what's going on with these guys, but I'll tell you what," and here Tate had to chuckle, "it almost makes me feel normal."

"No kidding," agreed Moller shaking his head slowly. "If these guys weren't so well connected, they'd probably be locked up somewhere. So what do we do?"

"I don't know," said Tate. "I went to see Father Miles, and he was going to try to talk to each of them, but, beyond that, I'm stumped. If we try to pull back too much with either of them, we run the risk of losing contact with them altogether, which is probably more dangerous than anything. I almost feel like the best plan is to go on with business as usual—on the surface you know—but wising up to the situation."

"Maybe so," said Moller thoughtfully. "Certainly the Light Show should be safe enough, but I'm suspicious as hell about this Get that Allie is working on."

"No kidding," said Tate quickly, then he paused. "But you know how hard it will be for us to steer things in the least when it comes to a major Get. That's just never been much of an option with Allie."

"That's true," said Moller, and then he pulled his hair back with a frustrated tug. "Damn," he said. "It's a tight spot. And just when I thought we were getting somewhere on the deeper things."

"Yeah," said Tate, "it stinks. But what can you do?"

"What, indeed," said Moller.

"Come on," said Tate as he sat up straighter and began pulling his books into a pile. Let's get out of here. I think Allie and Joey are working on the Lightshow downstairs. We could at least offer to toss the Frisbee around."

"Yeah," agreed Moller. "That's probably the best idea. A little Frisbee therapy. A little Light Show therapy. And if that doesn't help, what the hell, bring on the electro-shock therapy: let Allie have his Get."

When Tate and Moller found Allie and Joey, however, their friends were calmly at work in the school audio-visual room, quietly laboring over a slide sequence of their own for one of Tate's new songs. As Tate and Moller stood at the back of the room, watching the images projected on the screen and listening silently to the gentle banter between Allie and Joey, they could feel their concern for their friends dwindle—it was clear that Allie and Joey were still in command of at least one part of their lives.

"Well," said Moller to Tate, "maybe it is business as usual."

With some deep misgivings, Tate agreed. It was easier to believe everything would be all right. "Oh well," he finally sighed. "Maybe we should hold off on the Frisbee therapy and just go for the Light Show."

"Right," said Moller, and then he carefully broke into the aura of calm creativity by lifting his voice to his friends. "Hey, boys, what's happening?"

"Moller," said Allie spinning around, "and Tate—just the guys we want to see. Come on and have a look at this stuff."

"We've been spying already," said Tate as he and Moller approached their friends. "It looks good."

"Good?! Man, it looks great . . . here, sit down and watch this all the way through. Joey, cue the projectors while I rewind the tape. Okay, now get a load of this."

Poised over the projectors as he was, the light from below lit up Allie's grin like the bizarre Cheshire cat he was, and Joey huddled in the warmth of their collaboration. Tate and Moller sat down as ordered and watched as the efforts of their friends met up with Tate's song in a perfect match. It was another of Tate's songs about death, and the images put together by Allie and Joey made it clear that they were on the case. The purity of Allie's vision and the earnestness of Joey's assistance were suddenly stronger than the anxieties amplified by the girls' reports. When the song ended, Tate broke into a smile. "Okay, Allie, it was great."

"That's more like it," said Allie standing tall behind the projectors. He shook hands with Joey and then turned back to his friends. "So what's been going on with you two sleuths?"

Moller looked at Tate who gave him a shrug of "why not?" and then said, "Well, as a matter of fact, we have run into something rather interesting."

"Well, then," said Allie, sensing Moller, indeed, had something, "let's have it, lads."

Instinctively, Michael Moller stood up to begin his presentation. What followed caught even Tate by surprise. For although less than an hour had passed since Moller's meeting with Jane Quinn and his quick report to Tate, by the time the words began to roll off Moller's lips in front of his other friends, the implications of this latest development had taken on the cosmic proportions of the most monumental Full Report of his young life.

With the cool reserve of a college professor and the moral authority of an Old Testament prophet, Michael Moller found himself describing all of history as the spokes of a wheel, the hub of which is Calvary. "It's the cross, boys," he was saying, "the old rugged cross, and from this central hub emanates not only all of earthly history, but all eternal fate as well. Infinite evil performs the most dastardly and undeserved execution of all time, only to play right into the hand of the Universal Keeper of the Get. The cross was the biggest Get of recorded history."

Having sufficiently stirred the curiosity of his friends, Moller then told of his meeting with the Queen of Arts, and explained the discovery about the image of the mousetrap. "The joke was on the devil, boys," he said. "Think about it: if God sent Christ into the world for the very purpose of dying for our sins—whatever that means—then somebody had to do the dirty work. God tricked Satan himself into stirring up all those power-hungry leaders into performing the very sacrifice necessary for atonement. It was a trap, boys, a mousetrap."

Allie sat poker-faced as Tate allowed himself a smile and Joey began wiggling with the concept. "Don't you get it?" continued Michael Moller. "Primordial man falls—it's the 'sin of Adam?' in Smiles's church lingo—there's Father Miles telling us all these years that the same God who said, 'the soul that sins shall surely die' is the same God who loves us and promises us eternal life but he's also perfect Truth, so He can't change His word and, therefore—" and here Moller slowly held out his hands as if waiting for an invisible drum roll to play out—therefore he had to come up with some kind of holy loophole, a way past death without contradicting Himself. The soul has to die; someone has to die . . . and here's where our endless Sunday School stories and everything Miles has been trying to pound into us in his beautifully eloquent, passive/aggressive way . . . all this is conspiring to get us to see that Jesus allowed himself to be murdered so that He could satisfy the Death penalty and somehow come through the other side. The cross was a mousetrap, boys, it was a Get . . .

Jesus was the bait, the devil went for it, and a hole was punched through Death—"

"Assuming that Jesus rose from the dead," interrupted Allie suddenly. Moller froze at Allie's words. He had been so deeply entranced in his own oratory that he scarcely realized how close to the edge of his own beliefs he was treading.

"Well, yes," said Moller, almost stuttering. "Assuming that Jesus rose from the dead."

"He did," said Joey quietly, and it was just what the others would have expected him to say, but there was an indescribable force in his words that caught everyone off guard. He suddenly had the authority to stand up to Allie. It was as if the bloody image of Joey after he had been beaten up for his friends had left some untouchable imprint on everyone's conscience. In any event, no one challenged him. "He did rise from the dead," Joey continued, "and Moller is right—He had to do it to satisfy the sentence against the soul that sins. And, yeah, He did it for us. He did it so that we could—"

"Identification," interrupted Tate suddenly. "That's it. He did it so that we could make it through death by identifying with Him. Forget Romeo and Juliet and the Third Reich and pro football and whatever else," Tate laughed. He felt as if a pair of muddy goggles had just been lifted from his eyes, and he could see how obvious it all was. "Bolo knew," he smiled to himself, "Bolo knew exactly what I was looking for, but he wouldn't he spill the beans."

Allie, meanwhile, was back on Moller's initial point. He had been captivated by the concept of the cross as the greatest Get ever pulled. Seemingly oblivious to Tate and Moller's more studied hope in the issue, Allie suddenly appeared to be ready to believe just for the sake of the Get itself.

"Yeah, that's great," he was saying. "A mousetrap! Shit, that's great! A universal Get . . ."

And soon the wheels spinning on Allie's newly planned Get were gaining energy from the larger wheel of the grand Get described by Moller.

Joey was off in a daze, happy but distant. Tate tried to catch his eye but was instead interrupted by Allie's sudden outburst. "I've got it!" he nearly shouted. "Man, this is great. I've got our Get against Death."

Bolting around the projector tables, he grabbed Michael Moller and shook him and then hugged him. "You're a genius, Moller, a genius . . .

tell the Queen I want to marry her . . . a mousetrap . . . Jesus Christ is the bait . . . genius stuff . . . genius stuff . . ."

Releasing Moller, he turned his excited gaze towards Joey. "Okay, Joey," he blurted out, "come with me. You've got to hear me out on this . . . Tate, Moller, hold down the fort. Joey and I will get back to you after school. Tate's house at four o'clock. Come on Joey, let's get out of here . . . you're going to love this . . ."

Tate and Moller were mute as Joey happily followed Allie out of the room. After a long pause, Moller went falsetto for his Dorothy imitation and exclaimed, "My! People sure come and go quickly here in Oz!"

"No kidding," said Tate. "Now what were you we saying about shock treatments for Allie?"

"Gee," said Moller, still in his Dorothy voice, "do you suppose the Wizard could give him a lobotomy . . . I've heard that he is very powerful and kind..."

Tate laughed and then let out a sigh and slowly began drifting back to his new understanding. "So, Michael," he said, "I think I've got the picture on the identification deal."

"Yeah," said Moller without hesitating. "I got it too." Pulling his hair back from his face he gave Tate a small smile. "Hey," he said, "we may be blind and lame, but we're not dumb."

"Right," said Tate. "So come on. I'll buy you a burger before Allie leads us off a cliff."

"Sure thing," said Moller. "It'll be a Last Supper kind of deal, in an identification sort of way . . ."

CHAPTER FIFTEEN

EASTER WEEKEND

Michael Moller pushed his hair back from his eyes, placed both hands on the pulpit, and looked down at the huge book opened between his hands.

"The first reading is taken from Second Kings," he began, "verses thirty-two through thirty-seven." His hair already drooping back in his face, Moller cleared his throat and read:

"When Elisha came into the house, behold the lad was dead and laid on his bed. So he entered and shut the door behind them both, and prayed to the Lord. And he went up and lay on the child, eyes on his eyes and his hands on his hands, and he stretched himself on him; and the flesh of the child became warm. Then he returned and walked in the house once back and forth, and went up and stretched himself on him; and the lad sneezed seven times and the lad opened his eyes."

Michael Moller closed the book, pushed back his hair again, and looked up at the congregation. Smiling imperceptibly at Tate and Allie, he said, "This ends the first reading."

Father Miles nodded as Moller pushed away from the pulpit and skulked back to his seat. From a second pulpit, on the other side of the main altar, Father Miles continued the service. On one side of him was a young priest from the main church downtown, on hand to assist in the high service celebrating Good Friday. On the other side of Father Miles was his conscripted acolyte for the day, which happened to be Joey.

THE LAST GET

As one of only three required chapel services for the year, the Good Friday service brought the entire school together—excepting the Jewish students and teachers, of course—for the somber side of the Easter Weekend. The sheer size of the congregation, along with the fact that this was arguably the most dramatic service of the Episcopal calendar, tended to bring out the most intense side of Father Miles. There was no room for joking here and little room for human error, as evidenced by the nervous way Joey approached his simple tasks of acolyte service.

Michael Moller, meanwhile, responded to the drama of the hour differently than Joey, approaching his job as reader with a fearless enthusiasm. After a few more prayers and proclamations by Father Miles, Moller was bounding back to the main pulpit and reopening the book.

> "The second reading is taken form the epistles of Paul: 'Now I say this brethren, that flesh and blood cannot inherit the kingdom of God; nor does the perishable inherit the imperishable . . . For this perishable must put on the imperishable, and this mortal must put on immortality . . . Then will come about the saying that is written, "Death where is your victory? O death where is your sting? The sting of death is sin, and the power of sin is law; but thanks be to God who gives us the victory through our Lord Jesus Christ."

This time the slightest trace of a smile on Father Miles' face acknowledged the animated reading by Moller, as the priest nodded to his reader and took up the next part of the service. After a few more of the proclamations and responses that Allie liked to call ecclesiastical duck calls, Father Miles lifted an even larger Bible from the altar, pivoted toward the congregation and stepped forward, his assistant priest and Joey faithfully flanking him all along.

"This is the Gospel of the Lord," he announced.

The congregation came to their feet as Father Miles paused in the power of the moment and then proclaimed: "A reading from the book of John." He paused again and then read:

> "I am the resurrection and the life; he who believes in Me shall live even if he dies, and everyone who lives and believes in Me shall never die . . . And when he had said these things he cried out with a loud voice, 'Lazurus, come forth.' He who had died

came forth bound hand and foot with wrappings and his face was wrapped around with a cloth. Jesus said to them, 'unbind him and let him go.'"

Father Miles looked up at his audience, paused, and announced again, "This is the Gospel of the Lord."

"Thanks be to God," responded the congregation. Tate Henry's lips moved along with the others, but his mind had strayed to other things. These may have been answers to his deepest questions, but in this familiar setting, and owing also to the strange new turn of events occupying his thoughts, the words sailed silently past him.

The night before, the Mayor had received a bizarre visitor at the hospital. Dressed in the robe of a priest, the impostor had apparently snuck past the nurse's station and entered the Mayor's room. By the time an attending nurse happened into the room, the stranger had unhooked the I.V. from the Mayor's arm and was praying in a loud voice, his hand pressed against the patient's chest, as he emphatically thanked God for healing the Mayor. Startled by the nurse, the intruder fled quickly, saying only that, "God's will has been done." As he had listened by phone to the account of these things, Tate's heart had sunk with sadness and anger. He knew it had been Joey.

Watching his frail friend sitting nervously behind the pulpit as Father Miles began his sermon, the anger Tate felt slowly melted away before a rush of new sympathy for Joey. Every twitch and fidget by Joey sent a fresh impulse of compassion through Tate. Joey's deer-like gaze and his posture of earnest attentiveness to Father Miles' words brought renewed understanding and even admiration to Tate. Joey was such a lone soldier, Tate was thinking. If Joey's insecurities made him quick to follow the herd, Tate realized, his convictions made him even quicker to leave the pack entirely, even go against it. Pondering the incidents in the hospital, Tate even managed a smile. Imagine the look on that nurse's face, he chuckled, as she walked in on this high school faith-healer performing Pentecostal rain dances around the bed of the former Mayor. And, with visions of malpractice suits dancing in their heads, the hospital administrators had been quick to inform the family that no medical harm had been done. "Well, what the hell," thought Tate finally, "maybe it even helped."

As Tate's thoughts on Joey settled down, he began to pay more attention to the service. As he did he began to realize what he had been missing. Father Miles was by then deep in some of his usual British-intellectual extrapolations of the scriptures just read, and it was suddenly familiar territory. Tate quickly tried to back-track through his brain to the parts of the service he had heard but not listened to. This was all about death, he realized, and he had been tuned out. Side-tracked again, he thought, but he was slowly able to recall parts of the readings. ". . . anyone who believes in Me shall not die . . . even if he dies he shall live . . ." Now what is that supposed to mean?

Father Miles, meanwhile, was pressing on in his illumination of these things. Allie had once compared Father Miles' style of preaching to jazz music. "The man has a way of working in and around the main point the way most jazz players work around a melody. You get just enough of the essence to fill in the blanks yourself." And such was the case this day, as the illusive little priest teased the listeners with innuendo and inside jokes and pummeled his audience with indirect blows. "Modern society—" he was saying, "a circus tent filled with an audience ready to be entertained about life. Whoever can give them true life, enjoyable life, fulfilling life, let him come forward. And so three rings are filled with the daredevils and clowns and entertainers who promise life. But what about life forever? Ah, easy enough, says the Master of Ceremonies, bring forth the philosophers and the clergy, the modern masters of religion-without-suffering, the prophets of positive thinking. They will tell you about life forever, even as the leave out the very death that makes it all possible."

Dropping his metaphor like the handkerchief of a magician moving onto his next trick, Father Miles relaxed his tone of voice slightly and continued. "It's hard to talk about faith in Europe and America these days," he said. "Faith in eternal life is difficult to discuss at present, but I shall tell you it's not because we have trouble believing in a life of endless joy—no, that concept is peddled to us nearly twenty-four hours a day by our advertisers and entertainers. The implication of every ad and frivolous entertainment you see is that the sort of satisfaction brought on by the latest cola or cigarette will indeed do so forever. The pitch is not, 'oh, this will temporarily relieve you from your boredom and pain' —no, it is rather, 'drink this, smoke that, watch here, listen there, and you will be happy forever and ever.' You see? The problem with talking about true faith nowadays is not in getting people to believe in life, the problem is getting them to believe in death. No one has bought that one for so long, I'm afraid, that hardly anyone is to be found peddling it. Death is scarcely an option these days. And that's the rub. Resurrection without death is impossible. To find true faith, you have to first believe—and I mean really believe—that death is a serious and inevitable enough reality to demand new thinking."

Tate closed his eyes and soaked up every word. Here it was again. This was the problem. Nobody believed in death. They buried it under their good deeds and diversions and hoped that it would all go away. Tate leaned back in the pew to let the words sink in, to take stock of what it all meant for him and his friends. Beside him Allie scratched busily away at his pad, absorbing the sermon and pouring it back out through the point of his pen. Looking down at the pad, Tate watched the black shadowy lines of ink etching away at creating believable tombstones and graves. At the top of the page hung a harrowing skull and cross-bones. As Father Miles continued to talk, Allie's hand moved to the bottom of the page and began working on some lettering. Tate glanced over occasionally, trying to make out the words being fashioned by Allie's bold eerie letters, as Father Miles concluded his sermon.

"Want to believe more deeply in life? Then deal with death. Want to know more about the power of the resurrection? Study, then, the power of the cross."

Allie chirped an audible "Amen," as his hand scratched a final few lines into his letters and Father Miles turned to continue the service back at the altar. As Allie lifted his hand from his work, Tate looked over at the words he had etched onto the page. The three-word message lay on the page beneath his drawings like a cartoon prophecy that sent a strange shiver through Tate. The words read:
"THE LAST GET"

"Good evening, ladies and gentlemen and welcome again to the Eighth Wonder of the World Music and Light Review. We invite you tonight to travel with us to the boundaries of your own beliefs . . . journey to the edge of your deepest fears . . . boldly go where you have never gone before . . . It's Good Friday Night, there is Death in the air, and it's time you realized "—here Allie paused, nodded to Tate behind him on the stage, and finished his introduction with the title to the band's opening song.

The catchy bass line accompanying Allie met up with a crash of drums and wall of guitar and piano, and the Easter Weekend show exploded into the bright lights of the Keepers' final musical performance of their prep school careers. What followed first was forty of the most intense minutes ever produced by the engineers of the Light Show. It was all the new material, and it came through the speakers and projectors with a force and density that overwhelmed even the performers.

The opening images on the screens panned from panoramic shots of military cemeteries to close-ups of mourning families and flowers beside graves. The songs charted a course through various life callings, with death waiting at the end of every line. "Nobody gets out of here alive," warned the chorus, and again the visuals made the point even more inescapable than the blunt lyrics. And for this show, the Keepers had departed from tradition and set up three hundred chairs in the front of the auditorium, making for a concert setting as opposed to a dance format. "They were trapped," chuckled Allie later. Even the late arrivals and the more socially-oriented visitors who stood behind the first three hundred listeners could not escape the message of the opening set. "You could've heard a pin drop," observed Michael Moller, "if only we hadn't had the amps cranked up to ten!"

By the fourth song, it was becoming clear to the audience that the band was not letting up. "This Is What's Called Death" unrolled like a slow-moving thunderstorm, and a follow-up song drilled the point home even harder. Just when the audience was about to grow restless with the convincing but potentially depressing point being made, the band's music took one of its trademark turns into brighter areas. A rich passage on Tate's piano signaled the change as he introduced a song called, "The Other Side of the Coin." Tate's lyrics and the mysterious visuals hinted at an ultimately hopeful outcome. The finale of the set was a rollicking and unabashedly happy song that proclaimed,

> "It isn't what you think it is, it's better,
> "It doesn't last a long, long time, it lasts forever..."

The powerful melody of this final song took the audience gracefully past the deep dark sentence of death executed so convincingly earlier in the set. The contrast gave the song an unquestionable authority, even as the chorus offered a gentle hope:

> "And if you're thinking life is just a dream, look again—
> There's something hidden in between these things you've been..."

Some of the Queen's visual arsenal showed up in the finale, exposing the Keeper's most recent research on the issue. The various Christ images waged a humble war against the heroes of classical mythology in a barrage of images that somehow played out with the emerging sympathy the Keepers were having for the subtle teachings of Father Miles. The music and lyrics continued to tread lightly, however, making it all easy to swallow. If there was advice, it was there with an air of "still subject to review" which was a part of the final refrain of the opening set.

> "It's just some pieces of the puzzle
> I found inside a shoe;
> It might well be worth the trouble
> If you can find a fit or two…

During a short intermission, the chairs were taken up and stacked at the back of the room. The rest of the evening was a celebration of the best of the Keepers' earlier work. The band sounded great and the crowd was more than ready to dance to the lighter side of their music. Tate had long explained the basis of rock and roll as having its power in the dynamic of tension and release. In this respect, the great tension of the first set made for a powerful release in the latter parts of the show. "They went nuts," laughed Allie afterwards, and it was true. And, whatever the dynamics, the Good Friday Show would always be remembered by the Keepers as their finest musical hour.

The week after Easter, spring weather arrived with a dazzling series of bright, warm days. Dogwood trees and azaleas seemed to pop into bloom overnight, converting sunshine into lush colors against the rapidly greening grass and new tender leaves of shade trees and bushes. The birds and squirrels appeared in great numbers, and the occasional rabbit could be spotted on the early morning drives out of the neighborhoods and out to school.

Still riding the feeling of success on Good Friday night, the Keepers were greatly energized by the happy blue skies and lingering twilights and cruised through the week enjoying something of a respite from their respective wars and struggles. Then, as if to signal an end to their time of peace, a powerful rainstorm rolled in on Friday afternoon, darkening the skies to a night-like black as the students let out for the weekend. Making a mad dash for cars suddenly lost in a sea of rain, the four friends were separated from one another by the weather and traffic until making an appointed rendezvous at Tate's house late that afternoon. By the time

THE LAST GET

they arrived, soaked and inspired by the tumultuous downpour, there was war in the air again.

"It's time," Allie announced after they had dried off and settled in the clubroom, "for our promised Get against Death."

Laid across the various sofas and easy chairs surrounding the huge oak coffee table, no one disagreed. "Three weeks left of school," Allie continued, "then a week of finals and it's over. It's time we went to work."

Pulling himself up from his padded leather throne at one end of the room, Allie began pacing the floor like a British officer at a flight briefing. "Gentlemen," he began "I have in mind a Get that has its roots in the deepest literary tradition of our young nation. Inspired by one of the great American patriarchs of the Get, our stunt will be based on the most beloved prank of our most beloved prankster, Tom Sawyer. I refer, my friends, to the funeral prank. For those of us who have at least partial recall from the depths of our freshman reading list, we remember a certain adventure climaxing with Tom having the rare privilege of attending his own funeral. He was able to enjoy the remorseful attitudes of all those who should have treated him better, a well-deserved vindication, I might add, for someone who, like us, had to suffer through the lack of appreciation of his contemporaries. Above all, it was a great Get."

Perceiving that the imaginations of his three friends had been sufficiently stimulated, Allie paused with a wry smile and proceeded. "It is upon this literary foundation I propose to build; it is against the same backdrop of the great middle-American scenery, I suggest we paint our masterpiece. And what Mark Twain may have only hinted at, I say, let's proclaim: a direct look at death will change everyone's attitude. To perceive someone's life in context with their death is the only fair way to see that person. I propose to demonstrate this principle by way of a rather elaborate Get."

Tate sat in a pleasant daze as Joey wiggled in his seat. Michael Moller slowly leaned back hair and said, "Okay, maestro, you've got our attention. So let's have the specifics."

Giving Moller his famously wide, close-lipped smile, Allie took up his orator's brush and proceeded to fill in the details of his scheme. The plan called, first of all, for turning the tables on one of the school's oldest traditions. The farewell event known as the "Junior Class Lynching Party" involved the reading of the Senior Class Will, where-in certain incriminating items from the lives of the seniors were "willed" to the appropriate member of the junior class. This was followed by the ceremonial hanging of a stuffed effigy dubbed the Senior Class Dummy. It all took place at the end of the Awards Ceremony on the day before graduation.

"We're gonna turn the tables on 'em at the Awards Ceremony," said Allie cryptically. "We're gonna let 'em string up Joey."

"What?!" exclaimed Tate suddenly awakened from his daze.

"That's right," said Allie calmly. "We slip Joey into the dummy's clothes before the ceremony, and we let them string him up." Before Tate and Moller had time to object again, Allie had pulled something out of his satchel and held it out in front of himself. "Exhibit A," he said.

It was a new rope tied in a hangman's noose. "Alright, boys, here's the deal." Tugging on the rope to punctuate his words, he explained. "It looks like a slipknot but it isn't. And it's got this hitch, here, that slips under Joey's armpits, and all we have to do is recruit an insider, someone from the old guard in the Junior Class who talks his class into letting him be the guy to rig up the dummy, only it's not a dummy, of course, it's Joey. But nobody knows that until he's way above the floor and suddenly this hooded dummy takes off his hood, and it's Joey, and he starts kicking and flailing like he's choking to death. He's yelling stuff like, 'you did this to me . . . you're killing me', and stuff like that, and it really looks for the world like it's choking him to death."

"The ultimate gag," pointed out Moller.

"You've got it," agreed Allie. "And by the time they've got him back to the floor it's too late, Joey's a proverbial goner. One of us runs for the phone as if to call an ambulance and we've got one rented from that company they use for the football games and it shows up real quick. Meanwhile Father Miles is in on it, and he's keeping everyone back from getting a good look at Joey. He also finds this phony suicide note on Joey's chest, explaining how hard life was for him—and his last request is that Father Miles be allowed to give the graduation address the next night. Then we whisk Joey out to the ambulance and drive off, and a couple hours later send word back that he's dead, which of course he isn't."

"Well, everybody is so torn up they can barely make it to Graduation anyway, so what else are they gonna do but let Father Miles speak for Joey? And what's Smiles gonna do but give them the ultimate Full Report of all time, the Full Dose, Joey-style, if you get my drift, and just when he gets to the part about identification and resurrection and victory over death, in walks Joey! And we just sit back and watch the biggest revival since the Second Great Awakening. By the time everyone figures out that it was all a Get, we've got our first revival under our belts."

Tate looked up at Allie and just smiled. This was crazy, he thought, this was really crazy. But it was such a great idea. Moller was shaking his head, too, but his own chuckles betrayed the fact that he, also, was finding the scheme hard to resist. Could they really pull it off?

Joey, of course, had earlier been swept completely into the plan by Allie and was watching eagerly for the reaction of his other two friends. For Joey, this was perceived as his last chance to do something dramatic on behalf of his spiritually endangered classmates, a point of view Allie had certainly done nothing to discourage. For Allie, it was perhaps his last chance to do anything dramatic on behalf of his disappearing way of life.

"I don't think so," said Tate, at last. "It's just too crazy."

"Too crazy?!" shrieked Allie. "Come on, Tate. I mean, this is it. You've been moping around for months, and then you finally get onto something brilliant, and just when you're about to follow it out to its logical conclusion it's suddenly too crazy. Think about it, man. This Get is superbly designed to get to the heart of everything you've been talking about. Death is what everyone is afraid of. Death is what everyone is hiding from. Death is what makes everyone take themselves so seriously. That's the deal. But death can be defeated—according to your latest theory it already has—and the more people you can get to buy into that idea, the less power death has and then, guess what, it's no more Mr. Serious, which is what we've been going for all these years."

"He might be onto something, Tate," said Moller gently.

"Of course I am," said Allie, treading lightly. "And anyone can see that. Given the proper demonstration, I'm convinced that anyone can see where they've been missing the boat. Identification is the key, man, you said it yourself, and what better way to show how all that works than having everyone tricked into transferring their hatred onto this dummy named Joey, only to find out that it should have been love. They'll see their stupid Awards Ceremony mock-hatred literally kill a guy, and when Joey walks back in alive, it will all become obvious. Next time around, then, they might not be so stinking serious about this stuff."

Tate did not know what to say. The plan had a logic of its own. And the message, as Allie insisted, did indeed go right to the heart of the matter. But something deep inside of Tate said it was too late. Too late to change anyone at Somerset school; too late for the Mayor and his old way of life; too late for the Keepers. But, even as these things became clearer than they had ever been, Tate also realized it was also too late to stop Allie.

With Joey squirming in anticipation and Michael Moller calmly straddling the fence, Tate swallowed a whale of resignation, somehow pulled off a convincing smile, and cast the determining vote.

"Alright," he said at last. "It is crazy. But it's too good a Get not to try."

CHAPTER SIXTEEN

THE LAST GET

Tate pulled the door closed behind him and walked across the cold, tile floor to his father's bed.

"It's me, Pop," he said, resting his fingertips on his father's chest. The slightest alteration in his father's breathing was taken as an answer, and Tate pulled a chair over beside the bed and sat down.

"It's getting so strange, Pop," said Tate slowly, "things at school and all . . . I don't know what to think of it anymore." The sheets over the Mayor's chest rose and fell in a perfect, peaceful rhythm. Tate felt better already.

"It's like the administration has completely lost touch with the past, just like that. A new school building, a bunch of new students and WHAMO—instant change. It's really weird." Tate paused for a moment, as if the words needed to sink in, as much to himself as to his father, then he continued. "And I think Allie may be losing it, I really do. His jokes are getting way too strained a lot of the time and it's almost scary, like he's becoming obsessed or something—but then he'll turn right around and come up with something perfect too, so it's very confusing really. And then there's Joey—'

A quick nausea churned in Tate's stomach. He had not really discussed the strange incident in the hospital room a few weeks before with his father, and now he felt like he should.

"That guy who was in here the other night," he began, "you know, praying for you and everything . . . I didn't know if you knew that was Joey . . . I mean, if you're kind of awake and tuning into all this, it might have been pretty strange, but that's the side of Joey you've never seen and we've kind of gotten used to it but the only thing is, he's getting worse, too, he definitely is getting worse, and I hope it wasn't too weird because he really is sincere and . . . well pretty harmless when you really get down to it . . . which is why we've always cut him so much slack because he really isn't hurting anyone but himself . . . which is sad, but no reason not to be friends with the guy, so I hope it wasn't too weird . . ."

Tate looked at his father almost forgetting for a moment that there wasn't going to be an answer, then he let out the rest of his breath. "Anyway, it feels good to tell you all this stuff because I really am kind of scared and I . . . and I . . . " Tate's eyes and throat went suddenly hot, and he felt tears welling up from inside. He choked them back as he realized what his next words were going to be. He took a deep breath and tried to relax as he said, "and I am really looking forward to getting you out of here, Pop. Okay? I want you to wake up . . . I really need you to wake up." A huge sob escaped from Tate, and then the dam was broken. He sobbed again and then again and then he was crying out of control. But it felt good. He stood upright beside his father's bed and cried for a long time. Then a few laughs appeared between the sobs and slowly it all subsided. "So anyway, Pop, there you have it. I guess I've been holding that in for a while. And I know you're doing the best you can, so don't take it personally." He reached down and stroked his father's arm. So you hang in there, okay? And I'll be seeing you later—I've gotta meet the guys at Tolstoy's, okay? So I'll see you later."

The weeks before graduation flew by like the last cars on a train. More accurately, the individual days dragged on inside the train cars as the scenery outside poured past at high speed. Long days of sunshine alternated with beautiful spring storms as the four old friends faced their last set of finals and the barrage of ceremonies awaiting the graduating seniors. Tate was often accompanied by Moller as he tried to spend as much time as he could by his father's side. At the end, they would bring their school books and notes and quiz each other across the Mayor's bed in preparation for their tests. "Not only is he going to wake up," Moller joked one day, "but he's gonna wake up smarter than he's ever been."

Meanwhile, the notion that Allie might best be kept under control by allowing him his last Get was proving to be true. Joey, too, focused all his nervous energy on his heroic task ahead. The arrangements for the ambulance and various other details seemed to be going well. Still, Tate was not without reservations. "Just relax, boys," Allie would say. "We've got this thing under control," as if the Get itself was all they had to worry about. But that had always been the deal: big turning points in their lives had always been diffused by the right stunt or wisecrack. Why should this be any different?

Or so Tate told himself as he watched Allie pacing the floor the night before the Awards Ceremony. On top of the steadily building anxiety about the Get—and about life in general—there was suddenly some sobering news: Father Miles was out of the plan. Allie had failed to mention to the others that Father Miles had been completely against the idea all along. If he had not exactly been lying, Allie had at least been pathologically optimistic, as he continued to assure his friends that Father Miles was "coming around to the plan" and so forth. Instead, Father Miles had actually been trying every angle he could to talk Allie out of the idea altogether. He had assumed that Tate and Moller were actively pursuing the same course, and was shocked to discover that they were actually going along with the Get.

"Have you lads all gone crazy!?" Father Miles exclaimed when he realized their intent and summoned the foursome to his office. "Tate, Michael, have you given leave of your senses altogether? Joey, are you really going to give in to this heroic-martyr heresy?! And, for the love of God, Allie, will you not rest for one moment and see what you are doing?"

There had been a painfully long pause. Tate and Michael Moller felt too weak to defend their positions either way, and Joey just stared straight ahead, his lower lip quivering as he mumbled something inaudible. Only Allie seemed unshaken by their sponsor's stern rebuke. And there was a surprising power in his almost-whispered response. "Pause for one moment?" he repeated. "One moment is all we have left." Sensing their resolve, Father Miles quickly decided not to waste his words. "Very well, then," he said, "you lads are on your own here. May God have mercy on your stubborn souls."

And so they had returned to Tate's clubroom, there to lay the final plans for their last Get of high school—without blessing of Father Miles. Allie had quickly re-distributed assignments to cover for Father Miles' absence. "You guys may have to help hold the crowd back a little bit," he said, "and I'll read the phony suicide note. Once we pull that first part off—at the Awards Ceremony, I mean—I know Smiles will come around. I know he'll come through with that Graduation speech . . . he can't resist a crowd and he'll see for sure what a perfect set up it is . . . I mean, it's perfect . . . and he'll see that and it'll be great and we don't have to worry about . . ." And on and on went Allie in his final monologue as Tate and Moller and Joey rode along on the sound of his voice, pretending one last time that such things were all they knew.

At first everything went well enough. The Keepers' recruit from the junior class was a Somerset Lifer named Jack Raider. He had let his best friend in on the scheme, and together they had convinced their classmates to let them "do the honors" on the dummy. The rope had been rigged, and Jack Raider had practiced all week, putting it around Joey just right. On the morning of the Awards Ceremony, Joey had hid in the Junior Class conference room until the ceremony began and then slipped into the dummy clothes.

When the Ceremony began to build to its climactic rendezvous with tradition, however, something seemed to cloud the atmosphere. As veterans of scores of nerve-wracking stunts, Allie and the others could begin to sense the presence of something stronger than their usual nervousness. There was a feeling of danger and dread in the air. Allie began looking rapidly about the room, and Moller took to roaming the back of the Commons, his eyes scrutinizing every development. By then Headmaster Martin had yielded the floor to the Junior Class president who was kicking off the lynching party by reading an allegedly humorous indictment of various members of the senior class. Jack Raider and his accomplice slipped from their seats and disappeared through the door to the Junior Class meeting room. But just when the class president was wrapping up his debut in the world of stand-up comedy, there was suddenly a loud commotion in the Junior Class meeting room. Recovering quickly from the commotion, the class president announced the beginning of the lynching party just as the door to the meeting room swung open and two guys stormed out, dragging the dummy behind them. But the two guys were not Jack Raider and his assistant.

"It's Hoagley," gasped Allie. "What the hell is he doing?"

"This could be bad," said Tate out loud. By then the whole place had come to its feet. As was the tradition, the excitement in the room was hitting a fever pitch, but the panic in Tate, Allie, and Moller was something else again. Moller was already fighting his way to the front of the room and Allie and Tate were in the aisle, but the crowd had closed in tightly and the wall of people was suddenly the most oppressive obstacle the scared friends had ever encountered. In a moment, they knew they were too late.

"String him up!" shrieked the shrill voice of Dale Hoagley. Instantly the rope grew taught in mid-air. At the far end of the rope, the huskiest members of the junior class gave a great tug and the pulleys began squeaking as the dummy rose ominously over the heads of the students. They gave another great tug and the dummy rose halfway to the ceiling. Peals of adrenaline-filled laughter ripped at the air like daggers as Allie, Tate, and Moller caught a terrible glimpse of the truth: Joey's head was held tightly in the rope—Hoagley had changed the knot or, at least, had not slipped the rope under Joey's arms.

"He's choking to death!" screamed Allie. For an instant his voice was heard just above the others, but it made no impression. Just another of Allie's incredibly believable melodramas, thought those closest to him, and the rest heard only another excited scream.

"Let him down!" shrieked Tate.

"Cut him loose! screamed Moller. But, still, it only looked like a group performance.

The dummy jerked and kicked with Joey's terrified movements but even that was hardly distinguishable from the tugging on the rope the other end. And Joey's hands had been tied by the maniacal Hoagley, so he could not pull the hood from his head as planned.

After an eternity of futile screams, Allie came to his senses and began fighting his way back to the guys pulling the rope. Moller and Tate quickly followed, but the resistance at that end proved just as strong. The junior class henchmen were well primed for a fight and were in no mood to listen to Allie's desperate pleas.

"Sure thing, asshole," said one of them as he jabbed an elbow into Allie's face.

Moller figured things out quickly and circled around behind the rope. With Tate charging straight ahead and Allie coming up from the floor with absolute rage in his eyes, the three of them managed to emerge from the furious struggle with the rope. As they let off on it, Joey's body began its long descent to the floor.

From the other side of the room, Father Miles had helplessly witnessed the tragedy. Not sure at first what was happening, he had eventually fought his way to the center of the room, in anticipation of the body coming down. With a jerk Joey fell the last few feet onto Father Miles, knocking them both to the floor. Father Miles quickly scrambled around and pulled the noose from Joey's limp neck.

By the time Tate reached the two of them on the floor, Father Miles knew the bitter truth. His heart cracked and broke and broke again. His eyes filled with the compassion of a soul who knew more about suffering that any human could. Allie and Michael Moller crashed into Tate's back as Father Miles looked up at his three most precious friends. His eyes were suddenly the eyes of Jesus Himself, and they looked silently into the deepest reaches of each their hearts. Only such gentle eyes could mercifully deliver the most devastating news they would ever know.

Joey was dead.

CHAPTER SEVENTEEN

IDENTIFICATION

Michael Moller threw a stone into the dark pool of water before him and listened to its entry into the pond. It was just approaching dawn and he and Allie and Tate had been up all night, driving from one end of their lives to the other, crying silently against their respective windows, banging fists against the nearest objects, howling at the non-existent moon, asking the unanswerable questions, staring into the darkness, feeling alone together.

As the sky had begun to gray they had found themselves at Tate's pond where they had laid in the damp grass and watched the stars disappear into the blurred atmosphere of the dawn. The unfamiliar sounds of early morning played strangely against their weary souls, as did the light to their tired eyes. "Doesn't even feel like morning," said Tate at last. "It feels like the twilight zone."

"Yeah," said Allie, "it should be night for a lot longer . . . they shouldn't let morning happen for a long time."

It had been less than twenty-four hours since Joey had been wheeled out of Somerset School, face covered with a white sheet, but it had seemed like days. Time had gone into a tailspin as the sirens had come screaming up to the school and the paramedics and police had stormed into the school in a dynamic foursome that looked like some bizarre double-date on their way to the prom.

Dale Hoagley and his friend had left with the police, Joey had disappeared into the back of the ambulance, and everyone else had drifted away in various states of shock and dismay. Tate and Moller had followed

Joey's body all the way to the ambulance. They had wanted to ride with their friend but instead had stood with legs of lead as the ambulance pulled away with cruel speed, creating an ever-widening gap that felt like it would never be closed. Allie had stayed behind in the commons, plastered to the floor by the same weight that paralyzed Tate and Moller, and flanked on either side by Sarah and Emily, who were crying hysterically. Father Miles had stood there silently beside Allie and then left without a word.

By the time the three friends ended up at the pond, they were numb. With the sound of Moller's stone breaking the silence, Tate looked up, following the ripples in the water until they touched the other shore. There his eyes wandered up over the trees into the orange clouds and a sky already turning blue. "How can it be a beautiful day?" he asked.

A long silence followed. Michael Moller tossed another stone out into the water and Allie let out a sigh. "I'm sorry you guys," said Allie.

There was another long silence and Moller threw another stone into the pond. Tate began to sob as Allie's words sank into him. In the midst of their grief, it seemed, Allie had returned to his senses. But it was too late.

"Yeah," continued Allie, "I get it now. You can't stop this stuff when it's coming on, can't slow it down even. We were so stupid—no, *I* was so stupid—"I know now that you guys were catching on, but I just wouldn't let go, would I?" Allie's mouth twisted into a pain-filled version of his crooked smile. "I just wouldn't let go."

Michael Moller threw his last stone into the pond and turned around. "We probably didn't want you to, man," he said. "We're just as much to blame as you." Somewhere near the center of his shattered heart, Tate agreed. They had been only too glad to play along.

"Yeah," said Tate, "we're actually more to blame than you. We knew it was time to call it quits and we went on anyway. We had all the pieces laid out on the table and—just when it looked like they were all falling into place—we pitched it all away for one more shot at high school immortality. We knew the way out was a cross and not a Get, but we didn't want to go through that yet." He paused a moment and winced with his next thought. "Except for Joey," he said. "He was only too willing . . . shit, man, he probably knew it was coming. For all we know he could have baited Hoagley into it, mouse-trapped the guy into making Joey into a martyr . . . oh, great."

"Naw," said Allie. "Joey was just going along for me. I talked him into it, and he just figured it would be a great gag and a great way to

IDENTIFICATION

make some sort of evangelical statement. I was the guy who canonized the deal for him—and that's terrible, man, just terrible."

There was a tone in Allie's voice that Tate had never heard before. There was fear and remorse, and there was a loneliness that he suddenly recognized as the undercurrent to huge parts of Allie's life, to all of their lives. As if to break the spell of that loneliness, Tate reached over and put his hand on Allie's shoulder.

"It's okay, man", he said, "we're all in this together."

Allie looked at Tate for a brief instant and then looked away. "Yeah, sure," he said. "I know."

There was no sarcasm in Allie's weak words, no defenses for his sudden vulnerability. The facade had been shattered. The actor and genius that were true enough parts of him gave up their charade that hid the rest of Allie. In the wake of Joey's death, it seemed, these noble liars were ready to lay down to die. "God, how I need help," said Allie with total disgust.

Tate pushed the palms of his hands against his eyes and then wiped the tears on his jeans. "Don't we all," he sighed.

Behind them, the sun began to peak between the tall trees bordering the Henry's estate. The orange hues of the clouds on the horizon soaked the trees in rich sunburst tones. The grass all around shimmered deeply in green beneath the heavy dew. And slowly a most tangible feeling of relief engulfed the three friends. From within each of them almost simultaneously and from an invisible source somewhere in the very midst of the lifelong bonds between them, there arose a warm feeling of deep comfort. As if things would be all right.

The stillness around them slowly stirred with the whisper of a breeze. Gaining power slowly, the wind rose in unmistakable cadence with the rising hopes of the three friends. Within a few short moments the breeze was strong enough to blow the hair across Michael Moller's face. The three friends looked at each other with widening eyes, marveling as much at the inner changes as the outer ones.

"What's the deal?" smiled Tate, referring to both.

"Looks like a little change in the weather," said Allie with a grin.

"No kidding," said Moller. Then they all fell silent again as the breeze grew into a steady wind and the feeling of overwhelming contentment increased until they were all on their feet, shuffling about like a group of freed prisoners not sure where to go. "Man, let's take a drive," said Allie at last, and they were off.

By now it was full morning and the houses everywhere were filled with activity. Moller had taken the wheel and was steering the car through the old neighborhoods with no destination in mind. The inexplicable feeling of peace had traveled with them to the car and continued in their midst, rolling and cresting in a pleasant wave as the three friends glided through the early morning world. This was the strangest feeling they had ever known: complete inner calm in the wake of the worst outward experience of their lives—and the fact that it made no sense whatsoever only added to the wonder of it all.

As their car glided past houses and other cars busy with their days, Tate began trying to place where he had ever tasted these feelings before. After a while, he broke into a silent smile as the chapel services of Father Miles came to mind. After a long moment of consideration, he was sure of the implications. "You know," he said quietly, " this must be the peace of God."

Moller nodded his head thoughtfully and Allie just smiled. "Must be," said Allie, "cause it doesn't make any sense at all".

"And it's the power of God, too," added Moller. "Something's definitely up."

The power of God, thought Tate to himself. Moller had accelerated a bit to dramatize his point and, with the neighborhood scenes pouring past him, Tate began recalling the readings from the Easter service. "And Elisha went in and behold the lad was dead" . . . and Jesus said, 'Lazarus come forth' . . . Oh Death, where is your victory, Oh Death, where is your sting? . . . I am the resurrection and the life . . . " The goosebumps began at Tate's ankles and rolled all the way up his legs and body until they shivered through his neck. "Maybe it's not too late for Joey," he heard himself saying.

"What'd you say?" asked Moller calmly.

"Maybe it's not too late for Joey," he repeated. "Maybe he'd want to come back from the dead."

Moller and Allie looked straight ahead as Tate's words reached them. The wind blew against the car in gusts that somehow brushed away normal doubts. It did not surprise Tate when no one disagreed.

"Well now," said Moller finally, "There's an interesting thought."

The sense of peace and power in the car moved about somewhat until it seemed to hover over and around Allie. He sat up straighter, still looking straight ahead. "Well, yeah," he said. "Joey might be crazy enough for something like that."

Without another word, Moller took the next left turn and then went left again. It was understood that he was heading for the funeral parlor.

The sprawling white mansion on the edge of the business district was flanked on both sides by one-story office buildings. In front, beneath the long portacashire, three black limousines were parked end to end. A wide green lawn separated the stately former residence from the concrete and brick now surrounding it. "Here?" said Moller as he approached the entrance to the grounds of the funeral parlor.

"Yeah," said Tate, deep in thought. "No, wait. Pull around back."

Tate and Allie eyed the building carefully as Michael Moller steered the car around the block to where the narrow rear exit poured out into the street. "Here we are," said Moller, and he drove up the long drive and pulled the car into an inconspicuous parking space next to the house's large garage. Shutting off the engine, Allie punctuated the sudden silence with a gentle wisecrack. Tate stared straight ahead and silently waved away Allie's joking. Moller looked over at Tate, and then shot Allie a quick glance to let him know that their old friend meant business. "Okay, Tate," said Allie. "What's the plan?"

"You need to keep the manager of this place busy, Allie," said Tate at once. "And Moller, you've got to watch the foyer. There's a set of outer doors and the foyer and then the doors to the main chapel. Your job is to stall anyone in the foyer while I'm . . . while I'm in the chapel."

There was something in the way that Tate had paused in mid-sentence that did away with any further questions. Whatever Tate had in mind was better off left unsaid.

"Okay," said Allie quietly. "You can count on us. We'll keep you clear."

Three car doors opened and the Keepers of the Get moved in perfect unison across the parking lot to the back door of the funeral home. "Give me a couple minutes," said Allie. "Then you guys slip on in." Letting the dusty screen door shut behind him, Allie pushed open the back door and disappeared inside.

From the back porch, Tate and Moller could hear the muffled voiced of Allie and an older gentleman. After a few inaudible exchanges, the voices trailed off slowly, until finally there was no sound at all.

"Okay," said Tate. "The coast is clear." He opened the door for his friend and then followed him out of the bright morning light into the dark interior of the funeral parlor. Thick, dark carpet and ancient wallpaper absorbed what little light managed to come through the heavily draped windows and lamps covered with thick shades.

"This way," whispered Tate. He had made several trips to the funeral home a few years before when his grandmother had died, and he remembered a back hallway that he had used several times to avoid the clinging hugs of his relatives. Tugging Moller down that hallway now, they were soon out in the main foyer.

"Okay," said Tate to Moller. "NOBODY gets past you, man."

"Alright," said Moller, swallowing hard at the reality of his task. He was counting heavily on no one showing up, but he tried to be convincing in his resolve to handle anything. "I've got you covered," he said.

With a final look at this friend, Tate turned towards the doors to the chapel. He suddenly felt more alone than he had ever felt in his life. Huge waves of nervous nausea passed through him and he wanted to forget the whole thing, but something even deeper within him moved his feet through the doors of the chapel and up the long aisle towards the casket set at the other end of the room. Striding slowly forward, Tate began to be more aware of his body. The floor felt very hard to the soles of his feet and it seemed somewhat unique the way his frame moved through the air by way of bones and muscles. He was suddenly aware of what it was like to be alive—to be a human moving on the face of the earth. As he reached the edge of the casket, he realized Joey no longer had that strange privilege—or sentence—and he could practically touch the veil that separated himself from Joey. He stared down at his friend's still face, stark but serene, perfect but for a certain lack of color and subtle movement. Perfect but for a lack of life.

"Joey," Tate heard himself saying, "do you want to come back?" Staring at his friend's peaceful repose, Tate was shocked by the sudden and absolute sense of an answer. No, Joey did not want to come back. He'd had enough.

Suddenly knowing beyond all doubt that Joey was alive somewhere else, Tate replayed the terribly painful highlights of Joey's suffering pilgrimage on earth. The Czar, Joey's mother and step-father, all the cruel kids at schools past and present, even the well-meaning kidding of his only friends—all these played like perverse cartoon villains against the images of life in a far better place. "No, I guess you don't really want to come back," said Tate sadly. "Then he sighed. "But we need you," he said. "We need you . . ."

All the fear and loneliness Tate had ever known rushed to the pit of his stomach and cried out for Joey. "Come back, man," he cried. "Joey, come back!"

The most profound sense of loss throbbed through Tate's body and sent what was left of his mind reeling. Through the blurred confusion and pain there slowly emerged something like a template of clarity. It took the form of the words and images from the Easter service readings: "And Elisha lay face down on the lad . . ." Otherwise numb to his mind and senses, Tate followed a strange sense of peace and direction as he slowly placed his left hand on the casket and pulled himself off the floor, swinging one leg up to the cold, hard edge of the casket. Then he lowered himself down onto Joey, face to his face, chest to his chest. For a frozen minute he lay there, life against death, then he pushed himself up and lowered himself back to the floor where he stood looking for a long moment at Joey's body lying still as granite.

"You're not coming back, are you?" said Tate calmly, but the fear and sense of loss were gone completely. Joey was alive somewhere, and Tate was alive on earth. "Okay, Joey," said Tate quietly. "I get it . . . I'll see you later, man."

The doors of the hospital elevator popped open and Allie and Moller quickly stepped in. "Eight," reminded Moller and Allie pushed the button. The doors closed, and they stared straight ahead. Tate had led them out of the funeral home without a word and walked silently to the car where he got in the back seat. When Allie and Moller had taken their places in the front seats and turned around for a report, Tate had looked at them with clear eyes and the trace of a smile. "Joey's not coming back," was all he said, "but I think something else is going on." Then he had asked Moller to take him to the hospital to see the Mayor.

Moller and Allie had dropped Tate off at the front door of the hospital, planning to go to Allie's house to get some sleep, but by the time they made it there, Allie's housekeeper had an urgent message for them. "Tate says for you boys to come back to the hospital right away," she said. "It sounded awfully important."

When the doors to the elevator opened again, the halls on the eighth floor were full of activity. Allie recognized some of the Mayor's relatives, and he could see Tate's mother down the hall near the door to the Mayor's room. Nodding to the nurses at their station, Allie and Moller walked gingerly down the hall towards the Mayor's room.

"Uh, hello, Mrs. Henry," said Allie sounding very awkward.

"Oh, hello, Allie," said Tate's mother. She seemed pre-occupied as always, but she smiled at Allie and Moller. "Tate told me you boys would be coming. He's in his father's room."

Taking a deep breath, Allie and Moller smiled again at Mrs. Henry and then slipped by her into the room. They could see Tate first, standing at the foot of the bed, talking away as if in the throes of a Full Report. A few steps further and the two boys could begin to catch sight of the Mayor.

He was sitting up, eyes wide open.

"Allie, Michael," exclaimed Tate. "He woke up! He's back!"

The Mayor smiled at Allie and Moller with the charming smile they had almost forgotten. "Hello, lads," said the old gentlemen, giving them the patented tilt of the head and chin. "The Mayor, it seems, is indeed back."

"And not a moment too soon, your Mayorness," said Allie happily, and he extended his hand for a handshake that was heartily, if somewhat slowly, met with by the Mayor.

"Welcome back, your Mayorness," said Moller in his turn. And he, too, gently shook the Mayor's hand. The laughter and amazement filled the room until, just as Allie was about to announce that it was time for a Full Report, a doctor came in to check on the Mayor, and Tate took the opportunity to pull Allie and Moller back into the hall.

Once in the hall, Tate steered his friends past his mother and other well-wishers to an alcove near the end of the hall. "Allie . . . Moller . . . " he said in a raspy whisper, "the Mayor came out of his coma at exactly 9:15 this morning."

"Great," said Allie, not understanding what Tate was driving at.

"Allie—9:15! Don't you get it?" exclaimed Tate. "Don't you know where we were—at precisely 9:15?"

Allie raised his eyebrows as her remembered seeing a clock in the office of the funeral home director. The clock had said 9:10. "Okay, so we were in the funeral home," he said. "So what does that have to do with it?"

"Allie," said Tate, "I went in that chapel, and I prayed for Joey to come back from the dead. I got in there and I felt like he didn't want to come back, but I just felt like we needed him so badly that I prayed for him to come back. And I mean I prayed serious." He paused to make sure

Allie got his drift. "Well, Joey never woke up, see, and that's fine because I can see why he wouldn't want to come back anyway, but don't you get it? The Mayor woke up right then. This orderly guy was in the room, and he said he was sure it was 9:15 and—get this!—the guy told me the Mayor woke up sneezing."

Allie looked at Moller, who just smiled. "That was part of the reading, man," Moller explained. "The little guy sneezed seven times when he woke up from the dead."

"Exactly," said Tate. As if on cue, the doctor came out of the Mayor's room and headed off the other direction down the hall. "So come on," said Tate happily, "let's get the Mayor caught up on this stuff."

* * *

"I am the Resurrection and the Life," read the beloved Father Smiles. "I was dead and, behold, I am alive forever-more." Four hundred people were packed into the grassy outdoor chapel, hoping for consolation, understanding, some sort of relief from their pain. It was graduation day, but it felt like a funeral. Father David Miles stood at the simple podium and took a deep breath. He made a few token remarks about the occasion of graduation. Then he began a slow and loving tribute to his young friend, Joey.

He told, as no one else could have, the story of a frightened kid who had learned to believe in a God of love. "But that faith," he explained, "though it gave him a reason to live, also profoundly raised the stakes in a life already being played to the limits of his emotions. I'm not sure if any of us realized how much Joey worried and travailed about the people he loved. Instead, we saw the awkwardness and defensiveness as a sign of weakness or insecurity rather than the immature attempts at caring for those he knew would probably reject him. And reject him we did.

"How many of us played along with Joey when it was convenient, when we had nothing to lose, when we could even gain something by his presence? And why not? Joey had developed a knack for being the perfect fall guy, the perfect butt of anyone's jokes, especially his own. How familiar was his wheezy little laugh of excruciated angst. 'You're killing me,' he would say as he held onto his chest and cracked up at the latest insult directed at him. Well, dear people, as demonstrated so blatantly by this most tragic turn of events, it seems quite obvious to me that we were. Day by day, little cut by little cut, we were killing Joey Liptisch."

This was too much. It was all too true. And it was too gently delivered for the Keepers or anyone else to escape by feeling unfairly accused by Father Miles. It was too obvious that the broken priest considered himself as guilty as anyone. They had all played along with Joey's self-effacement. They had all participated in the slow annihilation of what was left of his battered self. And, in the end, he had become a pawn in everyone's game.

"So it's the comic's crucifixion," said Father Miles. His voice cut through the air like a sword, the incredible silence being sliced by the sharpest of words. "And we are all the traitorous mob known today as the audience. We all helped put that noose around Joey's neck, and there's no use trying to place blame for how it all backfired. We were all guilty long before Graduation Day. We were all ready for the right gag. We've always wanted some Joey to take the dive for us. How strange that we should be surprised that he did."

The amplified voice of David Miles richoteted away from Allie, Tate, and Moller. It was good to hear such things spoken aloud. Though they cut deeply, it was better that they should come forth in the light of day. But at some point the words began to fail, especially for Tate. So much had happened that was so far beyond words, that it was not long until Father Miles' eloquent words ceased to reach Tate's ears. About then, Tate's eyes were drawn to the distant hillside over-looking the outdoor chapel.

There, somewhere near the borders of the Unexplainable, stood two figures. The short, full frame of an older gentleman was recognized at first, jerking Tate back from his gentle musings: it was the Mayor. Though Tate's father had awoken from his coma, the doctors had informed him that it would be a few weeks before he was back on his feet, so this was impossible. But the pin-striped figure of the Mayor was unmistakable. Just then, Allie suddenly jerked in his seat and grabbed Michael Moller, and Tate knew without looking over they had just seen it, too. Eyes glued to the scene, Tate focused on the other figure. Instantly his chest began to pound and his hands started shaking. Smaller, frail of frame and even more relaxed than the Mayor seemed to be, the second figure slowly shifted into better view. Suddenly a glimmer of sunlight caught a shiny object on his face. "Eyeglasses," said Tate and then the breath went out of him: it was Joey.

The silent mention of Joey's name caused the second figure's head to lift slightly. Could Tate make out a smile from this distance? Allie and Moller sat frozen in their seats as they gazed into the same impossible scene. By then, Joey was saying something to the Mayor who proceeded to reach into the front of his pin-striped suit-coat, pulling out an object of some kind and handing it to Joey. For a frozen moment Joey seemed to be looking directly at Tate and the others. Then he stepped away from the Mayor, reached back with the object in his hand, and gave it a mighty fling. The tiny dot left his hand and sailed out in an arc that reached well above the horizon before it began its gentle descent many seconds later, growing slightly larger all the while. It was coming towards them.

The droning voice of Father Miles came back into focus for a moment as the dot drew nearer. His sermon had made the mystical turn from perfect tragedy to some sort of victorious homologue and—though his words had long since ceased reaching Tate and the others—it was clear the chaplain had found true hope for the situation. As if to punctuate some marvelous point in Father Miles' eulogy, the specifics of which have long fallen from memory, a flat, round object suddenly whizzed by his ear, sailed gently down the tail end of its arc and landed squarely in the lap of Michael Moller.

It was a Frisbee.

EPILOGUE

An open hand pounded the window of Tate's car with a single thud. "Wake up, Tater-head!" shouted Allie as he jerked open the car door. Tate caught himself from falling out of the door and sat upright, but, before he could speak, Allie was melodramatically shaking him and shouting, "Rise and shine, buddy, it's time for the new millennium . . . I've got your caffeine pills here and you better down 'em quick 'cause we're late for work at the Robot Factory."

"Okay, Comrade, okay . . . " said Tate dreamily. The last images of his long journey of thought dissolved into the abrupt scene change surrounding him. "I'm up . . . I'm up."

Tate and Allie had spent most of their last twenty-five years in their hometown. Each had made the four-year trek to universities on the East Coast, keeping in touch through the school year and then regrouping each summer for three months at home. Michael Moller had gone to college on the West Coast, traveling home for a couple summers and then drifting off to various more exotic destinations. A few years after their graduation from college, the three friends had traveled together to Europe and North Africa. By then Moller had taken a job in Amsterdam doing research and development for an optical tools manufacturer, and Tate and Allie had begun dabbling in the various oil and real estate activities of their respective families. Without ever completely growing up, the three had each managed to raise families of their own. And, without ever forgetting about Joey, they had quietly lived their lives without him.

Father Miles, meanwhile, had remained on at Summerset School for all those years. His plans to return to England for the second half of his ministerial life somehow never materialized. Instead he had become in Allie's words, "an institution himself" through his work at the school and, as it turned out, his administration of a trust fund set up by Joey's parents. At the suggestion of Father Miles, the proceeds of this trust had been used to establish and operate an Episcopal mission school in Paraguay.

Throughout the years Father Miles had maintained a limited but unwavering relationship with Allie, Tate and Moller. He would send them a Christmas card each year with a personal note of some kind and, more significantly, on the anniversary of Joey's death, he would also send them a card. Though the date always fell several weeks after Easter, the card would nevertheless announce the Resurrection.

"Easter in May," Allie originally wrote to Tate and Moller, "you know that cheapskate Miles is getting a discount on these cards." And Tate and Moller had, of course, played along, but there was no mistaking the message. In subsequent years, the old friends would exchange phone calls or letters or, of late, emails, each time the cards arrived. "It's like a sacrament," one would say about Father Miles' ritual regularity.

"As unavoidable as Lent," would be the reply.

In this year's card there had been a poignant announcement from Father Miles. After some thirty-five years of service, he was retiring from his post at the school. Enclosed was a formal invitation, prepared by the school, and a hand-written note from their beloved priest. Repeating the opening line of the formal invitation, "The Honor of Your Presence," Father Miles had underlined the word "Your" and added "would be especially appreciated." Then he wrote, "Along with the opportunity to celebrate the end of my illustrious career, I also have, it seems, one final clue with regard to the mystery of Joey."

It was the first time in all the years that his note mentioned Joey by name.

Allie and Tate were met at the edge of the parking lot by Michael Moller. "The honor of your presence," Moller said with a wry smile.

Taking turns shaking his hand, Allie and Tate each replied in the familiar drone of an acolyte, "No, the honor of *your* presence."

Inside the school, the three friends were immediately enveloped in a moment outside of time. "It's like we never left," said Allie.

"It's so great to be seventeen again," said Moller.

A few familiar faces and a sea of perfect strangers slowly surrounded the threesome, gently pulling them into the human stream funneling into the chapel. Dodging the ushers, the Keepers slipped into their old spot in the back pew. "No place like home," said Allie.

As the retirement ceremony began, Tate, Allie, and Moller swiftly drifted away into the memories of their years at Somerset. As always happened, they ended up at the mystery of Joey. "One final clue," would indeed be nice.

EPILOGUE

The usual array of accolades and anecdotes played like a pleasant pre-game show to the three pilgrims on the last leg of their quest. They nodded their heads in sincere "amens" as the present Headmaster listed the qualities of the venerable Father David Miles. They had no trouble finding laughter for each of the humorous stories being recounted by the various speakers from the faculty and board of directors. But there was no mistaking the anticipation in the air above their little corner of the chapel. Respect for Father Miles notwithstanding, the three old friends were completely preoccupied with the promise of a clue about Joey.

In the years since the event that had become known among the Keepers of the Get as "The Miracle of the Frisbee," there had been much debate and speculation over what had actually happened. Though the Mayor later claimed to have experienced nothing, Tate was certain that some combination of his father's spirit, soul and body had been present on the hill with Joey, even if the Mayors' conscious mind was not included in the mix. For Tate, the experience changed his life. His casual faith was transformed into the centerpiece of his existence and, though he never transferred his membership from the elegant if sleepy sanctuaries of the Episcopal Church to a more radical kind of Christianity, he would always regard his final week at Somerset School as the point at which he actually became a believer.

Allie, on the other hand, could never quite say how he felt about those same events. In some ways, his role in Joey's death had made it harder for him to accept the simple miracle of Joey's presence on the hill after his death. "I hope it's that easy," he used to say. And there were signs in Allie's life just after Somerset—some over-the-top collegiate drinking and, later, some stints with cocaine—that more than hinted of some deep pain he may have carried away from his last official Get. Within a few years, however, he found a great wife and some apparent peace of mind as he began to live out a seemingly happy life as a family man and investor. Still, one had to believe that memories of Joey were never far from him.

As might be expected, Michael Moller had the most elaborate response to the events of that graduation week. On their trip to Europe and North Africa, the three old friends had endless discussions about their years at Somerset, many of which involved, of course, their final days at the school. There was one night in particular when the events surrounding Joey's death and "re-appearance" came up for review. They were in Morocco at the time, and had found themselves at a desert campsite that was, as it turns out, better outfitted with alcohol and drugs than with food and other provisions. It was well after midnight and Michael Moller was listening silently to Allie and Tate banter about their various theories and interpretations of the now-legendary Miracle of the Frisbee. Just when it seemed their friend was about to doze off into some kind of chemically induced reverie, Moller sat upright and slowly launched into what may have been the most powerful and poetic Full Report of his life up to that point. "It was the long distance connection," he began.

Allie and Tate immediately fell silent as their old friend took his turn at explaining the events. "It was just like when Joey and I walked into the Cricket Cathedral that last summer night before our Senior Year," he continued. "We hadn't tossed the Frisbee together all summer but something magical had happened and we were unstoppable as a team. We had made the long distance connection; we were growing closer together even while we were apart and when we got back together there was no stopping us. It was two on two in the Cricket Cathedral, winner-take-all and it was the long distance connection, and after that, well, it never went away . . . even after he died."

By now Allie and Tate were mesmerized. They had always been aware of an unspoken closeness between Moller and Joey—especially by their senior year—but they had never been able to get Moller to acknowledge it with more than an elfish smile. Suddenly, after several long years, he was ready to talk.

"I don't know how deeply that kind of feeling is buried inside of you guys, " he continued, "but for me, I can usually get in touch with the idea that Joey's not really gone. I mean, he isn't right here, but he isn't really gone. So, my big gripe is, why should that be such a big deal? I mean, how is it that we've got this enormous, two-thousand-year-old civilization based on the reality of the resurrection of Christ, but when someone is lucky enough to get near the notion in our day and age, well it's time to call it all into question? Think about it. You've got millions of churches and choirs and all kinds of holidays—shit, you've got entire cultures and nations, for that matter, and all that stuff is built from the ground up on the assumption that a certain historical figure named Jesus of Nazareth literally came back from the dead and spent forty days and nights hanging out with his old friends and followers. And the idea is that he punched this hole through death that any one of us can walk through, and, if you don't believe that, then it's time to bulldoze every church in the land, and, if you do believe that, then what's the big deal about one little wheezebag of a guy showing up in the neighborhood after his own crummy death

EPILOGUE

just to lob a farewell toss of the Frisbee to his old friends? I mean, why is that suddenly the Twilight Zone or something. I mean, what's the big deal? Do we believe this stuff or not?"

Moller shook his head in dismay and then took a deep breath. His voice had been at a fever pitch but now he spoke more quietly, if just as fervently. "I say: of course it was Joey on the hill!" he continued. "And if you're wanting to place bets, I say he'll show up again some day and lob another Frisbee into our midst right out of the Third Heaven or wherever. It's just no big deal. And if he doesn't show up again, it's only because he's got better things to do out there in the eternity than to put on one more dog-and-pony-show on behalf of a few knuckleheads like us who should have believed long ago. That's the way I see it anyway," said Moller quietly. "And that, I guess, is the Full Report from this quadrant."

At the time, Moller's words had been deeply regarded by both Tate and Allie. To hear such a testimony from their most trusted empirical friend was powerful indeed. And whether Moller had since then even "darkened the door of a church" as he used to say, Tate would always consider him the truest believer he knew.

With their various 25-year takes on the situation, then, it was little wonder that Father Miles' promise of new information was all that was necessary to re-unite the three old friends. There was still such an air of mystery about it all. By the time Father Miles took the podium at his Retirement Service, the aging Keepers were as restless as a group of prep school seniors in hot metal chairs. "Come on, Smiles," whispered Allie aloud. "Let's have the goods."

As had always been his style, however, the unflappable chaplain was taking his sweet time. He began with general comments about his tenure at the school, citing the various changes in the school through the years, laying out a few anecdotes of his own and, in general, charming his audience this one last time.

"Cut the British charm bullshit," whispered Allie. But Tate and Moller elbowed Allie from each side and Allie calmed down quickly. Soon they sensed that the chaplain was about to begin his real message. As the laughter from one final story dissipated, Father Miles took a deep breath and looked out on the congregation with a more somber air. "We've had our share of difficult times as well," he said.

Without a word between them, the three friends shifted in their seats. As expected, Father Miles began the story of his earliest years at Somerset, paying homage from the very outset to the "delightful bands of princely pranksters" that had once ruled the school. He spoke of arriving at the original campus and encountering the charming sons and daughters of the city's fine American aristocracy. "It was as if England itself had been transported here," he said, "passed through a car-wash, as it were, and laid out in the middle of this huge continent to have another go at civilized life, this time with central heat and air conditioning."

"What a poet," whispered Allie sincerely.

"No wonder we liked the guy," said Tate.

After painting his portrait of the Somerset Old Guard, Father Miles endeavored to explain the essence of that unique brand of humor he had come to know as a "Get," and then he went on to explain the station and role of the "Keepers of the Get" themselves. Throughout the room, various members of the audience nodded with deep understanding while others smiled with this formal account of a phenomenon they only knew from other stories of a Somerset before their own time. Meanwhile, in the back of the chapel, three of the most revered of the Keepers of the Get were riveted to their seats.

After further engaging his audience with well-told accounts of some of the Keepers' most hilarious and beloved Gets, Father Miles eased slowly into a description of the tragic turns taken in the transition from the old Somerset to the new. With surprising detail, he told the story of Joey.

As Father Miles laid out his version of the events of that fateful year, Allie, Tate and Moller were suspended in a state just this side of a trance. For a long period of time, they listened to the story as if they are only observers, as if the events had taken place in lives quite separate from their own. Most likely, this was their old chaplain's intent. As he spoke, he artfully balanced his oratory between the mythic and the mundane. Yes, these characters were real individuals, he seemed to be saying, but their story is such a universal one that their terrible pain can best be shared with a huge community of kindred souls. "This was a tragedy," he said, "on an epic scale. It can only be endured by a part of humanity much larger than ourselves. And it can only be answered by a triumph of equally epic proportions."

These words stirred the Keepers out of their journeys of thought. A triumph? What could Father Miles possibly mean? Sitting up straighter, their quizzical angst was immediately put on hold by the rapidly unfolding performance of their former mentor. "The tragedy of Joey Liptisch was met with an outpouring of kindness unequalled in the history of this school," he continued. "His formerly estranged family honored Joey

EPILOGUE

in death in a way that had seemed impossible to them in life. Knowing of Joey's tortured empathy for those in deepest poverty, his parents and extended family established a fund for a mission school in Paraguay, which was the country to which Joey had been somehow most drawn. For the past twenty-five years, then, the proceeds from a generous trust established by Joey's family have been used to establish and operate the "St. Aidan's School" in central Paraguay. Over those years, a total of more than 3,000 students from some of the most desperately impoverished families in Central America have been able to attend this school, putting each one of them on a solid path to a new life."

By now, the famously stoic priest was beginning to show some emotion. His voice wavered for a moment and then he regained his composure. Taking a deep breath, he proclaimed, "And now, I am delighted to announce that my last official duty as chaplain of Somerset School is to introduce to you the first participant in our long-awaited, student-exchange program with St. Aidan's School. This student will be joining our sophomore class next fall but I have made arrangements for her to be with us this morning as she has just joined her host family for the summer, in preparation for her year at Somerset."

The three old friends were beginning to be moved by strange emotions. They had known about the school that Joey's trust fund had established, but they had never made good on their plans to visit it. To now encounter a human emissary from this distant land was both exhilarating and somehow frightening. Father Miles, meanwhile, was having great difficulty containing the tears burning at his throat and eyes. Taking another deep breath and drawing on the last ounce of his deeply engrained British restraint, he was able to calmly say, "Please join me now in welcoming Isabella Vasquelero to Somerset School."

As the angelic figure of a wispy, dark-haired girl appeared from somewhere near the front of the chapel, Father Miles and his three old friends may as well have been alone in the chapel with her. The shoulders and heads in the rest of the pews dissolved into a lush impressionistic painting as Father Miles and his three acolytes connected from across the room. The chapel had given rise to a warm chorus of applause that continued long after the young Isabella had reached the side of Father Miles. She looked shyly out over the loving welcome she was receiving and then lowered her head and moved a step closer to Father Miles. The chaplain put his arm gently around her as his eyes continued to be fixed on Allie, Tate and Moller at the back of the room.

With the applause ending, Father Miles broke the silence with yet another dramatic turn. "We are also honored this morning by the presence of three of Joey's closest friends." The audience stirred with more excitement as the Keepers began to shake their heads and smile with gentle trepidation.

"Oh, man, what's he up to?" said Allie.

"These three lads," continued Father Miles, "well, these three *aging* lads, were kind enough to attend this ceremony this morning out of respect for their former chaplain and sometimes mentor." Then he smiled, "Or just as easily, they might be here because I enticed them with the promise of a bit of news. In any case and without further fanfare, I'd like to ask them now to come forward to accept a gift from Isabella. You know who you are, lads . . . and, the rest of you, please welcome now, Masters Allie Reed, Tate Henry, and Michael Moller, faithful Keepers of the Get."

A spirited round of applause erupted, including a few renegade cheers from different part of the congregation, as Allie, Tate and Moller rose with only some faint grumbling. They moved up the side aisle to the front of the chapel and gathered themselves beside Father Miles, feeling almost as shy as the girl from Paraguay standing on the other side of the priest. There were no wisecracks here. This was holy ground.

Father Miles smiled benevolently at his three acolytes of old and then turned to the girl standing at his right hand. "Isabella, dear, can you tell these old friends of mine something of your story?"

In a sweet, lyrical voice that was soft but strangely confident, this girl of fifteen or sixteen began to talk about her journey from terrible poverty and abuse to a place at the mission founded by Joey's family. Her lush, Central American accent graced her voice with the gentle emotion as she described her battles with what she called the "great sadness" and the "night terrors" that haunted her long after she was safe at the school. She told how the Headmaster of the school had helped her "stare down her demons," and she explained in some detail how her final bouts with the "great sadness" would surely have ended in her taking her own life, had not the Headmaster intervened again and again, refusing to give up on her.

Hardly aware of the large congregation before her, the girl seemed to be talking directly to Allie, Tate and Moller. "Then one day," she explained, "when the Headmaster was speaking like always, saying all the same words he was always telling me, suddenly all the darkness began to just flee away. I felt the terrible weight being lifted, this terrible weight

EPILOGUE

which I was carrying so long that I no longer had noticed it until suddenly it was being lifted. And inside I felt such joy as I cannot describe, and I was filled with such peace as I had never known, and I knew that I had been delivered to the kingdom of eternal life. In my heart I just knew it, and the Headmaster said that it was so, and I do not doubt it ever since. And this is what has happened to so many of the students who come from places even more terrible than my own. And this is the wonderful work that your friend's family has brought to our people. All this healing and sometimes miracles and always the education that can lift us up out of our old situation. And sometimes, too, for those with ojos a veer—with eyes to see—this doorway into eternal life. And it's because of the life of your old friend and the way that his family has chosen to honor him, and it is something that you should be very proud of, to have known one such as this. And it is because of your friendship with him, I think, that the Headmaster has sent this gift to you . . . "

At this point the girl lifted a black velvet bag off the floor beside her and held it gently in front of herself. "He sends this gift and he tells me to be sure that I tell you that we pray for you every day. And it's true and it's because of this I know your names already for these are the names which are written into our prayer books, when it says to 'pray for all the saints especially insert here the names of your beloved' and the names are 'Allie and Tate and Michael and Joey'. And I know that Joey is the one who went before you in death and is seated, as the Headmaster always says, at the left hand of God."

By now Allie and Tate and Moller were beside themselves with emotion. Tears blurred their vision and their chests heaved with a great burning sensation. All around them, though, there was a strange sense of wonder that elevated the mood in the chapel. A strong breeze had been building outside since the girl began speaking and was now bouncing some tree branches against the window of the chapel, sending deeper chills through the three of them. Isabella's head was turned by the sound and she quickly collected herself.

"But I am speaking too much," she said, "because you all must already know all these things because you knew Joey himself. And the Headmaster asked me only to give you this gift and to tell you that we are praying for you every day. So here, from Brother Joseph, Headmaster of St. Aiden's Episcopal Mission School, is the gift he asked me to give you."

Pulling her hair back from her face, the beautiful young girl reached into the black velvet bag and pulled out a box made of a rich, dark wood.

She handed it to Tate and stepped back quietly. Tate's mind was swirling with the words that had been pouring from the girl's innocent lips. "The night terrors . . . the left hand of God . . . the Headmaster's prayers . . . Brother Joseph . . . " and then there was Allie's voice whispering gently, "Open it, man."

Tate watched as Michael Moller leaned over, pushed the metal latch on the box, and began to lift the lid. Tate looked down and suddenly began to feel a terrible weight being lifted from himself too, a weight that he didn't even know he had been carrying since long before this sweet Isabella had even been born. He looked into the box and saw the punch line at Custer's Last Stand, the wink at the world's end. "It's the Last Get," he was thinking, but no words came to his mouth. His legs were shaking uncontrollably.

As he lifted the object from the box, Allie and Moller were instantly overwhelmed too, as they quickly comprehended the meaning of the gift. But they were as dumbstruck as Tate, so it fell upon the venerable Father David Miles to give voice—this one last time—to the event. He looked intently at the gift in Tate's hands and then into the faces of his three most treasured disciples, who looked back at him, expecting to see the same shock of revelation in his face. Instead, however, they were greeted by a strangely knowing look that slowly revealed the trace of a smile. Before they had time to react, however, the wily old chaplain lifted his outstretched hands to the congregation in the familiar pose that announced the service's final benediction. Holding the round and shining gift over his head like some strange Eucharistic host from another dimension, he took a deep breath and uttered the last proclamation of his long and storied ministry.

"It's a Frisbee," he declared. "Go, now, in the peace and joy of the Lord."

That night Tate had a dream. In it he saw a frail figure in a hooded brown robe walking in the moonlight atop a forested mountain ridge. The face was covered by the hood, but Tate could clearly see a pair of wire-rimmed glasses peering out from the thick folds of cloth. A stern voice, like that of an older priest, called out, "Brother Joseph", but the figure did not turn in the direction of the voice. Instead, the feet beneath the robe moved a little faster, in the process kicking up the bottom of the robe to reveal a pair of worn sneakers.

EPILOGUE

"Joey!" screamed a more menacing voice and this time Tate recognized the voice of Joey's father, the infamous Czar. Again the robed figure picked up the pace, quickly turning into a lilting trot, playfully running away from the voices behind it.

When a third voice cried out, "Hey, Joey, wait up!", Tate's heart began racing: the third voice was Tate's own.

At the sound of Tate's voice, the robed figure instantly stopped. Turning around slowly, the figure of Brother Joseph was soon facing directly at Tate. A hand appeared out of one of the sleeves of the robe and reached up to pull the hood away from the face: it was Joey.

Smiling earnestly, Joey wheezed a joyful, "Come on, Tate, it's the Cricket Cathedral, winner take all."

As his one hand pointed further up the mountain ridge, Joey's other hand appeared out of the robe holding a Frisbee. Tossing it straight at Tate, Joey then turned and ran up the hill. Instinctively, Tate took a quick step to the side and jumped as high as he could, but the Frisbee caught a burst of breeze and sailed just beyond his reach. As Tate landed back on the ground, he turned to watch the Frisbee sail down the mountain into the outstretched hand of Michael Moller. "It's the long-distance connection," said Moller with a smile.

"Keepers of the Get," shouted another voice from behind Moller on the mountain. "Seize your destiny!"

Tate turned around to see Allie running full speed up the mountain trail towards him.

"It's the Cricket Cathedral!" chimed Moller as he rushed past Tate, "And it's winner take all . . ."

Again by pure instinct, Tate stuck out his foot and soundly tripped Moller, sending his friend sprawling and freeing the Frisbee to go rolling directly into Allie's grasp.

"Nice work, Tate," laughed Allie, "and nice hand-off, Moller."

"Hurry up, you guys," shouted Joey from above them on the mountain. "Quit clowning around, would you? . . . The light up here is perfect . . ."

"We're coming, you wheeze-bag," shouted Allie, and by then Moller was back on his feet in hot pursuit of Allie.

Tate took a last look behind himself at the distant lights of a small city far below them in the valley. He bid a fond farewell to the shimmering Magic Empire and then turned and began to run to catch up to his friends. Allie and Moller were now running shoulder to shoulder up the steep slope of the mountain where, at the top of the ridge, the silhouette of Joey stood against a brilliant sky of blue and orange. He was surrounded by light—it seemed to shine right through his body—and he was calling to them and waving them on, earnestly beckoning from the top of the mountain, just a Frisbee toss away, it seemed, from the left hand of God.

Made in the USA
San Bernardino, CA
21 August 2016